MYSTERY AT SADDLE CREEK

A SADDLE CREEK BOOK

MYSTERY AT SADDLE CREEK

Shelley Peterson

Illustrations by Marybeth Drake

KEY PORTER BOOKS

Library and Archives Canada Cataloguing in Publication

Peterson, Shelley, 1952-
    Mystery at Saddle Creek / Shelley Peterson.

ISBN 978-1-55470-268-8

I. Title.

PS8581.E8417M97 2010   jC813'.54   C2009-905176-1

ONTARIO ARTS COUNCIL
CONSEIL DES ARTS DE L'ONTARIO

The publisher gratefully acknowledges the support of the Canada Council for the Arts and the Ontario Arts Council for its publishing program. We acknowledge the support of the Government of Ontario through the Ontario Media Development Corporation's Ontario Book Initiative.

We acknowledge the financial support of the Government of Canada through the Book Publishing Industry Development Program (BPIDP) for our publishing activities.

Key Porter Books Limited
Six Adelaide Street East, Tenth Floor
Toronto, Ontario
Canada M5C 1H6

www.keyporter.com

Text design: Martin Gould
Electronic formatting: Alison Carr

Printed and bound in Canada

10 11 12 13 14 5 4 3 2 1

Mixed Sources
Product group from well-managed forests, controlled sources and recycled wood or fiber
www.fsc.org Cert no. SW-COC-002358
© 1996 Forest Stewardship Council
FSC

99%

ANCIENT FOREST ™
FRIENDLY

To every person whose life has been touched by mental illness:
those who suffer, and those who try to help

If you stand high on the cliffs behind Saddle Creek Farm, the shape of the river below forms the outline of a saddle. The water twists and winds its way through the rocky, dramatic landscape of the Niagara Escarpment in Caledon, connecting all who cross its well-worn path.

Wild animals—deer, raccoons, squirrels, porcupines, coyotes and fox—come to drink. Hawks and owls compete for field mice, and songbirds trill in the treetops. Beavers dam off sections to build their homes, and fish are plentiful in the cold, deep pools.

If you were to paddle a canoe down the creek from the Grange to King Road, you'd pass Owen Enterprises, Merry Fields, the Malones, Hogscroft, Bradley Stables and, of course, Saddle Creek Farm. It is a tightly knit community—a place where people care deeply for one another, and for the land around them. It is also a community that is passionate about its horses.

And what horses! Those in the area are famed for their talent and strength: the legendary Dancer; Sundancer; Moonlight Sonata. All were foaled within walking distance of Saddle Creek, and all have carried themselves and their riders to victory—both in the ring, and beyond. Some wonder what secret the area holds, to bring forth such amazing creatures. Some say it's in the water.

MYSTERY AT SADDLE CREEK

PROLOGUE

Tanbark was very hungry. He hadn't eaten a thing all day. The walls of his stomach rubbed together, screaming for food. Worse, it had been raining steadily, and he was soaked and shivering. Darkness was rapidly descending. He needed a fire to warm himself, and to cook the rabbit he'd killed with his slingshot.

Tan pushed his matted, dull brown hair out of his eyes and leaned over a pile of wet twigs. His numb hands shook uncontrollably as he tried to ignite the cardboard match. He concentrated as hard as he could, willing his hands to be still and do as he bid. On the third try, the match bent in half. Tan grunted in frustration. He hurled the matchbook as far as he could and fell backward, spread-eagled on the ground.

Life wasn't fair.

After a couple of minutes he opened his dark, hollow eyes. He gazed up through a canopy of maple leaves into the swirling sky. Drops of rain bathed his face and filled his eyes to overflowing. He clenched his fists.

Nobody understood.

His friends had long since deserted him. They all believed he'd gone insane. They didn't say it, but he knew. They looked at him with stupid pity, and Tan couldn't stand it. They were the ones to pity! They wanted him to be the same guy he used to be, but why? That whole life, everything he'd done and thought before the change, was fake. Sports, jobs, school, clubs—all of it fake. Just like them and their lives—they were hamsters running thoughtlessly on their little wheels. But they couldn't see it.

People were fools.

Even his own mother was no better. She wanted him to get help. Help? What did help mean? Medication to make him normal. As if becoming a drooling zombie was normal. And being locked up in a mental hospital? Just until he was sorted out, she'd said. Right. Like he wanted to be imprisoned with crazy people. Tan felt a familiar panic rise in his chest. His heart pounded.

And anyway, help for what? He liked the way he was now. He was so much happier, so much better. And way smarter.

Tan jumped to his feet and spun, looking in all directions. He would never be found. Nobody would take him away and lock him up. He'd rather die. He searched for the book of matches and bent to his task with renewed vigour.

He'd show them.

Soon, very soon, they'd discover how much he could teach them. They'd recognize his brilliance. Then they'd all want to know him! People would line up around the block to hear his words. They'd pay any amount of money to sit at his feet and glean his wisdom. He was so close to finding what he needed to find. So close. He just needed a little more time to figure things out. And he needed his freedom for that.

Freedom was everything.

Tan smiled as the match caught fire. It was an omen; things were going to be all right. He shielded the tiny flicker carefully with his cupped hand and held it to the dry leaves under the twigs. He watched with satisfaction as the leaves curled, contorted, then burst into flame.

He sat on his haunches and sighed. Here, finally, among the rocks and trees of the Niagara Escarpment, he'd found a home. Here, he had the peace he needed. Here, he would discover the real purpose of his life.

Here, he could find out about the other half of his family.

1

BACK AT SADDLE CREEK

Tan ran as fast as he could through the dense underbrush, back toward the safety of his makeshift camp. Somebody had seen him! He stumbled on a root and fell to his knees, panting hard. He had to get away, get back to safety. There'd been so much blood! He scrambled to his feet and ran on. So much blood! He had to get the sight of it out of his mind.

TEN WHOLE DAYS!

Alberta Simms wiggled her toes and shivered with pleasure. She and her sister were staying at Saddle Creek Farm with their Aunt Hannah for ten whole days while their mother and Stuart were on their honeymoon. The girls had returned to the farm on Saturday night, after the wedding, and Alberta was already loving every minute of it.

Everybody called her Bird. Her long, dark hair was lightly brushed and needed a trim. She had tawny skin and sparkling, somewhat mischievous, deep brown eyes. Her graceful, slight limbs gave her a younger appearance than some other girls of fourteen, as did her ripped denim shorts and old white tee. But Bird didn't care. It was the perfect outfit for a day on the farm.

Ten. Whole. Days. Bird could think of nothing better in the world as she sat on the top step of the kitchen stoop, taking in every detail. Sunday's persistent drizzle had greened up the fields.

On this perfect Monday, late in June, the sky was pure blue and songbirds chirped madly. Bird took a deep lungful of sweet air and stretched like a cat.

As she waited for her Aunt Hannah—they had to get groceries, then pick up Julia from a friend's house in Inglewood—her eyes absorbed the peaceful scene across the driveway. Two horses grazed in the front field, sleek and shiny in their summer coats. Charlemagne, Charlie for short, was jet black with a white blaze and four white socks. Sundancer was a tall, coppery chestnut.

The chestnut's head shot up. *What're you looking at?*

You, you handsome son of a gun.

Can't blame you for that.

Sunny, you never change.

Bird smiled broadly at the horse's enormous ego. Last summer, against all odds, she and Sundancer had won the trophy at the Haverford Fair. It had been a total upset. Sunny's clean, careful jumping skills and quick turns had rendered the competition speechless. And out of luck.

Sundancer was a champion jumper; there was no question about that. More importantly, though, he was her best friend.

Bird picked absently at a scab on her calf as she waited; a mosquito bite gone bad. Aunt Hannah could take her time. She'd happily sit here all day long.

Life hadn't always been this good. Her mother, Eva, had gone from job to job and man to man, and Bird had never known her father. He was a rodeo star whom Eva had met at the Calgary Stampede, and he'd left town long before Bird was born. She had been named Alberta after the province.

Bird knew she'd been a difficult child. At first everything had seemed fine, but that all changed when Bird was six. That's when she'd stopped talking. The doctors called it Elective Mutism, but for Bird it just meant that she couldn't get the words out of her mouth. Soon enough, she'd stopped trying—at least with humans. Animals, on the other hand, were no problem. Bird had always had an exceptional ability to communicate with them.

Eva probably would've had trouble coping with a perfectly "normal" child, but there was no way she could handle a girl who refused to talk. In desperation, she'd sent Bird off to Saddle Creek Farm to live with her Aunt Hannah. It was a good decision for the entire family. Bird found what she needed to start speaking again. Eva found Stuart Gilmore, the local school principal, and fell in love.

Bird licked her finger and wiped the blood from her leg where she'd dislocated the scab. Rays of light shone through the leaves, glistening on Sundancer's sleek, coppery coat. She breathed in deeply and sighed with pleasure.

The screen door opened suddenly. Hannah appeared, followed by a young dog. Bird glanced up at her aunt—a tall, slim, middle-aged woman in jeans, a mint green blouse and flip-flops.

"What are you waiting for, Bird? Let's go!"

Bird jumped up. "Sorry to keep you waiting!" she shot back.

"I know, I know. But the phone rang again just as I was almost out the door." Hannah walked briskly to the white Ford truck. "It was Paul. Vaccinations, worming, papers, entry forms for the show ... you know!"

Bird followed at a more leisurely pace. She opened the rear door of the truck and motioned to Lucky. "Get in, boy," she said aloud, catching her aunt's pleased glance. Hannah still worried that Bird communicated too much with animals and too little with people, even though she'd been speaking aloud for a year.

Bird silently asked Lucky to bark. *Speak dog-talk, Lucky.*

"Arf arf arf arf!" he obeyed cheerfully.

Good boy! "He told me we're out of dog food," Bird said.

"Remind me to smack you about the ears." Hannah shook her head and chuckled as she stepped up behind the wheel and started the engine. "Have you got the list?"

Bird waved a yellow sheet of paper in the air and jumped in. As they started down the lane, the impatiens and bluebells in the farmhouse gardens caught Bird's eye through the truck window. Vibrant reds and purples and blues. Hannah sure loved colour.

Sundancer looked up as the truck moved past. *Where are you going?*

To the store. Let's go for a ride when I get back.

Maybe. It's kinda hot and the grass is delicious.

We have to practice.

Practice, shmactice. I can do those baby jumps with my eyes closed.

But I can't.

You're such a perfectionist.

See you in an hour. Get your saddle on and wait by the mounting block.

Ha ha ha.

Bird laughed with him, ignoring Hannah's questioning look.

"I saw Cody this morning," said Hannah. "Somehow he knows you're back at Saddle Creek."

Bird smiled. The small coyote was very clever. Of course he'd known that she was back. He knew everything.

"I'm so glad you and Julia are around for a while," continued Hannah as they drove down the hill, past the badlands and over the railway tracks. "Like the old days! But the time will go by fast. Your mother and Stuart will be back before we know it."

Bird didn't want to think about it.

"Is there anything you especially want to do while you're here?"

Bird shook her head and grinned. "Just ride and ride and ride. And go to horse shows."

Hannah smiled broadly. "A girl after my own heart. But you've got a lot of catching up to do if you want to take Sunny this Friday."

Bird nodded. "I'll start as soon as we're back from the store."

She could hardly wait to get riding again. Since Bird's speech had come back last summer, she'd fit in at school for the first time in her life. Suddenly, there were friends to hang out with, sports to play, clubs to join—*and* a new boyfriend—as well as schoolwork. Her days had been full and she'd ridden only sporadically since last summer, a fact that she now regretted. There was so much to do!

"Are you and Alec still dating?" asked Hannah. "Tell me if it's none of my business."

Bird blushed. It was all so new. "It's none of your business, but yes ... if he doesn't forget all about me over the summer." She was joking, but she really wasn't happy that Alec would be away for three whole months. He had a job as a counsellor-in-training, or CIT, at Camp Kowabi, teaching kids how to canoe and make fires. Some of her other friends were CITs, too, but Bird hadn't applied. She'd wanted to stay close to home so she could go to horse shows with Sunny.

"How could Alec forget about you? You're an original."

Bird grinned. Original was a nice way to put it. She thought about their last date, just a few days ago. She'd invited Alec to her mother's wedding. Bird was busy being a bridesmaid, but after the vows, they'd danced the night away. She hugged herself and tingled with the memory of their kisses under the trees.

Hannah turned off the road and parked the truck beside the Inglewood General Store. They got out, leaving the windows down for Lucky.

Get me a treat?

I'll see what they've got, Lucky, but you can't have a treat every time we stop somewhere.

But can I have one this time?

Bird patted his furry brown head and ran her finger down the white on his nose. She smiled. Lucky was indeed lucky to live with Aunt Hannah.

Inside the store, Hannah took the grocery list from Bird and began gathering items while Bird looked through the movie selection. She'd seen a lot of them, but some new releases had just come in, and a few looked intriguing.

Suddenly, the door burst open and a middle-aged woman rushed in. Her face was red with exertion and her bleached blonde hair was flattened with sweat. It was Ellen Wells, a neighbour.

"Call 911!" Ellen ordered. "A woman is lying on the road up at McLaughlin and The Grange. She's bleeding badly, and my cell went dead!"

Roxanne, the store's owner, calmly picked up the phone and dialed. "Who is it?" she asked as she waited.

"I don't know her name." Ellen was beginning to catch her breath, but she was still flustered. The other customers stopped what they were doing and listened. "She lives in the new housing development in Inglewood. I've seen her around."

People started murmuring, and Roxanne held up her hand for silence. She gave the information to the 911 operator clearly, listened quietly, then put the phone back in the cradle. "They're on their way. Here, Ellen, sit down and drink some water." Roxanne took the excited woman by the arm and helped her into a chair. "Tell us what happened."

Bird, Hannah and the others huddled around to hear.

"There's blood everywhere!" Ellen started shaking. "There's a huge gash on her head!"

Roxanne spoke soothingly. "Help is on the way, Ellen. Take your time. How did it happen?"

Ellen's face was so flushed that Bird wondered if she was going to have a heart attack. Or explode.

The woman started talking again, making a great effort to speak slowly, but her speech got quicker and quicker as she went on. "I was driving east. On The Grange. A car was pulled over on the side of the road. Up the hill in the woods I saw a young man running away. I wondered why he was running up there—no trails. And then, when I got closer to the car, I noticed it had a flat tire. And there was a ... a person covered with blood on the ground. I stopped my car and got out. I thought she was dead, but she was alive. She opened one eye and said, 'Help!' On the ground beside her was a tire iron—covered in blood! I thought to myself, what if that man offered to help with the flat, then hit her on the head with the tire iron and ran away! I asked her if that was what happened, and she tried to say something but then she passed out and I drove here to call for help."

A young woman Bird didn't know spoke next. "It sounds like that's exactly what happened, with the bloody tire iron and the man running away."

"Why would anyone do such a thing?" Roxanne exclaimed. She rubbed Ellen's shoulder as her tongue clucked empathetically.

"What is the world coming to when you can't trust a man who offers to help change a tire?" asked an older woman who lived up the hill.

"Who was he?" questioned the older woman's sister. "The man who ran away?"

Ellen shrugged. "I have no idea. I'm sure I've never seen him before."

"How old was he?"

"Young. And fit. With longish dark hair."

The sound of sirens stopped the conversation dead. Roxanne hurried out onto the porch and waved at the first vehicle. It was an ambulance. The driver slowed and rolled down his window. "The Grange and McLaughlin!" she shouted. He nodded and sped off, followed by a fire truck and two police cruisers.

Ellen got up from her chair and headed for the door. Roxanne stopped her. "There's nothing more you can do, Ellen. She'll be looked after and taken to the hospital."

Ellen shook her off. "I found her. I need to make sure she's all right. And I'm the only witness!" The small crowd watched as she slammed the door and disappeared into her car.

"Wow," said Hannah.

"You can say that again," exhaled Roxanne. "What a shock."

Hannah nodded. "It's lucky Ellen was passing by right then, and stopped."

"She's the kind of person who would stop," said a young woman from down the road. "She brought me a casserole when George had his operation."

"That's Ellen for you," agreed Roxanne.

Hannah paid for her groceries in silence. Bird had lost all interest in renting a movie. They picked up their bags and started to leave. "Thanks, Roxanne," said Hannah absently.

"Bye, honey," answered Roxanne. "Bye, Bird."

"I hope they catch him soon, before he strikes again," muttered a young woman holding a toddler.

"And lock him up where he belongs," agreed an older one. "I won't be able to sleep until then."

Back in the truck, Hannah shuddered. "This is terrible."

"Let's go pick up Julia," Bird said. "I'll feel better when she's with us."

Hannah nodded. "Me, too. But we have to drive right by the scene of the accident. I'm not looking forward to that."

She could see that Hannah was upset, but Bird was more curious than anything. She wanted to see for herself what was going on.

She didn't have to wait long. Up ahead was a police barricade, set up around a small blue sedan. Bird watched while the medics rolled a loaded stretcher into the back of the ambulance. As soon as the doors were closed, the sirens began to wail. The vehicle raced off, lights flashing.

Hannah and Bird drove in silence until they reached the cozy white clapboard house where Julia had spent the night. As they pulled into the lane, Liz and Julia came running out, all flushed and excited.

"Aunt Hannah! Bird!" shouted Julia. "What's going on? We heard all the sirens, but we didn't want to bike down to see because you were coming." Her blonde hair was pulled back in a messy ponytail and her pretty face was strained with worry. "What happened?"

Hannah chose her words carefully. "A woman was hit on the head. She's gone to the hospital now. The police, ambulance and fire truck were there—that's why there was so much noise." Hannah turned to Liz. "Is your mom home?"

The diminutive girl shook her shiny black curls. "She'll be b … back around four. The neighbour's home."

Bird looked at her watch. It was only two o'clock. "Why not come with us?" She looked at Hannah for approval. "Julia and I are going out on the trails this afternoon and we need someone to ride Joey."

Hannah nodded in agreement. "You'd help us out, Liz."

Julia chimed in. "Yes! Call and ask your mom!"

Without a word Liz spun around and raced into the house. She was back in less than a minute with her riding hat plopped on her head and her chaps under her arm.

A few hours later, Bird walked down from the barn, leaving Julia and Liz cleaning the bridles. They'd had a wonderful ride through the trails along the crest of the Escarpment, and had all but forgotten the upsetting incident on The Grange. Bird breathed in the smell of freshly cut hay. Tomorrow or the next day, whenever it was dried and baled, the hay would start coming in. Cliff Jones, the farm manager, was making preparations. They'd need more than two thousand bales to feed the horses through next winter.

Sundancer whinnied as she walked past his field. *Why didn't you ride me today? You said you would.*

I thought you said it was kinda hot and the grass was delicious.

True and true, but I don't like it when you ride another horse, especially one so inferior.

A little stuck up, are we? How about I ride you after dinner?

Maybe yes, maybe no. But more likely yes.

Bird laughed. It was nice to be back at Saddle Creek.

As Bird approached the farmhouse, Paul Daniels drove up and parked beside the door. He got out and stretched, then noticed Bird. "Hi there! What's for dinner?"

"If you're here it's going to be good, that's all I know. Aunt Hannah's still trying to impress you."

"I hope she never stops!" The veterinarian's face broke out in a grin. "Don't tell her that I'm already impressed."

Bird smiled broadly. "You just don't know how to play it cool, do you?" She was startled at her own cheekiness, and covered her mouth. Being able to speak again was part blessing, part curse. It was great to be able to say whatever was on her mind, but sometimes she needed to remind herself not to say everything she thought.

Paul, however, didn't seem in the least bit annoyed. "Why bother? Life is too darn short!"

Hannah appeared at the door, freshly bathed and radiant. Lucky slipped past her legs and ran to Paul, wagging his tail madly. The dog wriggled with joy as he jumped and yelped.

"Down, pup," scolded Paul with a wink to Bird. "Play it cool."

Liz and Julia came running from the barn. "Aunt Hannah, can Liz stay for dinner? Please?"

"Of course! Liz, check with your mom, and tell her I can drive you home after dinner, unless you want to spend the night."

The girls locked arms and rushed into the house. "Thank you, thank you, thank you!" they chanted.

Paul turned to Bird. "And you think *I* don't know how to play it cool?"

2

A Mystery

Tanbark felt so alone. More alone than he'd felt for a long, long time. He listened to the breeze ruffling the leaves overhead, and wished he had somebody to talk to. Somebody to tell about what had happened on the road.

He'd moved his camp since that morning, careful to erase any sign that he'd been there. But he couldn't erase the memory. The tire iron crunching the woman's skull. Her surprised expression. The shock in her eyes. The blood gushing. The woman falling. The metal bar clanging to the road. The man on the road, watching him run. And the blood. So much blood. He shook his head to clear the images out as a wave of despair flooded over him. He curled up in a ball and slept.

WHEN THE DOORBELL RANG, they had finished dinner and were trying to decide whether to go to Best's for ice cream or slice into the watermelon that Paul had brought from the Apple Factory. Two police officers stood on the porch, their identification in hand. Officer Ed Paris was in his mid-fifties and wide across his middle. Officer Patrick O'Hare was younger by two decades, and slim. Hannah invited them in, and Paul offered them something to eat.

"No thanks," Officer Paris replied. "We're on duty. Sorry to interrupt your evening, but you probably know why we're here."

"Is it about the attack on the woman in Inglewood?" asked Julia, her eyes wide.

"Yes. The witness was able to help our artist put together a composite sketch. We're going house to house, asking people to take a look."

The younger officer added, "If anyone comes to mind when you see it, go ahead and tell us. We're trying to find people to interview."

"Don't worry that it'll get someone in trouble," Officer Paris added. "Just take a look and say who it reminds you of."

He pulled an eight-by-ten sheet of paper out of his case, and turned it to face Hannah. "Remind you of anyone?"

Hannah took a good look at the sketch. "It could be half a dozen people up here! Dark, longish hair, unshaven, dark eyes, thin face."

"Anyone in particular?"

Hannah shook her head. "No." She passed it to Paul, who breathed in deeply, then shook his head. "Hannah's right. Wouldn't want to start any wild goose chases."

Officer Paris frowned. "You'll have to leave that to us. As Officer O'Hare said, we're looking for people to interview. Time is of the essence. The man who did this is out there right now and we don't want him assaulting anybody else."

"Can I see?" Liz looked at Julia and giggled. "From here it looks like my mother's b ... boyfriend."

Officer O'Hare grabbed the sketch from Paul and showed it to Liz. Liz and Julia pored over it.

"I see what you mean," said Julia, "but Phil isn't so skinny and his hair is much shorter."

"What is his full name?" The young policeman smiled encouragement. "Phil who?"

"Philip B ... Butler," answered Liz.

The two policemen exchanged a glance.

"But it couldn't be Phil! He's a really nice m ... man. He'd never hurt anybody." Liz blushed and stammered, something she did only when she was upset. "A ... And he used to be a p ... policeman!"

"Thanks for your help. What is your name please, young lady?"

Liz was turning white. "Elizabeth Brown. But honestly, I didn't m ... mean that I think it's him, the picture only r ... *reminds* me of him. A *little*."

"Don't worry. If he's innocent he has nothing to fear." The young officer turned to Bird. "You haven't looked at this yet, miss. Does it remind you of anyone?"

Bird looked from one policeman to the other. "Yes."

All eyes were on her.

"With shorter hair, it looks like you." She pointed to the young officer.

Liz and Julia covered their mouths, but the policemen were not amused. "This is not a joke," said Officer Paris sternly.

But Bird wasn't joking; she was making a point. The picture resembled any number of people, all innocent except for one.

Paul deflected the tension with a question. "Could we keep one of your sketches and ask the people who board horses here?"

Officer Paris answered, "No. We'll ask them ourselves. We need to gauge their reactions. Where does your staff live?"

Hannah pointed north. "I don't think they're home right now, but it's the house at the end of the next lane. Go back to the road, turn right, then go up the next driveway. The house there has an apartment upstairs, so knock on both doors."

"Thank you for your time." The two policemen stood up and left.

Once the door closed, they all took a deep breath.

Bird was the first to break the silence. "We'd better warn Cliff. That sketch looked like him, too."

Hannah nodded. "And Pierre Hall."

Paul turned to Liz. "Don't worry. Somebody else would've identified Phil if you didn't. It does look a lot like him."

"Anyone for ice cream?" asked Hannah brightly. "We can't sit here and stew all night."

"You all go ahead," said Bird. "I'm riding Sunny. I've got an hour and a half before it gets dark."

"Bird, a woman was attacked today and the man is still out there!" Hannah's voice was filled with alarm.

"You think a man can outrun Sundancer?"

"Your Aunt Hannah's right, Bird." Paul backed her up. "This is no time for you to be out there alone."

Julia piped up. "She won't be alone. Liz and I'll go with her!"

"Definitely not." Hannah was firm. "And definitely not for you, too, Bird. Your mother would never forgive me if something happened. And she'd be right. It's not safe."

"I'll be perfectly safe," Bird said calmly. "And I need to ride Sunny. Besides, the man's probably lying low. Hiding. He knows the police are everywhere. He wouldn't dare make a move tonight."

Hannah and Paul looked at each other. Paul raised an eyebrow and motioned to the jumping ring outside the house. "There's mocha fudge ice cream in the freezer."

Hannah looked Bird in the eye. "I don't like this one bit, but if you must, Bird, practice in the paddock where we can see you. Do you hear me? And be back inside within the hour."

Bird grabbed an apple from the fruit bowl on the table and pulled on her boots. "Thanks."

Before Hannah could change her mind, Bird ran out to Sunny's paddock.

Come on, horse. Time to rock and roll!

Give a horse a chance to think!

We've got to hurry before Hannah changes her mind. There's a bad man on the loose.

Just one? We can take him.

That's what I told her. Here's an apple.

That's my girl.

We have to stay in the ring.

Come on!

Hannah said.

Can we warm up on the trails? Please? It's so boring in the ring!

Bird thought about it. She ran a brush over Sunny and threw on the tack. She glanced at the house. Through the kitchen window, she could see Hannah making ice cream cones for the girls.

Quickly Bird mounted, and soon they were trotting down the path toward the back. She knew she was disregarding Hannah's instructions, but it was such a nice time of day! She loved the trails on summer evenings, after the hot sun had cooled. The perfect time to ride was after seven-thirty and before the sun set at nine. She'd just warm up on the trails, like Sunny had suggested, then work in the ring.

The smell of fresh-cut hay and thyme wafted on the warm breeze. Bird had been desperate to get outdoors after the policemen's visit, and she could think of nothing better than breathing in fresh air while sitting on the back of her horse.

"Ah," Bird said aloud. "This is the life." The trail led to the back of the farm, then down the Escarpment. She eyed the cool forest below with yearning. Decision time, Bird thought. Obey Hannah or go down the ridge.

Hannah didn't have to know.

Bird and Sunny carefully descended the winding, rocky path. The shade of the forest embraced them. Sunlight played through the leaves, and little creatures scurried for cover. Bird relaxed. The ride was having a therapeutic effect on her—it was washing away the stresses of the day. She was sure they'd made the right decision.

Suddenly, a man stepped out of the bushes and waved frantically. Bird and Sundancer were caught completely by surprise. Sunny reared up on his hind legs in fright and spun. Bird managed to stay on by a hair. She turned her head and looked hard at the man who'd materialized out of thin air. He seemed ... wild. He was around twenty, with matted dark hair and scrubby facial hair. He was naked except for a pair of old gym shorts and ripped sneakers. But it was his eyes that really caught her attention. They were full of worry and need.

Easy, Sunny. He wants to tell me something.

Sunny reared again and took off at a gallop. *I don't care. We're going home.*

Whoa! I want to know what he wants. Whoa!

Don't pull that "whoa" crap. My heart is racing so fast I can't see.

All the more reason to stop running!

Bird, he's chasing us! Hold on to your hat!

There was nothing Bird could do but hang on. Sunny was in full flight, teeth clamped tight on the bit to avoid her efforts at control. He was covering the ground faster than he ever had before. Trees, bushes, the trail—everything was a blur. He stopped only when they reached the Saddle Creek barn. His sides were heaving and he was covered in sweat.

Bird slid down from the saddle, out of breath. She glared at him.

You could have killed us both!

That man could have killed us both!

He only wanted to talk to me.

Yeah? In the middle of the woods, smelling crazy? I know crazy and he's crazy.

You're crazy! You ran off like a lunatic. I'm so mad I could, I could ...

You could what? You never hit animals so don't pretend. And Hannah said there was a bad man out there.

Bird stared at him. "Good grief." She slowly sat down on the gravel driveway. The man in the woods looked just like the sketch. *What if you're right, Sunny? What if I'd made us stop and he'd attacked me?*

The big horse snorted and nuzzled Bird's hair. *Okay, maybe I didn't think of that 'til now. Maybe I ran because I was scared.*

But maybe your fear saved us. I guess I'll have to tell Hannah what happened.

She'll be upset.

You have no idea, Sunny.

3
THE WILD MAN

Tan had not intended to scare the girl with the beautiful horse. He'd only wanted to talk to her. The sound of something moving had woken him up. First, he'd listened to the noises of leaves rustling and twigs snapping. Then, he'd seen movement through the trees. A gorgeous chestnut horse was striding down the trail with a girl on its back. Tan had studied the girl's face; there was peace in her eyes. He saw something else, too—something that he couldn't define. Suddenly he knew that he could trust her with his secret. He wanted to tell her about all the blood, and explain how it had happened—he'd need her help if they caught him. And they'd try. People always blamed him. And that man. That man had seen Tan, and Tan had seen him, and the man knew it. Maybe they were stalking him now. He looked at the girl again. She wouldn't betray him. He could tell her about the morning. He must tell her. She would help. He'd stepped out of the bushes and—in an instant— the girl and the horse were gone.

HANNAH HAD BEEN every bit as upset as Bird had predicted. Maybe more. She'd yelled about safety and choices and reckless behaviour. And about breaking promises in general, and about her going down the Escarpment in particular. Hannah had never yelled at her like that, and Bird felt awful, mostly because Hannah was right.

But today was a new day, a fresh start, and Bird vowed to behave herself. Liz had ended up staying the night, and now Julia, Liz, Hannah and Bird were in the barn, saddling up for a light schooling and maybe a short hack. Bird was half listening to the younger girls' rambling conversation as she worked.

"So, want to hear something weird?" asked Liz as she bent down to pick dirt and pebbles out of Timmy's foot.

"Sure." Julia brushed Sabrina's thick white tail.

"When I called my mom this morning, know what she said?"

"How could I?" Julia grimaced at her friend.

"You're never going to guess."

"Just tell me!"

"You know that sketch the police brought here last night?" Liz straightened up and looked at her friend. "When they came to our house, Mom told them it looked like Phil."

"You thought so, too."

"I know, but at least I feel better now. And there's something else."

"What?"

"Jeremy, who lives next door, told *me* that his mother told *him* Phil didn't retire on purpose. He was *forced* to retire. He did something bad."

Now Bird was listening with both ears.

"What did he do?" asked Julia.

"I asked Mom. She said it was something that seemed bad but really wasn't. She said the person who accused Phil made it all up, but because it looked bad they made him resign."

"Wow." Julia stopped brushing her pony. "I wonder what it was."

Hannah had been listening, too, and now she offered a word of advice. "You know, girls, this is serious. Let's get the facts straight before we pass on gossip. Liz, your neighbour might have no idea what he's talking about."

"Maybe." Liz went on. "But now Mom's all worried. She thinks the police'll bring Phil in for questioning because of her."

Bird caught Julia's eye. "Did you mention that you'd told them the same thing? That you thought it looked like Phil?"

Liz shook her head and blushed. "No, but I w ... will."

The conversation was interrupted as Boss, a small white Jack Russell, started barking in his shrill, ceaseless way. A moment later, a police cruiser stopped beside the barn. Everyone watched as the two policemen from the night before got out.

"Excuse me, ladies," said Officer Paris as he entered the barn. "Is Cliff Jones here?"

"Is there a problem?" Hannah's voice was filled with concern.

Officer O'Hare spoke. "We have to take him in for questioning."

"Was he positively identified?" asked Bird.

"From that sketch?" Hannah put her hands on her hips defensively. "Who identified him?"

Officer O'Hare crossed his arms. "That's confidential, folks. Suffice it to say that she knows Cliff well."

"But that sketch could be any number of people."

"Maybe so, but if he's innocent ..."

"He'll be cleared." Bird finished his sentence. "But Cliff couldn't have hit a person like that. He couldn't even imagine doing that!"

"You'll have to let us do our job." Officer Paris glared at the still-barking Boss. The persistent noise was getting annoying.

Cliff came around the corner just then, pushing a wheelbarrow. "Boss! Hush!"

"Cliff Jones?" asked Officer O'Hare.

Cliff looked wary. "Yes?"

Officer Paris walked up to him, heavy-footed and straight-backed. "You'll have to come with us for questioning."

Cliff froze. His eyebrows rose quizzically.

Hannah stepped forward and patted him on the shoulder. "Don't worry about a thing, Cliff."

"He's innocent!" Bird stepped up. "Last night a man jumped out at me when I was riding. He looks exactly like the composite sketch. He lives somewhere in the woods and he had hardly anything on. *That* man is the man you need to arrest, not Cliff."

"He had nothing on, you say? A naked man?"

"He had shorts on," corrected Bird.

"And he jumped out at you?"

"Yes. From the bushes. He must live down there."

The officers gave each other dubious looks. Bird knew they didn't believe her. She appealed to Hannah to confirm her story.

"Bird came home quite rattled. She was worried that perhaps this man might be the one who attacked the woman." Hannah stepped closer to Bird. "And even if he isn't, I don't like the idea of a man living wild around here, jumping out of bushes."

"And why didn't you report this incident the minute it happened?" asked Officer Paris.

"I'm sorry." Hannah looked abashed. "I was going to call this morning, but I should have told you immediately."

"You certainly should have. We need all the help we can get." Officer Paris looked at his watch. "We'll get Bird's statement later. Right now, we need to take Cliff in. There are two more men to interview after him."

Hannah and the girls watched as the officers walked Cliff out to the cruiser and put him in the back seat, taking care not to bump his head on the door frame.

Before they closed the door, Cliff flashed a forced smile in Hannah's direction. "Don't worry, I'll be fine. Can you bring the horses in for me at four and feed them? Jules needs her mud fever treated—Bird knows what to do—and Sir Jeffery has to get one more dose of penicillin. Twelve pills soaked in hot water and mixed into his grain. And can you do night check if I'm not back?"

"Of course." Hannah shook her head. "I can't believe this is happening."

Cliff smiled with all the confidence he could muster, but Bird sensed his nervousness. She admired how he was being strong for Hannah's sake, and how he cared more for the horses than for himself.

The cruiser drove down the lane and away. Fine dust billowed up behind, obscuring the car from view.

They exercised the horses for over an hour, doing flatwork in the arena. Hannah was insistent on teaching horses to know their leg aids, bend into corners, flex their necks and stretch out their backs. After a good workout, the girls hosed down their mounts and put them back out in their fields. Then, like always after a ride, they soaped and oiled the tack. Finally, after checking the outside water troughs, they went to the house for sandwiches and milk.

Paul had just arrived, and he looked grim.

"What's the matter?" asked Hannah.

"It was on the radio. The woman died."

Hannah's hand shot up to her mouth.

Bird stiffened. Paul could only mean one woman—the woman who was mugged with the tire iron.

"She'd lost too much blood and they couldn't save her. She died in the ambulance yesterday, but the authorities only told the media today."

"All from the blow to her head?" asked Bird.

"They think she may also have hit her head on a rock when she fell."

Hannah grimaced. "It's a pity that Ellen came too late."

"Every second counts when there's blood loss," Paul said, speaking as a medical man. "There's more," he continued, as he washed his hands at the sink. "The woman's name was released. It's Sandra Hall."

Hannah gasped. "Sandra Hall? That's Pierre's ex-wife."

Paul nodded.

Bird knew who he was. Pierre worked next door for Guy and Bunny.

"And he definitely looks like the sketch," added Julia.

"Didn't Pierre and Sandra have ... problems?" asked Bird. "I used to see Sandra with bruises and stuff."

Hannah and Paul exchanged a look, but Paul answered Bird's question honestly. "That was always my impression, but it's impossible to know what really goes on behind closed doors."

"Maybe it *was* him," mused Julia.

"The jealous ex-husband," added Liz. "The prime suspect."

"Now we're behaving just like everybody else," chided Hannah, "putting two and two together and getting forty-four."

The girls looked sheepish.

"It's all that people are talking about," Paul said. "Everywhere I went this morning, everybody had a theory. Everybody's got a suspect."

"And everybody wants him caught," Bird said, thinking about the women in the Inglewood store. With all the talk and that sketch out there, she hoped the police would catch the right person.

"Is there anything we should do for Cliff?" Hannah asked Paul as he sat down at the table. She'd filled him in by phone, moments after the police had left. "Should we go down and vouch for him? Hire a lawyer?"

"Let's see what happens. If they question him and let him go, no harm done. If he's held there or arrested, that's another thing altogether."

"They didn't believe me," Bird told Paul. "I told them about the man in the woods and they thought I made it up."

"They'll be back," Hannah reassured her as she put a plate of chicken salad sandwiches on the table. "They'll believe you because it's true. When the truth is told, things always turn out fine."

Bird wasn't so sure.

"Something else was on the radio," Paul said. "There's a meeting tonight at the Inglewood General Store. The police are making themselves available for questions." He took a bite of his sandwich.

"What time?" Hannah asked.

"Seven. No children allowed." He glared in mock seriousness at Bird, Julia and Liz, trying to lighten the mood. "Not that you'd want to go, anyway. It'll be a bunch of worried grown-ups wondering if they'll be the next to get a tire iron to the head."

The phone rang, and Bird picked it up.

It was Patty Brown, calling to speak with her daughter. Bird handed Liz the phone. After a quick conversation, Liz hung up with a stunned expression on her face. "Phil's been t ... taken to the police station for questioning, and Mom's coming r ... right away to pick me up."

"Oh, Liz," cried Julia. "It's not your fault. You know that, right?"

"I can't believe this is h ... happening," whispered Liz, her eyes filling with tears.

Hannah crossed the kitchen and put her arm around Liz's shoulder. "It'll be all right, honey, you'll see. This'll all be over before you know it. Once the man is caught."

"If they can figure out who really did it," Bird added.

Hannah shot her a look, but Bird wasn't paying any attention.

Bird summarized, counting on her fingers. "There are four suspects that we know of: Cliff, the wild man, Phil Butler and Pierre Hall. I know for sure it wasn't Cliff."

"Or Phil," added Liz quickly.

Bird nodded. "Of course. So that leaves Pierre and the wild man."

"Pierre is creepy," Julia stated, "but the wild man really scares me."

Bird knew exactly what she meant.

After helping to clean up the lunch dishes, Bird put on her chaps and went outside, desperate to get in a practice with Sundancer. No matter how horrible the news of Sandra Hall's death, the show was only four days away.

The Palston Horse Show was a big one. Bird felt totally unprepared and more than a little nervous. She would be competing against some serious riders. Normally, she would've had several schooling shows under her belt by this point in the season, but this was her first time out in a year.

To duplicate the level of difficulty they'd be facing, she set up a course of jumps in the front field. Striding out the distances, hauling poles, measuring heights, Bird was concentrating so hard that she was startled by a nose on her arm.

Sunny! You scared me!

Cool.

I think it's ready. Let's get your saddle on and give it a whirl.

The triple is weird. Pace it out again.

It's perfect.

You want to risk it?

Bird thought for a second. She didn't want to ride through and crash. She took Sunny's advice and walked it again. Sure enough, she'd made a mistake. The first and second jumps were fine, but to get to the third was not an easy three strides, it was a messy two-and-a-half.

Bird looked at Sunny. He was gloating.

Okay, okay, so you were right.

Again. And you were wrong. Say it.

I said you were right.

Say you're wrong or you can't ride me today.

What?

I'll get all crazy. I still remember how to do that, you know.

Are you threatening me?

Maybe.

Bird certainly did remember how crazy Sundancer had been. When he'd first arrived at Saddle Creek, Hannah had forbidden Bird from riding him, and for excellent reasons. The horse was particularly sensitive and naturally suspicious. His first trainers had not factored that into his early education, and, as a consequence, Sunny had become confused, bitter and unresponsive. The situation quickly became a vicious circle—the more he questioned, the harsher the training methods became until finally Sunny was a danger to himself and to every rider who dared get on his back. Saddle Creek had been his last chance, and Bird had been his saviour. Her unique ability to communicate with animals had literally kept him alive.

I can't believe you'd do that again. She patted his neck gently, enjoying the feel of his healthy, silky coat. They'd been through a lot together. *Those were not good days.*

You're right. He rubbed his forehead on her shoulder. *I wouldn't really do it on purpose.*

I was wrong about the triple.

Then let's do this.

Bird and Sunny warmed up for ten minutes with a collected walk and trot that stretched out his back muscles and the tendons and ligaments in his legs. Soon his stride was long and low and loose, and it was time to begin the course. Just as they cantered around the corner toward the first jump, Sundancer spooked and leapt sideways.

Sunny! What's up?

A human is there.

Where? Bird scanned the edges of the field. She could see nothing.

Behind the trees along the fenceline. It's the same human from the trail.

The wild man?

He smells the same. Let's pay him a visit.

What? Last night you almost kill me running away from him and today you want to confront him?

Yes.

The pair trotted along the fence to the spot where Sunny had sensed the presence. Nothing was there.

Are you sure, Sunny?

Of course, I'm sure! My nose still smells him. Sunny flipped up his upper lip and snorted loudly. *Horrible.*

He's gone now.

I know. But he was here.

Puzzled and disquieted, Bird rode Sunny back to the grassy area where she'd set up the jumps. *Can we do this now?* she asked, unsure whether the man's presence had spooked Sunny out of his good mood.

I can. The question is, can you? You're trembling.

I'm fine. It was just a little weird.

They began the course again, cantering in the same as before, and this time there were no interruptions. They got their rhythm around the corner and took the first jump nice and easy, cantering four strides to the hedge, then six strides to the oxer. The triple combination rode perfectly, thanks to Sunny, with a two stride then a three stride and on to the water jump, which was really a kid's discarded wading pool rescued from the dump. Sunny took the skinny, then doubled back to an illusion jump constructed of jumbled poles. They finished by jumping the hedge from the other direction.

You did that really well, Bird.

Thanks. So did you!

No surprises there. You left my head alone so I could land easily and keep my hind feet up over the poles. And you didn't overdo the lead cues. I hate when you jab me with your heel when all you have to do is look where you're going next. I get that.

Bird slid off Sunny's back, laughing.

What's so funny?

Never mind. Bird could only imagine what people would think if they knew the conversations she'd had with this horse.

By four o'clock the chores were done, and Hannah, Bird and Julia started to bring in the horses for their dinner.

Boss had been out of sight all day, sulking. Now, however, he came racing out from under the sink in the feed room. "Arararararara!"

"Cliff must be back," said Hannah, looking out the barn door.

He's home! He's home! Hurray! Hurray!

Calm down, Boss. You're deafening us. Bird put her hands to her ears.

Hannah had guessed right. A police cruiser stopped at the barn, a cloud of dust catching up and engulfing it. Cliff got out and closed the door. The car turned around and sped away.

"Hi there, folks," said Cliff with a smile. Boss ran for him and jumped into his arms, licking his entire face.

"Are you all right?" Hannah ran out, followed by the girls. "What happened?"

"They asked questions. I answered them."

"That's all?"

Cliff put Boss down and patted the little dog's head. "They wanted DNA and I gave them some. They scraped some cheek tissue."

"Did you learn anything new?" Hannah was curious.

"No."

"Did you see anybody else? Any other suspects?" asked Julia.

"No."

"You were gone all day and that's all you can tell us?" Bird persisted.

"You should talk! You went years without uttering a word." Cliff looked at Bird with affection.

She smiled. "Guilty! Did you see Phil Butler? He was identified by that composite sketch, too."

"They bring a person in one door and another out a different way. Nobody sees anybody else."

"Well, we're happy you're back." Julia spoke for everybody. "You must be relieved they let you go."

Cliff nodded. "You bet, but it's not over yet. I'm not supposed to leave town, and if my DNA matches, I'm in deep trouble."

"It won't, because you didn't do it." Hannah gave him a quick pat on the shoulder. "I wonder who told the police the sketch looks like you."

Cliff cocked his head. "I've been thinking about that. Remember Laura Long? When she took her horse away she was pretty mad at me."

"She was mad because she couldn't have you on call twenty-four hours a day to change blankets and boots and bring her horse in at whim." Hannah threw up her hands. "Boarders! We need them and love them, but sometimes ..."

Bird and Julia chimed in unison, "... they can drive us bananas!"

Julia broke into a dance that reminded Bird of a circus monkey, and everyone laughed. Cliff laughed loudest of all, and Bird realized how very happy he was to be home.

Watching him scoop up Boss and join the monkey dance, Bird couldn't help but shake her head. How unfair that Cliff, of all people, would be accused of murder! What were the police thinking? There was only one way to find out: she needed to get to the meeting in Inglewood.

4

THE INGLEWOOD MEETING

Tan crept closer and closer to the farmhouse. He had watched the adults leave in the truck, but the girl with the horse was still at home. He would speak to her tonight. Tan quickly looked over his shoulder. His stomach rumbled. While he was here, maybe he'd get something good to eat. He'd feel a lot better once he'd eaten something that hadn't been scrounged from the forest.

He stepped into the shrubs and peeked in a window. Nobody there. He tried to open the window, but it was locked. He moved silently to the next one and looked through the glass panes. Nobody in the dining room either, and it was locked as well. As Tan stealthily made his way toward the kitchen door, the brown dog inside the house began to bark. He moved away, confused. Then he sensed a presence: a savage presence. A low growl sounded behind him, and suddenly, a small coyote with a snarling face and glowing eyes appeared. Tan didn't wait for it to bite. He ran.

BIRD LAY FLAT under a horse blanket in the back of the Ford pickup, wondering if this whole thing was a good idea. Oh well, she thought. If she was caught, Hannah would be mad. It wouldn't be the first time.

The truck slowed. Bird could hear people talking, tires crunching on the gravel and lots of activity. She lifted a corner of the blanket and peered out. Hannah backed into a spot close to the store, beside the hill that crested at the railroad tracks. Perfect.

"I hope this meeting doesn't run too late," said Paul, as he got out and closed the door behind him. "I'm up early tomorrow."

"We can leave any time," answered Hannah.

"The police think this will calm everyone down. Bet on it riling everyone up instead."

"I think it's more for information. Awareness." Hannah's voice grew fainter as they walked toward the store. "I hate leaving the girls alone with the attacker still on the loose."

Bird felt a twinge of guilt. Because she was here, Julia was truly alone—all by herself in the farmhouse. Bird had told Lucky to guard the place, but she really hoped her little sister wasn't afraid.

Nobody had noticed Bird slipping onto the back of the truck as it idled outside the kitchen door—she'd taken the opportunity when it had presented itself. Just in case Hannah asked where she was, she'd prepared Julia with an alibi. Julia was to fib about Bird being up in the barn nursing a cat whose tail had been stepped on by a horse.

Now Bird lay still until she was pretty sure everyone had gone into the meeting. She had a cramp in her leg and the horse hairs from the blanket were making her itchy. But just as she began to uncover herself, another car drove quickly over the gravel and stopped. She waited while the door slammed and a woman's running footsteps headed for the store.

Okay. All's quiet, she thought. Time to figure out how I'm going to hear what's going on. Bird climbed off the truck and circled the store. At the far side was a window that was open just a crack. Bird smiled as she settled into the bushes and waited for the meeting to begin.

In less than a minute, the man who raised chickens in Cheltenham appeared at her window and looked outside. She tensed.

"It's getting hot in here already," he said loudly. "Bea, get help opening all these windows. Roxy, can you put on the fans?" He hoisted open the window to let in the cool evening air. Bird smiled. Even better.

It took a moment for Bird's ears to sort out individual voices from the cacophony. She heard smatterings of assorted—but definite—opinions. Some were more forceful than others. Names were bandied about and people accused. The more Bird heard, the more she believed that people would be better off if they thought before they spoke. Or didn't speak aloud at all, like animals—like she herself had done for so many years.

Finally, Bird heard Roxanne introduce Officers Paris and O'Hare. She couldn't quite hear Roxanne over the voices close to her window, but as soon as Officer Paris began to speak, the crowd quieted.

"Thanks for coming out tonight, folks," he began. "Your numbers show just how much interest this community has in safety." There were murmurs of assent.

"We've been very busy since yesterday." Rumbling asides and whispers punctuated Officer Paris's words.

"Thanks to those of you who came forward with information, we've interviewed three men today and are looking for a fourth. Before you ask for names, I'll tell you right now we're not giving them out. These men are innocent until proven guilty."

"One of them isn't," a woman's voice interjected. Bird recognized her as the owner of the coffee shop in Erin.

"We already know the identities of the suspects," called out a man. "Her ex, the cop and the farmhand."

"Who's the fourth?" asked another. Bird guessed that this speaker was Jim Wells, Ellen's husband.

Officer Paris tried to keep order. "Please, folks, leave the police work to the police. If everyone co-operates, we'll have this crime solved in no time, and the perpetrator will be behind bars."

"Where he *should* be!" a woman with a shrill voice shouted.

"Amen," added Jim Wells. "So, who's the fourth? You didn't answer my question."

The young policeman cleared his throat. "The fourth suspect is an unknown man who is currently being sought by the police. We don't know much about him at this time."

"Where does he live?" the shrill woman asked.

"It's possible that he's homeless."

This admission caused an outbreak of discussion. Bird wondered if the meeting could continue with so much commotion.

"Quiet!" commanded Roxanne. "Really, people! We'll never get anywhere like this!"

Once the room was still, Officer Paris spoke again. "If we all follow basic good sense, like locking our doors and being aware of what's happening around us, there is no reason for concern. Keep us informed of anything out of the ordinary, and no matter how small it seems, tell us anything that worries you."

"You talk about worry? I can't sleep with worry," murmured someone, a younger woman by the tone. "And now you tell us there's a homeless man out there, too?" Bird strained her ears to pick up her words.

Another joined in. "This has always been a safe community. Now a woman's been killed! And you don't know who did it!"

"We understand your concern." Officer Paris tried to soothe their fears. "We're taking this very seriously. No one wants this solved more than we do, and we're doing everything we can."

"Is that true?" Ellen Wells's voice rang out above the others, and the room went quiet. "Sandra Hall was going about her day, minding her own business when this happened. If you'd seen that poor woman lying on the ground covered in her own blood, as I did, moments from death, exposed to the world and as helpless as a newborn baby, you'd stop talking about protecting the suspects' identities and all this stuff about innocent until proven guilty. You'd want that monster tarred and feathered!"

Bird shuddered. Ellen sounded like she was ready do the job herself.

Her husband spoke. "When you said this community cares about safety, you got that right. And justice, too. If this community doesn't get justice from the police, it'll get justice for itself!"

As the murmurs grew again to a roar, Bird felt goosebumps rise all over her body.

"Folks, please!" Officer Paris had to shout to be heard. "We're working night and day. We're following leads and searching for clues. I urge you all to remain calm."

An elderly woman spoke up. Based on her Hungarian accent, Bird figured it was old Mrs. Goose. "Thank you, officers. We appreciate your visit very much." She paused slightly, as if trying to decide whether to say more. "You have to understand, we all know each other here. We're good people, and we know the good and the bad about each other. We get used to things being the same—and safe—and we get worried when things change." She swallowed and cleared her throat. "I want to ask us all to listen to the police and not let things get out of control."

The whole store filled with noise. People began to talk to each other, speaking louder and louder in order to be heard. Bird's ears picked out comments.

"It's obvious! Pierre Hall attacked his ex-wife."

"He's such a hothead."

"Who saw this homeless guy?"

"I think Philip Butler did it."

"But Pierre used to beat Sandra. That's why she left, you know."

"Don't forget Cliff Jones!"

"What about the homeless bum?"

"First I've heard, but it scares me!"

"Please! May I have your attention!"

"What's all this about Phil's secret past?"

"Pierre's always been strange."

"Where do they think the homeless guy lives?"

"If he's not locked up, somebody else will be next!"

"People, please! Calm down and listen!"

Bird slumped down on the ground outside the window. She knew these men and women. They were good people, as Mrs. Goose had said, but Paul had been right. The meeting was not going well, and she'd heard more than enough. She wanted to go home. But how?

As if in answer to Bird's wish, Mr. and Mrs. Pierson chose just that moment to make their own early exit. They passed so close to Bird that she was amazed they didn't notice her hiding in the bushes. She watched, holding her breath, as they climbed into their truck. The old blue Chevy kicked into action, then stopped. Pete got out and returned to the store, mumbling about how forgetful he was getting.

Bird didn't hesitate. This was her chance to get back to the farm before Hannah and Paul. She quietly ran to the back of the truck and carefully climbed on. Pete must have been moving hay that day, because the floor of the truck bed was soft with chaff. She lay as still as she could, and tried not to sneeze. Pete returned, backed out and drove off.

Bird was thrilled. All she had to do now was stay where she was until Pete and Laura entered their house, then she could dash home. If she ran fast she'd make it in ten minutes, maybe fifteen, and be back at Saddle Creek before Hannah and Paul.

Bird had just finished congratulating herself when the truck stopped—in front of the Saddle Creek farmhouse.

Laura opened her door. "Bird, honey? You can get out now. We thought we'd save you the trouble."

Bird sat up, astonished and embarrassed. "I didn't think ..."

"I know, dear, but I was powdering my nose in the rear view mirror when you hopped on. It's all right. We won't tell."

Pete opened his door and got out. "I would've done the same thing if I hadn't been invited. Sure as heck! Did you hear everything?"

Bird sighed as she jumped down to the ground. "You don't miss anything, do you? Did anyone else see me?"

"Nope," answered Pete. "And we wouldn't have either, if Laura wasn't such a beauty." He grinned at his wife, who tossed her head sassily.

Bird chuckled. "Thanks for the ride. And if it's okay with you ..."

"We won't tell, dear. Promise." Laura gave her a quick smile.

Pete looked her in the eye. "What did you think?"

"Of the meeting?"

Pete nodded.

Bird paused before she spoke, weighing her thoughts. "I'm worried. People are really scared and angry. I just hope nobody does anything stupid, you know?"

"Perhaps they just needed an opportunity to blow off steam. Get things off their chests. Keep the cops on their toes. I hope that's so."

"I hope so, too," said Bird.

"Well, good evening, dear," said Laura as she closed the door of the truck. "We don't want dear Hannah and her lovely beau to see us."

"Good night!" Bird waved. "And thanks again!"

"We'll be at the show on Friday!" Pete called out as the truck rolled away. "We wouldn't miss it."

Bird smiled. She loved the Piersons.

As she turned toward the house, Julia burst out of the front door followed by Lucky. "I was so scared! Lucky barked and barked and I was sure that the wild man was walking around the house trying to get in! I've never been so scared in my life. I'm *so so so* glad you're home!"

"I'm sorry! I didn't stop to think how scared you'd be or I wouldn't have gone." Bird hugged her little sister tightly. "You're shivering."

A man was here! A man was here! I scared him away!

Good dog!

As they hurried together up the walk, Bird checked for signs of the intruder. There! Under the living room window. Footprints. Several of them were clearly embedded in the new loam that Hannah had put in the gardens that very morning. And under the dining room window, too. Julia and Lucky hadn't imagined things. Not wanting to frighten her sister further, Bird said nothing.

Once inside, the girls locked the door and turned on all the lights, even though the sun had not yet set. To keep busy until the adults returned, they decided to make hot chocolate and oatmeal cookies. They went into the kitchen and got out all the ingredients. Bird stirred the cocoa on the stove and Julia mixed the eggs with the vanilla, butter and brown sugar. As soon as the electric beaters started up, Bird yelled, "I'll be back in a sec! Keep it going for three minutes!"

Bird went into the hall and dialed 911. She instructed the police operator to come immediately—a person had been looking in the windows around the house and might still be there.

"Will someone be here soon?" she asked.

"As soon as you hang up, I'll pass it along."

"Thanks." Bird hung up without delay and entered the kitchen.

"That's enough, Julia!" Bird said over the noise of the beaters.

"It's not three minutes!"

"It's enough anyway."

The cookies took twelve minutes to bake. By the time Julia took them out of the oven, sniffing the delicious aroma, both Hannah's truck and a police car had arrived at Saddle Creek.

5

THE MOON AND THE STARS

Out of breath, Tan reached his campsite and darted under the rigged-up canopy, his back to the rocks. In one hand he held tightly to his slingshot and with the other he grappled for a heavy, large stone. That coyote had followed him, for sure. It was small but fierce. Tan distrusted all coyotes. They were sly and persistent and brave around people. They also stole his food from under his nose and killed rabbits before he had a chance. But this one was worse. It seemed to have a personal vendetta. Tan must not fall asleep tonight. Again.

THE TWO VEHICLES STOPPED in front of the house at exactly the same moment. Bird and Julia watched the action through the window. It was nine-thirty and the sun had just set. Hannah and Paul spoke with the two police officers, one male and one female. Bird guessed that Officers Paris and O'Hare were still at the meeting.

Hannah's gaze followed the beam of the female officer's flashlight to the footprints under the windows. Paul put his hand reassuringly on her shoulder.

Julia gasped as she realized why the police were there. "There really *was* somebody trying to get in?"

"Yeah. I called 911 when you were running the beaters."

"And you didn't tell me?"

"You were already scared enough."

"Bird! You should've said something!"

"And had you screaming in the corner until the police came?" Julia frowned. "Okay, maybe, but still ..."

"I should tell them where I really was tonight," Bird whispered. "They're going to freak if they find out I was alone!"

"But I can't lie to the police."

"They won't ask! And I lied, too. When Aunt Hannah asked me where you were, I told her you were in the barn with the cat. I don't want to get in trouble."

"You'd be in far less trouble than me, Julia."

"I guess."

"Okay. If they don't ask I won't tell, but if they do, I will. That way I don't lie, and there's a chance we don't get in trouble."

"Sounds good."

The front door opened and Hannah, Paul and the two officers entered. Hannah hugged the girls tightly. Lucky jumped all over them, wagging his tail.

"You poor kids! To think we were at a meeting about this horrible event and the man we're looking for was here, trying to get in. I don't even want to imagine what might've happened!"

"Hannah." Paul's voice was calm. "The police have told us not to jump to any conclusions. We don't know that this is the same man. It might've been an attempted burglary." He looked at the girls. "Are you two all right?"

Julia and Bird nodded. "I ... we ... didn't know he was out there," Julia said. "Lucky barked his head off for a bit, and then stopped. It was Bird who saw the footprints under the windows when she came back from ..." Julia stopped herself just in time.

"From checking it out. I went outside to see why Lucky was barking and I saw the footprints," Bird jumped in. "I didn't want Julia to be upset so I called 911 when she was busy making cookies."

The female officer—her name tag read Beth Richardson—spoke. "That was the right thing to do. You were also very smart to have locked the windows, which he tried to open. There are hand smears all over them. Most people lock the doors and forget about the windows." She took out her pencil and pad. "What time did the dog start barking?"

Bird looked at Julia. Julia hesitated. "Well, Aunt Hannah left around quarter to seven, so it was probably around eight o'clock?" She looked at Bird for support.

Bird nodded. "Probably." So far, so good.

"Eight?" the officer asked. "Why did you wait until nine to call?"

Bird opened her mouth to answer, but nothing came out. Oh no, she thought. Not this again. She tried again. Nothing.

Julia answered for her. "She didn't go out to look until then."

Bird wanted to hug her sister, but she didn't dare make eye contact.

"Is that why?" Officer Richardson asked Bird pointedly.

Bird nodded.

The male officer, Lou Polito, addressed Bird. "Your Aunt Hannah told us that you've seen a 'wild' man around. Can you tell us more about that?"

They were on safer ground now, and Bird relaxed. Her vocal chords worked. She spoke rapidly in case they stopped co-operating again. "Yesterday after dinner, when my horse and I were out on the trails, a man jumped right out of nowhere. He wanted to talk, I could tell, but Sunny spooked and raced home. Later I realized that he looked like the police sketch. I was so glad that my horse ran away! And, today, I think someone was in the bushes when I was riding out there." Bird gestured to the front paddock.

Hannah gasped. "You didn't tell me that! I would never have left you girls alone!"

Bird felt another stab of guilt. She *had* known, and she'd left her little sister alone.

"What made you think that someone was here earlier today?" asked Officer Polito.

"My horse ... spooked." She could hardly tell them that Sunny had *told* her.

Officer Richardson looked up from her pad. "Can you describe this man?"

"Yes. Well, he looked homeless. And lost. Wild. Dirty. Scruffy. Rough dark hair, dark eyes, dirty skin. He was mostly naked. Except for dark blue gym shorts and old white sneakers."

Officer Richardson smiled at Bird kindly. "Thank you."

Officer Polito finished the interview. "We'll look around outside the house, take footprint casts and dust for fingerprints before we leave. We may bring a dog over to follow the scent, if it's not too dry. Call if there's any reason, big or small. We can be here in minutes. Here's my card. Put it beside the phone. Call me directly at any hour."

"Thanks, officers," said Hannah as she walked them out. "We'll stay inside and keep all the doors locked. And windows," she added quickly.

Officers Polito and Richardson went to the car. They took their kits out of the trunk and began the careful work of retrieving evidence.

An hour later, the cruiser finally drove away. The family sat around the kitchen table with tall glasses of milk and Julia's cooled, freshly made cookies.

"How was the meeting?" asked Bird innocently, steering the conversation away from the evening's events at Saddle Creek.

Paul thought for a moment. "It may have done more harm than good. People got angry and upset."

"They're scared," added Hannah. "They fear for their safety."

"You were back sooner than we thought," said Bird. "I called the police because I didn't know when you'd be home."

"It was the right thing to do. If there's ever a problem, that's who to call." Hannah pointed at Officer Polito's card, stuck on the bulletin board over the phone. She put the empty glasses in the dishwasher and wiped the counter. "I don't know about you folks, but I'm beat. I'm ready for bed."

"Me, too," said Julia, yawning. "Bird, can I sleep in your room tonight?"

"Of course. I need the company."

Hannah motioned to Julia. "Come on. I'll help you with the futon."

They headed up the stairs, Hannah's arm around Julia's shoulders, leaving Bird and Paul downstairs to lock up. They let Lucky out, and stood together at the kitchen door. The moon was large and bright in the clear night sky.

"You know, when the moon is full, its brightness obscures the stars, even though they're up there, too," said Paul. "We see them only after the moon begins to dim."

"That's totally poetic!"

"I try." He smiled, then looked surprised. "Did you hear what I just said?"

"The brightness of the moon obscures the stars?"

"It just came to me! Sometimes what appears to be obvious obscures the actual truth."

Bird thought about that. "You can't see the forest for the trees?"

"Almost, but not quite."

"Okay. What are you talking about?"

"The meeting tonight. It looks obvious to most people that Pierre Hall is the culprit. He's got a violent reputation and it was his ex-wife who was the victim."

"And to us it looks obvious that it's the wild man. He's so weird. He's creeping me out." Bird shivered.

Paul put his hand on her shoulder. "And yet, neither one has been proven guilty. We might have to look past the moon and examine the stars before we find the truth. Just a thought."

Bird nodded slowly, thinking it out. "It's a good thought."

Lucky came back, wagging his tail and quite content. Paul locked the door behind him and began to turn off the lights.

"You go on up to bed, Bird. You've had a long day." He ruffled her hair fondly as she scooted past him to the stairs.

6

PIERRE HALL

Tan watched as the lights turned on, room by room, from the upstairs down. In spite of the coyote, he'd been drawn back to the farmhouse. He had to tell the girl what happened. He couldn't trust anyone else, and he would try until he succeeded. But a man—the man from next door who neglected his horses—was making a racket at the front door. The echoes of his fist against the wood reverberated in the still night air, and Tan covered his ears to block out the sound. Thankfully, nobody had come looking for him. Yet. He was still free. And freedom was everything. The coyote wasn't near, for the moment, and the night was young. He would be patient. He would wait.

JUST AS BIRD had slipped under her covers, a loud banging sound got her attention. She jumped up and looked out her bedroom window at the stoop below. "Julia!" she whispered. "You'll never guess who's at the door!"

"Who?"

"Look for yourself."

Julia crouched down beside Bird to see. She gasped. "Pierre from next door! What's he doing here?"

"Let's find out."

Bird and Julia waited until Paul and Hannah had hurried downstairs in their robes, then crept silently down the stairs. They hid behind the stairwell, where they could observe the action.

Pierre Hall pounded relentlessly on the door.

Neither girl knew Pierre well. He worked next door and lived in an apartment above the barn. They'd often seen him around, but there was something about him that they instinctively avoided. He was odd, simple as that.

Paul opened the door. "Pierre! What can we do for you?"

"I got something to show you." Pierre looked blurry-eyed and dishevelled. By his demeanour and his breath, Bird figured that he'd had quite a few beers. She could smell it from all the way across the hall.

Paul and Hannah ushered him into the kitchen and closed the hall door, probably hoping not to wake the sleeping girls. Bird and Julia crept closer to listen.

"They left me this." Bird heard paper crumpling. "Cowards! Didn't dare show themselves."

There was a pause. Bird assumed Paul and Hannah were reading whatever Pierre was showing them.

"It was tacked to my door. I was having a few with my pals at the bar. I found it when I came back."

"Have you called the police?" Paul asked.

"No. And I'm not going to. They think I killed my ex with a tire iron! They took DNA. I didn't do it! But I don't have an alibi." Pierre sounded miserable. "Let's have a drink."

Bird listened to Hannah's slippered feet cross the kitchen floor. The tap ran and a glass was filled. "This note is threatening," she said. "The police should know about it."

"They wouldn't do anything."

Paul's chair creaked. "You don't know that, Pierre."

The glass slid across the table with a rumble. "You have something better than this?"

Hannah answered, "Not tonight."

Paul's chair scraped. "Pierre, call the police about that note. There's nothing we can do that the police wouldn't do better."

"You could protect me!"

"How?" asked Paul.

"Let me stay here tonight."

Bird was taken aback. The idea of their smelly, drunken neighbour sleeping on the couch didn't appeal to her at all.

"Look, I'll be no trouble. Where's your can?" With no warning, Pierre pushed open the kitchen door and immediately tripped over Bird and Julia. They yelped in surprise and tried to scramble out of his way.

"Damn kids!" he yelled.

Lucky began to bark loudly, and he rushed along the hall to Bird and Julia. Pierre, who'd just got to his feet, was knocked over again by the dog.

"Damn dog!" He kicked out and missed Lucky by a few inches.

Lucky growled.

Hannah grabbed the dog by his collar and stood between Pierre and the girls. "Pierre, you're drunk. I don't want you staying here tonight."

"You read that note! They're coming to get me!"

"Call the police. They'll protect you."

"They think I'm guilty!"

Paul spoke. "You're frightening everybody, including the dog."

"What if Pierre stays in the barn tonight?" asked Bird helpfully. "We could give him that blow-up mattress and some blankets."

"The barn?" sniffed Pierre. "Like some am ... mi ... nal? Animal?"

"It's not so bad," said Bird. "We sleep up there lots of times, when we're waiting to help with a birthing—it's actually quite nice."

"It's damp and noisy, with all the snorting and farting of horses." Pierre drew himself up from the floor. "Seems I can't count on my neighbours. Thanks for nothing."

Paul opened the front door. "Pierre, don't make us the bad guys. The choice is yours. Call the police or stay in the barn."

Pierre walked outside with great dignity. He turned around, shook his fist and repeated, "Thanks for nothing!" He slammed the door behind him.

They all stood staring at the closed door.

"Holy smoke," said Julia.

"That was upsetting," added Hannah.

"What does the note say?" Bird asked. "Is it still in the kitchen?"

Paul nodded. "I think so. He forgot to take it."

Bird dashed to the kitchen and snatched up the note. She read aloud:

"Pierre Hall, you're a bully and a drunk. You're going to feel what it's like to have a tire iron across the head. Be afraid."

"This is awful." Bird dropped the note and wiped her hands on her pajamas, as if it was contaminated. "We have to call the police ourselves. Pierre won't."

Hannah nodded and picked up the phone. She punched in the numbers from Officer Polito's card and waited. The voice mail was on, so Hannah left him the details of Pierre's visit.

She put down the receiver with a worried frown. "That's all we can do tonight. Let's try to get some sleep."

Tan watched as the neighbour left the house, and the lights in each window were extinguished. He'd hidden himself in the horses' walk-in shelter in the paddock across from the front door, armed with his slingshot. He could trust the girl. He knew it. Adults could never hear what he said, and they never knew what he meant. That was always the trouble. Nobody understood him. But the girl would understand. She might even give him food. He would find a way to get to her tonight. He had to. Nothing would stop him this time. He could see that an upstairs window was open. This would be simple. All he'd have to do was climb up like Spider-Man, remove the screen …

All at once, hot breath whooshed across Tan's neck, and he spun. A huge creature was standing in the dark, so close that Tan couldn't even make out what it was. He screamed—a muted, harsh, stunted sound—but the creature didn't budge. Tan's eyes flicked around. There was nowhere to run. He was trapped in the shelter with a monster.

Sundancer moved a little closer. He contemplated crushing the man, then rejected the idea. This human was going nowhere. Let him sweat. He stomped his front foot hard, inches away from the man's legs.

Tan jumped in agitation and flattened himself against the wooden boards. He had to think of a way to handle this. Fast.

Sunny snorted. He leaned his neck forward and licked Tan's chest.

Tan fell to the ground. He'd made his decision. He would play dead.

Sundancer lifted his upper lip and shook his head. Yuck. The man tasted disgusting, even with the salt of his sweat. He tossed his mane and walked out into the cool night. The grass in the paddock was delicious.

7

PUTTING UP THE HAY

Tan awoke with a start. Where was he? He had to get back to his tent … it was already morning and he would be seen.

BIRD AWOKE EARLY the next morning. It was Wednesday. With all the goings-on the night before, she hadn't slept well, and her head felt thick. She lay in her bed and opened one eye. Julia had deserted the futon and was sprawled across her bed.

Outside, the sun was shining through the bright green leaves and the birds were chirping cheerfully. Without disturbing Julia, Bird slid out from under the covers, picked up her clothes from where she'd dropped them the night before and tiptoed downstairs.

In the kitchen, Lucky thumped his tail. His handsome brown face wore a sheepish expression.

Let me guess. Bird gave him a look. *I'm too late?*

One minute too late. I couldn't help it.

Lucky, you've got to tell someone when you have to go out.

I don't like waking people up.

We'd rather wake up than clean up.

Lucky hung his head.

Bark or whine like other dogs. You're too polite for your own good.

I'll try.

Where is it?

What?

The mess.

Lucky looked under the kitchen table and Bird's eyes followed. She sighed. *And do you still have to chew things? Your baby teeth fell out long ago. No more excuses.*

I'm ashamed, girl. Let me out?

Bird patted him on the head. The little guy was worried. *I'll clean up everything, never fear. And Hannah won't miss the oven mitt.* She opened the kitchen door and Lucky bounded out. But instead of heading for the bushes like usual, he tore off across the field sounding a sudden, shrill bark.

Bird followed his streaking form and saw what was causing his panic. A human figure was slinking away along the fence line, followed by Sundancer, prancing tensely with flattened ears. It was the wild man. Cody was stalking him, too, from the other direction.

With a clutching in her gut, Bird ran across the lane to watch. The small coyote was creeping out long and low. Step by step he neared the far corner of the field where the man was heading. Cody wouldn't hurt anyone unless he was attacked, but he sure wouldn't hesitate to scare someone. Bird watched as Cody sprang, and she cringed at the man's scream.

Sunny reared at the far corner of the fence, then spun and kicked out. Cody reappeared from the woods a moment later, and Lucky came bounding toward her. Bird took a deep breath. The man was gone.

Hopefully, he wouldn't come back, but that man had been around far, far too much. Who was he? What was he up to? Why did he keep showing up? And was he harmless, or harmful? Bird thought about it for a moment. He did such odd things, but for some reason she wasn't totally afraid of him. Should she be? She considered her reaction. He was creepy, and she was suspicious of him. She didn't like him lurking around, but she was more curious than afraid. Bird shook her head. This needed more thought.

Lucky reached Bird, wagging his tail wildly. *I scared him away, girl! I'm a good dog now!*

Yes, Lucky. Good dog! Bird gave his chin a firm scratching.

Sunny trotted up to the fence. *The wild man. He was here all night. In my shed. I licked him.*

You did what?

Never mind. He's scared, but he'll be back.

Why do you say that?

Just a feeling.

Is he dangerous, Sunny? Does he want to hurt us?

Maybe. Maybe not. He's crazy. You can't tell what he'll do.

He's weirding me out.

Me, too, Bird. Are we jumping this morning?

Good idea.

Bird went back inside the house, cleaned up Lucky's messes and grabbed her helmet and chaps. Cliff was in the barn when Bird arrived to get her saddle.

"You're up early, Cliff. It's only six o'clock."

"I couldn't sleep. Thought I'd get moving." Cliff spoke quietly, much more so than usual.

Bird stopped in her tracks. "What's wrong?"

"Ah, nothing. I don't want to worry you."

"I'm already worried. Tell me."

Cliff reached into his pocket and pulled out a piece of paper. "If you're already worried, this is not going to help."

"When did you get this?" she asked, taking the note from him.

"It was on my door. I found it when I let Boss in for the night."

"Did you call the police?"

"No."

Bird read the words aloud.

"*Cliff Jones, you are duly warned. You are going to feel what it's like to get a tire iron across the head. Be afraid.*"

Bird handed the note back. "Cliff, you're not the only one who got a letter like this."

"Who else?"

"Pierre Hall. He came over last night looking for protection. He wouldn't call the police so Hannah did. You have to, too."

"I thought about it, but they won't believe me. They already think I'm the bad guy. They'll figure I wrote it myself."

"Cliff, listen to me. You're innocent! How can the police prove that if they don't know what's happening?"

Cliff took a moment to consider Bird's advice. "They can't. You're right. I'll call them."

Bird smiled grimly. "It's the right thing. Meanwhile, I bet Philip Butler got one, too. And the wild man would've got one if they knew where he lived."

"Who's 'they,' do you think?"

Bird tilted her head. "Very good question."

That question was still on Bird's mind as she and Sunny worked in the ring. Who had sent the notes? They walked, trotted and cantered in circles, keeping a steady rhythm. It was boring work, but essential. To be ready for the show ring, a horse had to be fit and limber, and respond willingly to leg aids. Abby Malone had told Bird to think of the jumps as obstacles to a steady course on the ground. It was a helpful piece of wisdom, one that helped calm her nerves when she saw the size of the jumps.

Where are you, Bird? Your mind is all fuzzy. Sunny's thoughts broke into Bird's own. *What's up?*

I'm wondering who threatened Cliff and Pierre.

Oh. Can we jump now? Or go for a ride? I can't take much more of these circle exercises. My muscles are aching and I'm dizzy.

Bird shook her head and laughed out loud. *Why don't you complain a little more? It may be hard now, but you'll thank me Friday at the show.*

You're heartless.

You're complicated.

Complicated?

What other horse argues with its rider like this?

What other rider argues back?

Enough, Sunny! Concentrate.

As Sunny and Bird were finishing up their flatwork, a beige Toyota turned into their lane—Liz's mother. It was early; it seemed as if nobody had slept well. Regardless, it was as good a time as any to find out if Phil had gotten a note like Cliff's and Pierre's.

Bird waited patiently for Patty Brown to let Liz off at the barn. She made her move as the car drove back down the drive.

"Hello, Mrs. Brown," Bird called out from Sunny's back as the car slowed.

"Morning, Bird." Patty looked tired.

"Are you all right?" asked Bird.

"Not really." Bird saw a tear forming in her eye.

"I'm sorry." Bird knew this was her opening, and she jumped in. "But it seems that you're not alone. Cliff isn't all right either. A horrible message was nailed to his door last night."

Patty's eyebrows shot up. "No!"

"It was a threat. And Pierre next door got one, too."

"What did they say?"

"They were the same. Something awful about a tire iron."

"And that he should be afraid?"

Now Bird knew for sure that Phil had received the same note.

"Philip got home late and found one stuck under the

knocker," Patty continued. "I wasn't going to say anything, but now that I know ..."

Bird nodded. "You're absolutely right. The only thing to do is to call the police, or else whoever's threatening people will get away with it."

Patty nodded slowly. "Of course. I'll call them now."

Bird waved goodbye to Patty and continued up to the wash-stall with Sunny, deep in thought. Who had written the notes, she wondered again, and why? It was upsetting.

By the time Paul left for work and Hannah and Julia arrived at the barn, Cliff and Bird had finished cleaning the stalls and had organized the hayloft. They were expecting twenty-four wagons of hay—two were already on their way, and would arrive any time.

"I brought extra gloves and old cotton shirts," Hannah said. "Cliff, is there water in the tack room fridge?"

"Lots."

Cliff went out to the drive shed to get the conveyor belt. He pulled it with the tractor and parked it on the big orange tarpaulin, which was spread on the arena floor to catch the loose hay.

Liz rolled her eyes. "My luck that you're bringing in the hay on a day that Mom drops me off and I ... leaves me."

Julia laughed wickedly. "You have no idea how tough it gets. You get sweaty and prickly and so hot you get woozy. Strong men weep."

"And that's supposed to b ... be encouraging?"

"You don't *have* to help, girly-girl." Julia laid down the challenge with humour in her voice.

"Actually, it's girl-power time," said Bird. "Let me see your muscles."

Liz flexed her skinny biceps.

"First class. You'll have no problem. There's a reason why no men are around when the hay shows up."

Cliff popped his head around the corner. "Oh, really?"

Bird grinned. "Besides you!"

The hay wagons started to arrive, loaded with more than two hundred bales each. The hay farmers would drop off a full wagon and return home with an emptied one, which would go directly back to the field and get filled up again. To keep things going, the Saddle Creek team needed to have each wagon unloaded by the time the next one arrived.

Hannah and the younger girls positioned themselves in the hayloft. Bird stayed below with Cliff. Cliff plugged in the conveyor belt and it started up, making a racket of clickity-clacks. He and Bird began to send the heavy bales up to the loft.

The work in the loft was easy at first, carrying and stacking the bales tightly against each other. First row lengthwise, then next row across. Soon, though, as more wagons were unloaded, and the stacks got higher, it got much harder. Cliff sent Bird up to help, and continued the ground job himself. As long as the wagons kept coming there would be no break. Old farmers joked that their break was in winter, when nothing could grow.

Between wagon number five and wagon number six, Hannah brought out a huge jug of lemonade. They all sat outside on the front bench, grateful for the rest and the slight breeze.

"Your face is all r ... red and sweaty," said Liz.

"You need a mirror," retorted Julia. "You look like a lobster."

"And your shirt is stuck to your body! Gross."

"So's yours! You should talk, Liz-ard."

Cliff laughed. "Save your energy. Another load is coming."

Sure enough, the rumble of another hay wagon could be heard from down the road. The girls groaned.

"Drink up and man your stations." Hannah screwed the lid on the lemonade jug and put on her sweaty gloves.

Bird waited until the others had left for the loft. "Aunt

Hannah," she said quietly. "The wild man was around again this morning."

Hannah looked startled. "When?"

"Around five-thirty, when I came out to ride."

"What was he doing?"

"Running away as fast as he could. Cody and Sunny chased him."

Hannah shook her head slowly. "I'll give the police a heads-up. Which way did you see him go?"

"Toward the back, along the fenceline in Sunny's field. Cody and Sunny gave him a good scare. And Lucky got in the act, too." Bird knew that Lucky would want Hannah to think well of him. "Oh, and Phil Butler and Cliff both got those horrible threats, too, like Pierre."

Hannah was startled. "How do you know that?"

"Cliff told me about his note this morning, and Mrs. Brown told me when she dropped off Liz. They're both going to tell the police."

Hannah looked at her watch. It was just after twelve. "I'll call Paul. He'll want to know."

"What will I want to know?" Paul had come up behind Hannah, finger on lips to ensure Bird's silence. Hannah spun around to face him.

"Paul! You scared me." She gave him a hug. "Cliff and Phil got the same letter that Pierre got, and the wild man was here early this morning."

The broad smile disappeared from Paul's face. "Not good."

"It feels like we're right in the middle of this," said Hannah. "And I don't like it."

"Look, Hannah, I'll take over hay duty. I'm free for a couple of hours unless an emergency comes up. You go call the police. Tell them everything. These are important pieces of the puzzle."

Hannah stripped off her gloves again and handed them to Paul. "Five down. Knock yourself out." She smiled briefly and strode down to the house.

"Come on, Bird," said Paul. "Round six."

Cliff Jones, you are duly warned. You're going to feel what it's like to get a tire iron across the head. Be afraid!

8

FIRE!

Tan was back in his tent. The coyote was never far away, and that made him nervous. The animal was small and clever. Other coyotes wanted food. They would steal but leave him alone. But this coyote seemed to be on a mission. Like a watchdog. Tan would have to get rid of him before he could get to the girl and tell her what happened. Poison? A trap? A stone to the head with his slingshot? He'd have to do something, and soon.

But now he really needed to feed the horses at the barn next door to the girl's. On his scouting trips, he'd noticed that the man slept all morning, so now Tan gave them water and hay before he woke up. He liked this new feeling of being needed, even though nobody would ever know. Tan looked around for the coyote. He couldn't see him. Taking a deep breath, Tan sprinted as fast as he could.

THE HAY WAS FINALLY IN. Cliff was sweeping the barn, and Liz and Julia were lying in the wading pool that doubled as a water jump, discussing which boys at school were cute. Hannah and Paul were in the kitchen making a late lunch, and Bird was in her room, changing into clean clothes after a long, cool shower.

She slipped a soft white T-shirt over her undershirt, and pulled on her favourite green shorts. She was looking around for her running shoes when an acrid odour floated on the breeze through her open window. Smoke. Bird looked outside and

73

gasped. A split second later, she was thundering down the stairs, shoes in hand.

"Fire! Fire! Guy and Bunny's barn!" She raced downstairs. "Aunt Hannah! Paul! Call the fire department! I need to help Pierre!" Before Hannah could stop her, she was out the door and on her bike.

Bird pedalled as fast as she could, her legs aching from the work of putting up the hay. Bird knew that Pierre often slept all day. She feared that the horses might still be in their stalls, locked in and helpless. Bird remembered Hannah telling her that the smoke killed horses before the flames. They fainted from the smoke, then got burned. She pushed away the thought.

Bird raced up Pierre's driveway. Her feet hit the ground and she dropped her bike. Just to be sure Pierre was awake, she threw a rock at his bedroom window over the barn. Her aim was good and it smashed through. If he was still in there, Bird thought, he'd hear it.

She held her breath and threw open the barn door. Smoke billowed out, stinging her eyes and heating her face. She coughed and jumped back, reassessing the situation. The other doors were open on the far side of the barn, and through the smoke she saw a human figure opening stall doors.

"Pierre!" Bird yelled as loud as she could. "I'll help!"

Bird pulled off her T-shirt, dunked it in the water trough and wrapped it over her face. She took a deep breath and ran in, grabbing the first stall door latch she could reach. Instantly, pain shot through her hand. The metal was too hot to touch! She took off her shorts, swaddled her hand with the green cotton fabric and began again.

Get out! she messaged to the frightened animals. *Now! It's not safe in here! Get out now!*

This is my home! A big grey was panicking, his head weaving from side to side.

Your home is in danger. Go outside where there is no smoke and fire.

Fire? A tall, bony, older chestnut thoroughbred was alarmed.

Yes. Tell all the others.

The geldings stood there, frozen with fear.

Bird looked around for Pierre, but now she could see no one. She was alone, and the smoke was getting thicker by the second. The heat was almost unbearable. The roar of the fire was deafening. It was getting harder to breathe and Bird could barely see. She might have very little time before the barn would fall in on itself.

Bunny and Guy stabled ten horses. She'd opened stalls for six, but none wanted to leave the barn. She kept going. She thought some stalls were empty, but the smoke was so heavy that it was hard to tell.

A dark shape huddled against the wall in the next stall. Bird peered through the smoke. It was a small bay Welsh pony cowering in the corner, barely visible until he moved his head.

Bird waved her arms to get him going. *Get out! The barn's on fire.*

I can't! I'm afraid!

Frustrated, Bird tried a new approach. *What's your name?*

Bandito.

Good boy, Bandito. Bird tried to remain calm and unhurried. *I'm Bird. I live next door. It's time to go outside now.*

Hello, Bird. Outside now, is it? Okay.

To Bird's amazement, Bandito trotted out of his stall, down the hall and into his field. That was easy. Bird wondered if it might work again.

Did you hear, horses? It's time to go outside now. Outside.

One by one, the horses stumbled out of their stalls and staggered outside, heads to the ground and drooling. Bird was stunned. By calming herself down and simplifying the message, she'd made it possible for the animals to respond. Only two more to go and they'd all be safe.

But as Bird turned to the next stall, the stable swirled around her. Her knees weakened and began to buckle. She thought of the horses still trapped and fought hard against oblivion. Then it was dark.

Bird awoke to the sounds of sirens. She coughed. Then she coughed harder and harder, until she vomited. Rolling herself over onto her stomach, Bird retched into the grass. Now up on her knees, she trembled and shook and vomited again until there was nothing left in her stomach. When she finally lifted her head, she saw green through the slits of her puffed eyes. She was outside, hidden in a grassy little dip in the land, far from the barn. The last thing she remembered was being inside it.

With no strength left, Bird let her head flop back down, trying to avoid her own mess. Did she hear someone calling her name? She strained her neck. Her vision was blurry, but she began to count the horses through squinted eyes. They were lined up along the fence, staring at the burnt rubble that used to be their home. One, two, three, the pony, five, six, the grey, eight, nine, the bony old thoroughbred. All ten had gotten out. They'd all made it.

Bird welled up with tears of relief, and the salt stung her eyes sharply. Salt heals the human body better than anything else, Bird remembered, so she tried to ignore the pain. She sank back into the green grass and let her mind wander.

She'd once heard the story of a horse named Atticus, a strong young Dutch warmblood who'd fought his way out of a burning barn. The owner had arrived too late. He stood helplessly watching the fire eat up his barn. Tears rolled down his face as he thought of his eight beautiful horses dying inside. Then he felt a nudge on his shoulder, and when he turned to look he saw an amazing sight. Atticus, singed all over, with blood pouring down his face from a wound caused by a falling beam, stood there behind him. Alive. The only horse to survive. The man fell to his knees in thanks. Atticus became a legend that day. Nobody knows what kind of courage, ingenuity and strength he'd needed to get out of that burning barn. The owner claimed it was a miracle. There was even an article written about it in *Horse Sport* magazine.

Wait a minute, Bird thought, snapping back to the present. I *did* hear someone calling. She caught a glimpse of her body as she attempted to lift her head. Am I lying here in my underwear? Memories of hot metal and searing smoke came flooding back, but how had she gotten outside? Who'd closed the gate to the horses' field? When had the fire trucks arrived? Who'd gotten the last horses out? Nothing made sense.

She peered at the barn—or what was left of it. Black smoke billowed up from an unrecognizable heap of charred timbers, broken windows and jagged steel posts. The firemen held hoses that gushed streams of water, and debris hissed and smoked as the water evaporated almost before it hit the heat. A shiver passed through Bird's body. *I might have died in that fire.*

I wouldn't let that happen, Bird girl.

Cody. Bird looked around. There, standing behind shrubs and a fence post, was the small coyote. He was singed from head to toe.

You saved me, Cody?

It is my duty.

Bird's stinging tears reappeared. *Thank you, Cody. For the rest of my life I'll be grateful. But you're burnt. Are you hurt?*

No. It's only fur. But the man is not good.

What man?

The one with little covering.

The wild man?

Yes.

He's not a good man?

He is a good man, but troubled. He is not good now. He is in pain from the fire.

He was in the fire?

Yes. He helped get out the animals. Then he saw you. He could not get you away from the fire. He fell down.

He tried to save me?

Yes.

You dragged him away, too?

Yes.

Where is he now?

Gone back to his den.

Oh, Cody! He needs help with his burns.

He will not get help. He is like an animal. He's as wary of humans as my fellows.

Can you show me where he lives?

Later. Now, humans approach. Suddenly, Cody was gone.

Bird's head ached and her eyes stung. Who was this man? And where had Pierre been while all this was happening?

"Bird!" She recognized Hannah's voice before she could see her. "Oh, honey! We couldn't find you anywhere! We thought you were still in the ..." Hannah dropped down on the ground beside Bird, laughing and crying with relief and holding her tightly. Bird's arm felt the warm tears from her aunt's eyes.

Bird heard another familiar voice. "Medics! Over here!" Paul's commanding presence was a comfort. "Stand back! Make room!"

Bird closed her eyes and darkness fell again.

9

RESCUE

Tan was in agony. His skin was raw. His throat felt like a hot poker had been rammed down it, and he could barely see. He'd dragged himself over rough earth and stones to his tent, then passed out. Now awake, he wished for nothing more than to pass out again. He couldn't remember ever being so alone in his life. He wanted his mother.

But wait. He remembered something odd. The coyote—dragging him out of the barn onto the grass. Had that really happened? Could that be true? Tan touched his arm and flinched. He couldn't tell if the pain was from burns or bites. The coyote hated him! He wouldn't have saved his life—unless he saved him so he could get him later. Or maybe he was trying to eat him. Tan drifted off before he could figure it out.

BIRD DREAMED THAT she was upstairs in bed, and that Hannah and Paul were in the kitchen below, talking.

In the dream, Hannah said, "Sundancer won't calm down. There he goes again, Paul. Back and forth, back and forth along the fence." She sounded far, far away.

"It's almost as if he's worried about Bird." Paul's voice gurgled. Was he under water?

"I'd love to tell him that she'll be fine. And thank heavens, she will."

"It was a close call. She's lucky that she got out of the barn before it fell in." Paul's voice grew louder, then fainter.

"She has minor burns, but you're right, she's lucky. We're all lucky."

Bird dreamed that Lucky, lying on the kitchen floor, sat up at the sound of his name.

Then, Paul was saying, "When she wakes up I'll ask her what she meant about the wild man."

"I think she said he helped get the horses out."

"I couldn't make much sense of what she was saying."

"Me neither. Anyway, it can wait. We'll let her sleep as long as she can." Hannah clucked sadly. "Would you look at that horse tossing his head and hopping around. He's quite upset."

Bird began to wonder what kind of dream she was having. It sounded like a real conversation. Now, Sunny entered her hazy consciousness. His energy was intense.

Bird! It's me. Sundancer. The horse? Remember? Come on! Answer me! I know you're in there. I saw them carry you in. News flash: your hair's gone. It wasn't as nice as mine, anyway. Bird! Can you hear me? I'm worried! If you don't answer me right now I'll jump over the fence and kick in the door! One ... two ... three ... okay. You asked for it.

A loud, long whinny cut through the fog. Sundancer. Suddenly, a deafening "thwack" reverberated through the house.

Bird tensed, now fully awake. She heard people run outside. Hannah and Paul's voices carried up clearly through Bird's window.

"Sundancer!" scolded Hannah loudly. "What the heck are you up to?"

There was a slight pause. Bird heard hooves trotting quickly across the gravel, then landing on grass with a soft thud.

"Did that really happen?" asked Paul. "Did Sunny just kick in the front door, then jump back into his field?"

Hannah answered, "I think so. But if you weren't here with me, I'd think I was dreaming."

Bird carefully opened her eyes, confused about whose dream was whose. Her eyes were swollen and gooey, but she could see.

Sunny?

Bird! Finally! You got me in trouble with Hannah.

What do you mean? I'm in bed.

Forget it. You had me worried. Don't do that again!

Why is everything my fault?

Can you come out? I want to get a good look at your hair.

My hair?

I guess you haven't had a chance to admire yourself since the fire.

Ohmygosh. I can feel it. It's falling out all over my pillow!

Just throw on the riding hat and you're done.

I think it's still there at the back, but the front! Ohmygosh!

Settle down.

Right. It's just hair. Sunny, we have to go look for the wild man.

No.

Yes! Cody told me he helped get the horses out. And me out, too! Cody said he was burned, that he needs help.

He's a freak.

Maybe so, but he's a good freak if he helped those horses.

Good point.

Will you help? I can't do it alone.

Okay, but this will end badly.

Find Cody. He'll know where the wild man is. I'll be downstairs as fast as I can. Which isn't too fast. I don't feel that good.

You'll have a problem with the adults. They won't let you out.

You're right. Can you work on a distraction?

My pleasure. I'll fake colic.

Deadly stomach pain works for me.

Bird found the softest old sweatsuit she had and put it on. Everything hurt. Her eyes, her throat, her skin, her muscles.

Then she looked in the mirror. Her hair! Her thick, straight, dark hair. It had completely dried out and whole hunks at the front were missing. The hair that was left on her head was frizzled and yellowed. Bird gulped. Her eyes were swollen and red and she had no eyebrows. Pig eyes. She wondered how long Alec would be at camp. She hoped it would be a very, very long time.

I deserve that award for acting, Bird.

The Academy Award? I'm sure you do. What's the plan?

The adults are here saving my life. Sneak out the back and meet Cody behind the barn. He knows where the wild man is. I'll give you a head start, then I'll miraculously recover and follow your scent. They'll think you're still asleep.

Brilliant.

Not bad, if I say so myself.

See you soon. Bird went from the mirror to the window for a peek at Sunny's performance. *Sunny, from up here it looks a little over the top. Colicking horses don't do that.*

What?

Spin their tails and heads at the same time.

Well, what am I supposed to do?

Just lie down and groan and look at your tummy over and over again.

That's boring.

That's how colic looks. Do you want them to send you to Guelph for a total evaluation?

Right.

Bird snuck out of the house and made it past the barn without detection. Things hadn't improved since she'd left her room. Her head hurt, her eyes stung, her throat was raw, her muscles ached—but she was determined to find the wild man and get him help. She looked around for Cody as she advanced silently.

A bush rustled. *Girl. Come with me.*

Cody! Bird followed him down a thorny cliff. The further they went, the more Bird worried about Sundancer. Hannah and Paul were vigilant horse people. If he wasn't able to get away, how would she get the wild man home? It would certainly take some ingenuity.

She didn't have to worry for long. A moment later, Sunny came galloping. He stopped abruptly at the top of the ridge.

Sunny! How did you get away?

They lost interest in me when those men came asking questions, so I escaped.

What men? The police?

How would I know?

If it was the police, there must be new developments. Bird made a mental note to find out when they got back.

Come on down, Sunny. There's no time to lose.

It's too steep!

If I can, with two legs, you can with four.

I'll kill myself! The show is in three days, and I have to be perfect.

Sunny, I'm a swollen, burnt bag with bad hair. We're not going.

If you can climb down these hills, you can ride a horse around a show ring. I'll do all the work. As usual.

I'll think about it. Why don't you go around the long way and meet us at the bottom. Try to be quiet.

Like a rabbit.

Nearby, Cody had been listening in. *You two argue all the time.*

We do? Bird was surprised at his observation. *I guess we do. But we love each other.*

They continued down, one step at a time. Cody stopped moving, so Bird did the same. Then she heard it. A low moaning sound. Definitely human—and definitely in great pain.

That's him, isn't it, Cody?

Yes.

He needs a doctor. We'll get him up to the farm.

Good.

Sunny appeared at the clearing below the ledge. He looked up at Cody and Bird. *Where's the wild man?*

Follow the groans. Up on this ledge, a little to your left.

I can smell him. Now I hear him. Oh, now I see him. He looks yucky, he sounds yucky and he smells yucky.

Bird got a whiff of charred flesh. To her human nose it was bad enough, but for a more sensitive animal nose, it must have been close to unbearable. *We're going to bring him up to our farm. And you have to carry him.*

I'm not putting that thing on my back! He's filthy! You fix him!

I can't fix him! He needs doctors. And medicine and creams.

Then bring them here.

They can't get anywhere near here with an ambulance.

I don't care! I don't want him on my back.

Think about it, Sunny. We don't have time to wait until the ambulance comes with the paramedics, who'd have to scramble down here and get him. It's faster if we just carry him back ourselves.

Not my problem. I'm going home.

If you don't help, I'm not riding you in the show.

No fair! I'm going to win!

It's up to you.

The horse paced and fidgeted for a moment, then stopped. *Okay, I'll do it. But you have to give me a bath with bubbles and everything.*

Deal.

Cody slid closer and closer to the man until he was right beside him. He sniffed his face. *We don't have much time, Bird.*

Let's figure this out.

Bird forced herself to take a good look. Sunny had not exaggerated—it was not a pleasant sight. The man lay on a dirty wet blanket surrounded by debris. A rude tent made of stolen horse blankets propped up on rocks sheltered his bed, and the ground was littered with foul garbage. In the worst state of all, though, was the man himself. His entire body was blistering and caked in mud. Bird had no idea how they could lift him onto a horse without causing him extraordinary pain.

She studied the problem from all angles, and came up with a plan.

Sunny, move as close to the ledge as you can. Cody, you take that end of the blanket, and I'll take this one.

Bird gently pulled the blanket until it lay flat under the man. He was lying on his side, so Bird rolled him onto his stomach and gently straightened his arms and legs. He made no sound.

Now we'll slide him onto Sunny's back, legs first, blanket and all. Are you two ready?

Ready.

Ready.

Slowly, inch by inch, the coyote and the girl slid the blanket to the lip of the ledge. When it was in place, Bird scrambled down and stood at Sunny's side. She reached up over his back, and grasped the foot ends of the blanket. She started to pull. Cody took the head-end blanket corners in his mouth and lifted, allowing Bird to slide it over Sunny's back.

Sunny stood completely still as the blanket and comatose man were draped over him. Finally, everything was in place. The man was on his stomach with his feet hanging down Sunny's right side and his arms down the left.

Sunny was getting restless. *Can we go now?*

Soon, Sunny. I don't want him to fall off when we start up the hill.

It worried Bird that the man made no movement. His breathing was hoarse and shallow. She feared he was barely clinging to life.

Bird looked at their work and considered how to secure him. She couldn't tie his hands and feet together. If he slid around Sunny and hung down under his belly it would be horrible.

I know. I'll tie the blanket on so it doesn't slide off, then walk beside him all the way and hold his legs.

Bird took the rope from Tan's tent and, as quickly as she could, tied the blanket securely around Sunny's girth. She hoped they were ready.

Let's go.

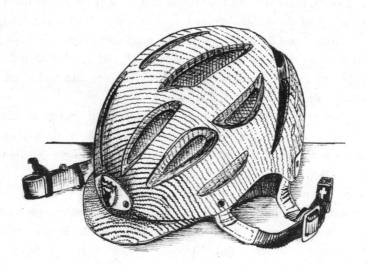

10

SPEECHLESS

Tan was deep in childhood memories, rocking on his old wooden horse. His mother held his leg so he wouldn't fall, and she was singing something very quietly—so quietly that he couldn't quite hear the tune. Back and forth, back and forth, rocking on his rocking horse. Back and forth, back and forth …

SUNNY FELT THE LIFELESS WEIGHT on his back and shifted a little to get comfortable with it. He took a step. He took another step, and another. Satisfied that the man was somewhat secure, and with Bird at his side holding the man's leg, Sunny began the steep climb up the Escarpment.

Bird, the way up is even harder than the way down.

We're going against gravity. Bird was already breathing hard, which made her throat hurt more. At least she didn't have to speak aloud.

I know nothing about whatever that is. All I know is this guy feels dead. I'm going to freak out.

Hang in there, Sunny. You're doing great.

I'd feel better if he started groaning again.

Cody was in front of them, then behind, sniffing and watching out for trouble. *Be cautious. This red mud is very slippery. Go around it.*

I know what I'm doing. I've walked on that red mud before …

Just then, Sundancer stepped into a patch of the brick-coloured clay and slid out, legs splaying. Bird held tight to the man's legs, but she was having trouble keeping upright herself. Oh, no, she thought. Sunny's going down. He was on his knees now, with his nose in the mud. The horse tried mightily to keep his balance.

Hold on, Sunny! urged Bird. *You can do it!*

All at once, the man's body pitched forward. Sunny threw up his neck to stop him from sliding off, but the action caused his hind end to skid under him.

Bird held on tight, and looked ahead. Solid ground was one step away. *Keep going. You're almost there.*

Sunny's left front hoof inched forward until it found good footing. He took a deep breath and moved his right front to join it. Now, with his two front feet out of the mud, he slid his back feet slowly forward until he was finally safe. Bird let out her breath. That had been way too close.

Good work, Sunny!

You try that with four legs, no toes and slippery ooze!

It took twenty-five long minutes of patience and extreme tension, but step by careful step, Sunny, Bird and Cody carried their human cargo up the steep slope. Thankfully, once they were on top of the ridge, the travelling was much easier. They walked silently along the trails and up to the kitchen door.

Bird ran into the house to call for help, but as she opened her mouth to shout out Hannah's name, she made a horrible discovery. She couldn't make a sound. Nothing. She tried again. Same result. Not a squeak, not a rasp. Her voice had shut down. She closed her eyes and rubbed her tender throat, hoping beyond hope that this was only temporary, maybe caused by the smoke. She'd worry about that later. The man needed help right now.

Bird ran through the house looking for Hannah. She wasn't there.

She ran back outside. *Cody, I need you to find Hannah.* Cody shot off with his nose on the ground to do the job.

Sunny began to fidget. *Can you get this guy off me, Bird? Now?*
I need help to do that. Can you stand still for a bit longer?
Look, Bird, I've loved every minute of this, but I can't keep it up. The blanket is itchy and he smells really bad.
I understand. I'll find something we can slide him onto, okay?
As long as it's now.

Just in time, Cody returned. *She's in the barn, Bird. With the good thin man and some others.*

Bird knew that Cody called Cliff "the good thin man," but she didn't know who the others might be. And she didn't care. She needed Hannah to call an ambulance, and she needed help getting the man down from the horse. Bird must get her attention.

The Saddle Creek truck was parked in the driveway. Bird opened the door and leaned on the horn.

Sunny planted his four feet and tensed. *You coulda warned me!*
Sorry, Sunny.
I'm a horse! We startle easily!
Thanks for not spooking.

In seconds, Hannah came running. "Bird! What's the matter? What's on Sundancer? What are you doing? I thought you were upstairs sleeping!"

Bird opened her mouth to answer. Nothing came out. She shook her head and pointed to her throat.

"Oh no, Bird! You can't speak?"

Bird nodded. She stepped over to Sunny and flipped open the dirty blanket that covered his back.

Hannah gasped. "The wild man?"

Bird nodded.

"He needs help! I'll call 911. Wait! The police are here, up in the barn questioning Cliff. Just a minute." Hannah ran back to the barn, calling.

Bird, I can't stand it. Get him off me! Really. I'm at the end of my tolerance. I'll do something I don't want to do.

I know, Sunny. I know. Look, they're on their way now. We'll get him off and I'll give you the bath I promised.

I don't want a bath! The second he's off I'll jump into my field and roll around for days. Just get him off!

The police, Hannah and Cliff quickly took over. Officer Paris had his phone to his ear, but the others expertly untied the knots and removed the man from Sunny's back using the blanket as a gurney. They laid him carefully on the ground.

As soon as Sunny's burden had been removed, he did precisely what he said he'd do. He galloped the few strides to the fenceline, jumped the split-rails into his field and rolled and rolled in the tall grass.

Thanks, Sunny. You were wonderful. I owe you one.

A big, huge, honking, fat one.

"The ambulance will be here in approximately three minutes," said Officer Paris as he snapped shut his cell phone. "Now, young lady, what is this all about?"

Bird shook her head and put her hand to her throat.

"Her voice is gone, officer." Hannah came to Bird's aid. "All I know is that this is the man we've been calling 'the wild man.' He's the one who's been coming around. I don't know anything more."

The officers stared at Bird. "You have a lot of explaining to do."

From the bushes beside the house came a low growl, startling the officers.

Thanks, Cody, but everything's fine.

Call me when it's not.

I will. And thanks for helping.

Good. I'm gone.

Bird smiled as Cody shot out from the bushes and sped away through the fields.

"That was a coyote!" gasped Officer O'Hare. "Too quick to shoot!"

Bird was horrified.

"That was Cody," said Hannah. "He's a pet. If you ever harmed him, we'd be very upset."

"A pet?" said Officer O'Hare. "Each to his own. What concerns us is this. Bird brings a badly injured man to your house with no explanation. There are a lot of unanswered questions, and Bird here can't speak."

Bird darted into the house, and quickly returned with a pad of paper and a pen. She began to write, and when she was finished, she handed the page to Officer Paris.

"*We call him 'the wild man.'*" The officer read aloud. "*We thought he was bad cause he looked in windows & scared us, but he dragged me out of the barn & saved the horses, so he can't B bad. I went 2 look 4 him cause I was worried. That coyote who U were going 2 shoot found him, & my horse brought him home 2 get him 2 the hospital.*"

After a few stunned seconds of silence, Officer O'Hare spoke. "Well, I never." Then he pointed a finger at Bird. "This just leads to more questions. Who is this man, and how did you find him?"

The sound of sirens cut off the questioning. Everyone watched as an ambulance raced along the road and came to a halt at the door of the Saddle Creek farmhouse. Three minutes exactly.

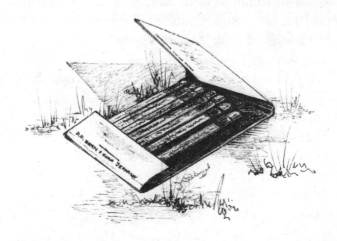

11

JUSTICE FOR THE INNOCENT

Tan felt no pain. He felt nothing. Was he dead? If he was dead, would he know? Pinkness was everywhere. Humming sounds. Was this heaven?

DINNER THAT NIGHT was very simple. Hannah, Paul, Julia and Bird sat around the table listening to the radio as they ate steamed hot dogs and a leafy green salad. Everyone was extremely tired, but most especially Bird. It had been a very long day. First the haying, then the barn fire, and finally the retrieval of the wild man. She was worn out. In spite of her afternoon nap, she was more than ready for an early night.

Lucky lay under the table, hoping for a sloppy or benevolent eater. Hot dogs were his favourite food in the whole world.

"Good job trimming Bird's hair," Julia said to Hannah as she squeezed mustard onto her bun. "She looks a whole lot better."

Paul grinned at Bird. "Almost normal."

Bird grimaced.

"It'll grow out before you know it," smiled Hannah. "I took off some singed parts, and the back is just fine."

Bird didn't really care, she was so tired.

"I've called Mundells to fix the front door," Hannah told Paul before taking a bite. "If they can't fix it, they'll replace it with something nice."

"And solid, I hope," replied Paul. "Sunny splintered it with one kick!"

So she hadn't been dreaming after all, Bird thought.

"Who's going to look after the horses next door?" asked Julia.

"Bunny and Guy are already home," answered Paul. "They got on a plane the minute they heard. The horses are happy living outside in their shelters, and the new barn will be built by the winter."

Hannah passed the salad bowl to Bird for a second helping. "They're very grateful to you for saving their horses' lives."

Bird was very grateful to Cody and the wild man for saving hers. When she saw Bunny and Guy, she'd tell them how the man had helped get their horses out. Or write them a note, she thought wryly. Unless her voice came back after a good night's sleep. That would be very nice.

An item on the radio caught their attention. Paul turned up the volume.

"Breaking news. CHKO has just learned that a man identified as Pierre Hall was seriously injured in the barn fire in Caledon reported earlier this afternoon. He has been airlifted to Sunnybrook Hospital in Toronto. The barn was owned by Guy and Bunny Linwood. No further details are available, due to an ongoing investigation. Arson is suspected."

"They think somebody did it on purpose!" gasped Julia.

"They came to question Cliff about it!" exclaimed Hannah. "The nerve! I told them I hoped they weren't suggesting that Cliff had anything to do with it. He was in the barn with us all day putting up the hay, and he would be the last person on the face of the earth to start a fire in a barn full of horses!"

Julia and Bird nodded with indignation. "The very last person!" said Julia.

Hannah's face flushed pink as she continued. "Cliff got a threatening note, just like Pierre. Philip Butler got one, too. I asked the officers if Cliff's and Pierre's lives were in danger as well! And is my barn next?"

"Good questions, Hannah." Paul spoke calmly, trying to settle things down. "We're all a little tense about this. You have to admit, it's been pretty unusual around here, but the police are working hard."

Hannah wasn't quite ready to calm down. "If it turns out that the fire *was* intentional, and Pierre dies, then it's another murder!"

"There are bound to be more reports," said Paul, switching to another station.

"This just in. An unnamed source reveals that a group calling themselves Justice for the Innocent has been threatening suspects in the Sandra Hall case. Sources close to police tell us that they are hinting at more violence."

"'Justice for the Innocent'? What the heck?" Paul muttered.

"*More* violence? Did this group set the fire?" Hannah asked.

Paul pursed his lips. "It sounds like people are wondering."

They continued to listen: *"Police spokesman Daryll Singh had this to say: 'Someone, or some people, burned down the Linwood's barn and injured Pierre Hall. We strongly suspect that this was arson. If you have any information, we ask that you come forward. If you were involved in this incident, police want to talk to you. Also, we are doing everything in our power to find Sandra Hall's killer. We have interviewed several people and have followed up hundreds of tips phoned in by the public. Search teams with helicopters and dogs have combed the area. We ask that people remain calm and leave both investigations in the hands of the police.'"*

Paul switched stations again. By now, they were all on the edge of their seats.

"A word from Police Chief Mack Jones." They listened to a short clip asking the citizens of Caledon for an end to the violence, and to do their civic duty by reporting unusual incidents.

The announcer continued: *"There you have it. A plea from the police. Now, just in, we have a taped interview with Guy*

Linwood, the owner of the burned barn."

Guy's voice sounded angry. *"This is ridiculous. If this fire has anything to do with some kind of revenge scenario, it's pure craziness. We're innocent people here! This fire was an abomination!"*

"Breaking news! An unidentified man who helped save ten horses today in the Caledon barn fire that threatened the life of local man Pierre Hall was taken by ambulance to get medical attention for his burn-related injuries. Sources at the Orangeville Hospital say he will not be released until he can be identified. The man is in stable condition."

Julia looked confused. "Stable? Like a barn?"

"Stable means he's not getting worse. That's good news," said Hannah. "Nice work, Bird." She smiled at her niece.

Paul nodded. "You're astounding. It's a mystery to me how you got him home on Sunny's back."

Julia nodded. "Sundancer, the terror of the show ring. And here he is, hauling bodies up the Escarpment like a pack mule!" She grinned proudly at her big sister.

Bird smiled back, warmed by all the praise.

"Speaking of Sunny and the show ring," interrupted Hannah, "Sunny showed signs of colic this afternoon. We'll have to keep an eye on him."

Paul crossed his arms thoughtfully. "It wasn't colic, Hannah. His temperature was normal and there was normal bowel noise. He wasn't sweating. I have no idea what the tail rotation was all about."

Sunny had certainly done a good job of distracting them, Bird thought as she busied herself with her hot dog.

"And the head tossing," added Hannah with concern. "Maybe wasps? I remember when Lady Olivia had wasp bites in her mouth. I thought it might be rabies."

"Hmm. There were no signs of bites. No swelling, no bumps, no stinger marks. But he certainly was in distress."

Bird looked hard at her plate. She fought to control her urge to laugh. She'd bring him an extra apple.

"Let's just watch him for a while," said Paul. "I'll check him tonight before bed."

"If there's anything at all wrong, he won't be able to show on Friday, Bird," Hannah declared. "And I know how much you were looking forward to it."

Now Bird had to turn away. This was too much. Her face darkened with suppressed laughter, and Julia noticed. Her eyes widened. "Don't cry, Bird! He'll be all right! He was well enough to carry the wild man up the Escarpment!"

Julia's concern brought Bird back from the brink. She patted her sister's arm and smiled, possibly too brightly.

"True, Julia. He's probably just fine. As I said, I'll check on him tonight." Paul turned very serious. "There's growing concern, though, about the man that Bird and Sunny rescued today. I'm hearing a lot of chat and speculation."

"From whom, Paul?" asked Hannah.

"He was the main topic at every farm I went to this morning." Paul put down his fork and wiped his mouth on his napkin. "You can't really blame them. Nobody knows him. He showed up when Sandra Hall was killed, and he lives in a cave or the woods or something. People are worried that he's the killer."

Bird knew that Paul was right. Why wouldn't people worry? Everybody is afraid of things they don't understand, and Bird had wondered the same thing herself.

The phone rang, and Hannah stood to answer it.

"Hello?... Oh, hi!" She looked at Julia and mouthed, "Liz's mother." Hannah listened, concern creasing her brow. "Oh, Patty! Is he all right?... For sure ... Look, why don't you all stay here tonight ... I understand ... Okay, sure, whatever works for you. Let me know how we can help."

Hannah slowly hung up the phone and turned to face her

family. "Phil went to the police station this afternoon to give them his threatening note. He was bumped by a car just as he came out. The car didn't stop. It was a close call, but he wasn't hurt. He went back in and told the police. Now they're looking for a beige, four-door, late-model sedan, North American make. Phil had his car keys in his hand and he's pretty sure he scratched the fender."

Paul nodded. "That'll help identify the car."

"Can Liz stay here tonight?" Concern for her friend was written on Julia's face.

"Mrs. Brown thinks they'll go to her mother's in Barrie, just for a few days."

Hannah sat quietly with her elbows on the table, chin resting in the palm of her hands. Bird had never really noticed Hannah's age before, but now her face seemed to sag with worry. Bird moved over and patted her aunt's shoulder. Hannah reached out and squeezed Bird's hand with her own.

The phone rang again, and this time Paul picked up. Bird could tell it was Patty calling back. "Sorry to hear about ... Right ... Do the police know?... Good ... Thanks for telling us ... You take care of yourself."

It was Paul's turn to relay the conversation. "Patty found a note in her mailbox. It said that next time Phil wouldn't be so lucky."

This is getting worse and worse, thought Bird. The hit and run hadn't been an accident, and she guessed that neither had the barn fire. Who were these people? Before, things had always felt so safe at Saddle Creek Farm. They'd never even bothered to lock their doors. None of the neighbours had, either. Now everything was locked up tight; now, everything was different. Bird hated this new uneasy feeling.

An awful thought jolted her. What about Cliff? Of the four suspects, he was the only one who hadn't had something bad happen today. Phil had been targeted by a car, and Pierre Hall and the wild man were in different hospitals, fighting for their lives. She grabbed a pen and piece of paper from the desk beside the phone and scribbled: *Is Cliff safe?* She showed it to Hannah, who passed it to Paul. Julia looked over his shoulder.

"You're right, Bird," said Hannah. "He could be in danger at this very moment."

Hannah and Paul got up from the table. "Julia," said Hannah. "Get the dishes done. Bird gets a break tonight. Then both of you get ready for bed. We'll try to persuade Cliff to stay with us."

Julia started clearing the table. Bird changed radio stations until she found one with only music and turned up the volume to the max. They'd had enough bad news for one day. Bird's battered body found new life as she moved with the music, and Julia danced around the kitchen as she worked. By the time Hannah and Paul returned, the dishes were done and Julia was wildly sweeping the floor as she shouted out lyrics.

"Turn down the radio!" yelled Hannah. "I can't hear myself think."

Paul grinned at the girls. "Cliff says he'll be fine. He refuses to sleep here."

"He told us that Boss wouldn't settle down over here and that he'd drive us crazy barking," Hannah added. "That's probably true. But he'll call if there's anything that worries him."

"He's stubborn, that Cliff," smiled Paul. "A true country man."

"And ingenious. He's rigged up a tripwire that sets off a siren. If anyone tries to get near his place, the whole neighbourhood will know! Now, get to bed, you two," Hannah ordered. "It's been a very long day."

Bird's body was exhausted. As soon as her head hit the pillow, she fell into a deep sleep. Around two in the morning, however, she awoke. Must be because I slept most of the afternoon, she thought. I'll just lie here for a while and drift back to sleep.

She turned onto her right side and breathed deeply. She turned onto her left and counted sheep. Then she rolled over onto her back, and flipped onto her front. She recited the alphabet backwards from *Z* to *A*. She counted backwards from one hundred.

At number forty-four, Bird heard a sound downstairs. It was Lucky, scratching at the kitchen door. Keeping her end of their bargain, Bird got up to let him out. She pulled her soft sweats over her nightie and crept downstairs.

Thanks, Bird. I don't want to make any more mistakes.

You did the right thing by scratching at the door. You can try whining, or barking, too, if nobody hears. She opened the door to let out the grateful dog.

That's when she saw headlights at the end of the lane. A car was stopped at their mailbox, facing north. Bird tensed. She couldn't see the car, only the lights. She wondered what she should do if it came up their lane, but when the car moved it drove up the road, away from Saddle Creek. No need to decide.

A second later, Bird stepped outside into the dark night. There were no stars out, and the moon was hidden behind clouds. She stumbled down the lane, feeling her way step by step until she reached the mailbox. She lifted the metal flap and reached inside. Her hand felt a letter. She pulled it out. The envelope was addressed to Cliff, in heavy ink. There was no address, just his first name.

Who would deliver a letter at two in the morning? Bird normally didn't open other people's mail, but this was different—lately, notes in mailboxes meant only one thing. She ripped open the envelope. In the dark, Bird could barely make out the words.

What happened to Pierre could happen to you. You're not safe until someone admits to killing Sandra Hall.

Just what she'd thought. Another letter like Pierre's and Phil's. Bird's head reeled. Were these people trying to scare all the suspects into admitting guilt? It didn't make any sense. They couldn't all be guilty! It was ridiculous and scary and wrong. Bird folded the note and tucked it into the pocket of her sweatpants.

She'd have to tell Hannah, of course. The only question was whether to wake her or wait until morning. Bird was still trying to decide when headlights shone from up the road. A car was coming. Bird jumped behind the fence and waited. She didn't want to take any chances, just in case it was the same car. Slowly, it rolled closer. Now, right beside her at the end of their lane, it stopped. It must be the same car. Who else would stop by in the middle of the night? Bird held her breath.

The driver's door opened, and a man got out. He walked around the back of the car to the mailbox. The headlights in Bird's eyes made it impossible for her to get a good look at him.

He was on a cellphone, talking. "I hear you now ... On the radio?... Okay, okay, I'm getting it." Bird could hear the sound of the man's hand searching around the mailbox. "Wait. It's not here."

Bird's skin broke out in goosebumps.

"I said, it's not here, pal ... What're ya saying?... Yeah, I'm sure I put it in. Less than five minutes ago!" He leaned over and felt around on the ground. "No, I didn't drop it. What do you think? I'm clumsy?"

Bird stayed as still as a mouse. The man walked in front of the car, and was suddenly lit by the headlights. Bird memorized his bulky shape and rough physical manner. Brown hair cut short, nondescript features, clean-shaven face. Nothing special or memorable, except for a surly demeanour and a sloppy way of walking.

"Look, pal, go easy here. The note's gone ... I don't *know* how ... This is getting a little too intense ... What, tonight?... I need sleep, too!... Which hospital? Orangeville?... Man!... Okay,

I'll do it after I find a gas station. I'm riding on empty, and I need a sandwich."

The man pocketed his cellphone, muttering to himself, then got back in the car and drove off.

The Orangeville Hospital. Bird shuddered. He could only be talking about one thing. The wild man was in the Orangeville Hospital. She'd saved his life once today; she wasn't about to let anything happen to him now.

12

THE ORANGEVILLE HOSPITAL

Tan drifted on a sea of white clouds and cotton. Faces appeared and disappeared. He imagined things: a girl with dark eyes stared at him; a coyote dragged him away from a blazing barn; his rocking horse carried him up a mountain. He was thirsty. Very thirsty. Water. Cold water. Water burst from a balloon that was smashed with a tire iron. The balloon became a skull and the water turned to blood. Tan screamed and screamed, but he couldn't make a sound.

FOR A FULL MINUTE after the tail lights disappeared, Bird stayed hidden. She'd paid close attention. The car was light brown. It was a four-door Chrysler sedan, about ten years old, she guessed. The licence was MNTN 3672. She repeated it over and over in her head until it was committed to memory.

When she finally felt it was safe, Bird jumped up from the ground and ran back to the house.

Should she wake Paul and Hannah? The memory of Hannah sitting slouched over the kitchen table with her chin in her hands came into Bird's mind. No. Hannah and Paul needed their rest. They were getting older. Plus, they'd insist on calling the police, and Bird didn't want to wait for them and have to explain everything. That man was on his way to the hospital now. She needed to get there as fast as possible.

Very quietly, Bird tiptoed into the kitchen. She tore off some paper from a pad and wrote a note to Hannah. She explained about the beige car at their mailbox, and included the licence plate number. She put her note beside the letter to Cliff that she'd found in the mailbox. Then she put the pad and pen in her pocket, and stepped outside.

Lucky was standing at the door.

Where are you going, Bird? Where are you going?

I have to protect the wild man.

How?

I'll know when I get there. Keep an eye on Cliff, will you?

Can I come with you? With you?

I need you here, Lucky. Can you help me out?

Lucky stood proudly, puffing out his chest. *I'd be honoured.*

Good boy. She patted his head. *Now, watch Cliff's house. If anyone shows up who makes you nervous, bark your head off and come back and wake Hannah and Paul.*

At your service.

Bird watched him race bravely toward Cliff's house, just as he said he would. Bird felt a pang of love for the awkward puppy. He would be a great dog one day soon.

Bird ran around the house to where her bike was propped against the wall. She hopped on and sped off toward the hospital, wondering if she had understood the cellphone conversation correctly. If the man really *was* driving to the wild man's bedside, it wouldn't be for a pleasant little visit.

Very soon, Bird's lungs began to burn and her leg muscles hurt. It was a slow uphill climb, and her body was already in a mess from the fire. Bird could hardly believe it had happened less than twenty-four hours ago—it had been an incredibly awful day. She tried to manage the pain by taking slow, deep breaths. There were almost no cars out this time of night, she noted, and few trucks.

Twenty-five long minutes later, Bird saw the hospital ahead.

She glided silently into the parking lot, taking care to stay in the shadowy areas unlit by the tall lamps. There were a couple dozen cars parked in the staff parking section, many fewer in the visitors' area. And there, across the lot, parked far away from the lighted section, was a beige sedan.

Bird rode past the car, pretending not to notice it in case anybody was inside. Empty. Licence plate MNTN 3672. She braked the bike and did a double take. The front left fender had a long, deep mark on it: a fresh scratch. This was the car that had hit Philip Butler, no question. She put her hand on the hood. Still hot. Good—he hadn't been here too long.

Bird rode up to the entrance and left her bike hidden in the bushes by the front door. She walked up to the doors and looked through the glass. There were lights on and a few people walking around—people who looked like they knew what they were doing. She'd better do the same. Expecting the door to be locked, Bird yanked hard. It opened easily, and for a second she was thrown off balance. Bird breathed deeply to collect herself. When she was ready, she strode in.

There was a friendly looking elderly woman at the reception table along the wall. Bird stood waiting until the woman looked up.

"May I help you, dear?" the lady asked with a pleasant smile.

Bird pulled out the pad of paper and pen, and wrote quickly but carefully: *Yes, thank you. A man was brought in with burns. He helped get some horses out of a barn fire. Could you please direct me 2 his room?*

The woman assessed Bird carefully. "Why don't you talk, dear? Sore throat?"

Bird nodded. She wrote: *The fire hurt my throat.*

"You do look like you've been in a fire! Your hair is completely singed." The woman's expression was kind, but Bird could see that she was no fool. "Why are you here at this late hour, and not in bed?"

Bird gave her an innocent look: *This is the first chance I had. I slept all afternoon recovering.* She wondered briefly if she should take this nice lady into her confidence. Maybe she should, but the whole story might sound too far-fetched. She decided to stick with the plan. Adults rarely believe you anyway.

"There's a gentleman with him now. When he comes down you can go on up. What is your name, please?" The woman opened the guest book.

Bird was alarmed. He was there! It might already be too late. She quickly studied the guest book. "John Smith" was the last name entered. Beside it was written Room 213.

When did he go up? Bird wrote.

"He's just gone up, but he said he won't be long. What is your name, please?"

Alberta Simms. Bird wrote quickly. *I must go now. That man is not nice.*

The woman's eyes narrowed as she read. "He's a *very* nice man. He brought me a box of chocolate mints."

It was just as she'd feared—the woman did not believe her. She hadn't wanted it to come to this, but she had no choice. With a quick look around, and another deep breath, Bird dashed for the stairwell.

"Stop!" the woman yelled from behind her. "You can't go up without permission!"

Bird flew up the stairs, two at a time, hoping the woman would call security. She'd need all the help she could get when she got there. She rushed down the second floor hall, checking room numbers as she went. No matter how hard she tried, her feet would not go as fast as she wanted them to. She made a wrong turn and doubled back, feeling more and more anxious with every passing second. There—finally! Room 213.

Panting for air and sweating, Bird looked through the small glass window in the door. Yes. This was the right room. The wild man was lying perfectly still in the dim light. His body lay under a white sheet, and his head was covered in bandages.

Bird gasped. The same man who had been at the Saddle Creek mailbox stepped out of the shadows and up to the bed, his back to the door. Bird watched as he reached down and began to violently shake the wild man's shoulders. She reached for the door handle to stop him.

But before her hand even touched the metal, two security guards grabbed her arms from behind. "Okay," said one. "You're coming with us."

Bird was aghast. She motioned frantically with her head and eyes, urging them to look in the window. She had to make them see!

"You're going to struggle, are you?" said the other. "There are two of us and one of you."

Bird tried to talk. "Arghhh …" was the only thing that came out. She kicked out hard.

"That's enough!" spat the guard. He twisted her arm and held her tighter.

Bird wiggled and fought. She couldn't explain things to them. The only thing she *could* do was make them see what was happening in the room. Through sheer force of will, she pulled them closer and closer to the door.

One of the guards cursed loudly as he hit his head on the doorframe. Bird cringed, waiting for the inevitable yank on her arm. It never came. Miraculously, the guard's attention was caught by a movement in the room. He released Bird's arm and stared in the window.

"Let her go," he commanded. "We have a situation."

As quickly as she'd been grabbed, Bird was dropped like a hot potato. She found herself alone on the corridor floor. Bird heard the intruder exclaim as he was pulled away from the bed. "Hey! What are you doing?"

"More to the point, what are *you* doing?" responded a guard.

"I'm visiting a friend, pal."

"You're roughing up a patient, *pal*. And you're coming with us."

Bird wiggled across the floor and peered into the room. She watched as one of the guards pressed the alarm button to call for the nurse. That was good—the wild man needed attention. He was still motionless, but now his arms and legs were in awkward positions.

Before the guards could remember that Bird was there, she slipped behind the open door next to the wild man's room, and hid. Through the hinges she watched the three men as they marched down the hall—the unhappy intruder in the middle with a stern guard at both sides. When they turned the corner, she made her move. She had to get back to the stairwell unde-tected. She had to get out.

Nurses rushed past her on their way to the wild man's room.

Bird crept along, keeping the sound of the guards' footfalls within earshot. If they came back for her, Bird planned to tell them she'd fainted. But with all the commotion nobody seemed to notice her. She heard the elevator doors open and close. The guards and the man disappeared.

She reached the stairwell and sank to the floor. With her head pounding and her arms sore from the struggle, Bird lay on the floor and caught her breath. After a few minutes, she felt well enough to walk downstairs. She had to get out of the hospital pronto, before anybody remembered about her.

Silently, barely allowing herself to breathe, Bird tiptoed down the stairs. At the bottom, she looked around the lobby for the guards and the lady in reception. All clear. She braced herself.

Very casually, she walked out the front door, and once out of sight, she raced to her bike.

But what was this? There was a dark shape lurking in the shadows. Bird's heart stopped. She became motionless.

Bird girl. Do not fear. It's me.

Bird slumped with relief. *Cody! How did you get here?*

I followed you. You might have need of me.

Oh, Cody. You are the best. Bird's heart was full of love for her loyal friend. She suddenly felt a whole lot less lonely as they began their trip back to Saddle Creek.

The road sloped downhill all the way. With the night air in her lungs, Bird felt better and better with every passing kilometer. She began to smile, then grin, then laugh aloud, in a raspy, squeaky, honking kind of way. Her escape had been exhilarating! Not only had she possibly saved the wild man's life again, but the hospital guards were holding the man who was planting threatening notes and who'd carried out the hit and run on Philip Butler. With any luck, the case would soon be solved!

Cody raced along beside her as she rode. Bird pedalled only as fast as he could run. Finally, they turned up the country road that led to Saddle Creek Farm. Her leg muscles were searing and her energy was spent. It was five-thirty in the morning, and Bird was ready for bed.

Lucky ran up to her as she parked her bike. *Bird! Bird! You're back!*

Did anything happen while I was gone?

Not a thing, Bird. Not a thing.

Good work.

Thank you! Thank you!

Good boy, Lucky. Bird rubbed his head and playfully grabbed his snout. Lucky wagged his tail and shook with glee.

Quietly, Bird and Lucky entered the kitchen. Making not a sound, Bird closed the door behind them.

"Bird." A voice startled both dog and girl. "I saw the note." Hannah turned on the lights. She looked terrible. At a glance Bird could see that she was in a foul mood. "I've been worried sick."

Bird pulled out the pen and paper. *A man left that in the mailbox & said on his cell he was going 2 the O'ville hosp. I went 2 save the wild man & it's good I did cause the man tried 2 hurt him but the guards stopped him & I came home. His car is beige & has a big scratch.*

Hannah's face changed as she read Bird's scrawled message. "You went all the way to Orangeville." It was more a statement than a question.

Bird nodded. *I'm very, very tired,* she wrote. *Can I go 2 bed now?*

Hannah gave her a gentle hug. "Yes. I'll call and leave a message for the police. You're a brave girl, Bird. It wasn't very smart, though. I've been so worried! You could've been hurt in so many ways I don't even want to think about."

Tell her what I did! demanded Lucky.

Bird gave him a dismal look, then relented. Like all dogs of his age and type, he needed lots of approval. She reached over and scribbled. *Lucky was on patrol while I was gone. Pat him & make a fuss.*

Hannah looked at her quizzically, then laughed. "I'll never understand you and animals." She knelt down and scratched Lucky's neck. "Good boy! You did a good job, Lucky!"

Lucky was in heaven. He rolled over and let Hannah rub his tummy.

Somberly she said, "Never do that again. It should have been done by the police."

Bird wrote, *I couldn't wait.*

Hannah didn't buy it. "You should have wakened me, Bird. I would have helped." She gave Bird another hug and a kiss on the cheek. "Now get to bed."

Bird dragged herself up the stairs, one at a time, followed by Lucky. She fell into her bed without washing her face or brushing her teeth, and was deeply asleep in an instant.

13

TANBARK WEDGER

Tan felt a quiet presence in the white room. It was gentle and loving. It was his mother. Mom. Mommy. His eyes burned with salty tears. He sighed in halting bursts, then completely relaxed for the first time in a long while. Everything would be all right now. Everything would be fine. He closed his eyes and slept.

BY THE TIME BIRD AWOKE the next morning, the clock read eleven. Her head felt fuzzy and her mouth tasted awful. She rolled over to take another look at the clock. Yep. Eleven. Light poured through the crack in her curtains. She threw off her blankets and stretched.

The events of the night before crowded her brain. The note, her impulsive ride to the hospital, what she'd seen there, her escape. She cringed, amazed that nothing bad had happened to her.

Bird tried out her voice, hoping that the deep sleep had cured her. Nothing. Not even a squeak. Maybe there was still a chance it was smoke damage, thought Bird. She vowed not to let it bother her.

From outside in the field below, Sunny's playful whinny brought her thoughts to the impending horse show. Today was Thursday. Her heart leapt. Tomorrow! Tomorrow was the Palston Horse Show and she wasn't in the least bit ready!

Jumping out of bed, Bird stubbed her toe on the frame. Her mouth opened to yell but not a sound emerged. She hopped on one foot to the chair where she'd left her clothes. She got dressed and ran downstairs.

Hannah was in the kitchen, taking a coffee break and reading the newspaper. Bird knew she'd already given ten kids riding lessons. Five at eight o'clock and five at nine-fifteen. Hannah looked up. "Well, rise and shine! You really needed that sleep, I'd say."

Bird nodded vigorously and grabbed her pen. *The show! Is it really tomorrow?*

Hannah nodded. "Do you still want to go?"

Bird was unsure. Was she ready? Maybe yes, maybe no. Was Sundancer ready? She'd made a deal with him. He'd carried the wild man up the Escarpment because Bird had promised that they'd compete. She owed him. Bird wrote one word: *Yes.*

"Well, then," said Hannah. Her tone was strangely flat. "Get some breakfast in your tummy and let's do a little work."

Bird looked at the newspaper, spread out on the kitchen table. There, in black and white, was a big picture of the wild man's face as he lay in bed in the hospital. Underneath, the caption asked, "Who is this man?"

Hannah followed Bird's gaze and smiled sadly. "I can answer that question," she said, her voice barely above a whisper. "I know this man, Bird. He's my half-brother. His name is Tanbark Wedger."

Bird's heart skipped a beat. She stared at her aunt.

"Yes. You heard right."

Bird plunked herself down in the nearest chair, her heart pounding now. His name was Tanbark? He was her mother's and her Aunt Hannah's half-brother? Did that make him her uncle? Half-uncle? Her mind whirled.

"Something about him was nagging at me—something I was missing. When I saw this picture, it all came clear." Now Hannah began her story. "Twenty-five, maybe twenty-six years ago, my father had an affair with a very nice woman who worked for him. Her name is Alison Wedger. They had a child—a son. Nobody knew about it for quite a while, but as the son grew he looked more and more like my father, and people talked. There were rumours. Alison was beautiful and my father was known to be a lady's man, so it made sense. My mother refused to discuss it." Hannah paused absently to sip her coffee.

Bird's head was reeling. The wild man was her uncle?

"Your mother and I met Tanbark one day by chance when he was about fifteen years old. It was just before Christmas, when the town lit up the big tree in the park. We knew right then that he was related to us. He looked like our family, somehow." Hannah stared into her cup as she remembered. "We had a great time that day. He was smart, charming. Lots of friends. He had a great sense of humour, and he teased us about being relatives— outlaws, not in-laws, he said. Eva even asked him to come to the family Christmas party. He declined." Hannah chuckled. "Good thing, too, because our mother would've had a coronary."

Bird studied the picture in the newspaper on the table, searching for the family resemblance. There was something around the eyes and brows. The forehead. Even the shape of the lips.

"Dad has never admitted to having a son. Never denied it, either. But I know it's true. I know Tanbark's my half-brother. And when my parents divorced, my mother confronted Dad with it. She believes it now, too."

Hannah inhaled deeply. "We never saw each other after that, but I always listened for news of him. He was a star in high school. Lots of sports teams and clubs. The girls loved him, and it seemed like he was a popular guy. He went off to university in Toronto and got his Bachelor of Arts."

Bird pictured the wild man, and tried to connect him to the person her aunt was describing. Could they really be the same? And was this why he was hanging around Saddle Creek? Was he looking for his family? It made sense. But if so, why now? It was odd that he'd turned up at exactly the same time as Sandra Hall's murder. Could he have done it?

Hannah went on. "It was after university that things started unravelling for Tanbark. He had some kind of mental breakdown when he was in his early twenties. His mother tried to get help for him, but he refused to see that there was anything wrong. He couldn't get a job. He borrowed money. He slept on people's couches and ate their food. He always said he was looking for work, but he never did. It didn't take long before he'd used up all his friendships. But Alison never gave up on him. She kept trying to get him some help, some guidance, but he ran away. That broke her heart. There were stories about him—sightings. Begging on the street in Toronto. Squeegee kid stuff. As far as I know, no one has heard from him, or about him, for years." Hannah shook her head in wonder. "Imagine him showing up here."

Bird wrote: *Why did it happen?* She still couldn't fit the person Hannah had described with the man who'd been scaring them.

Hannah raised her eyebrows and pursed her lips. "Some people say it's genetic, that it runs in the family. Some people say it's a chemical reaction to drugs or something. The answer is that there's no clear answer."

Bird knew she'd have to settle for this, at least for now. *We'd better tell the police.*

Hannah nodded. "I've already called. They're on their way now. I gave them Alison Wedger's name, too. I didn't say anything about my father, since he's never owned up to it. He's got enough on his plate, anyway, with his insurance fraud case coming up." Hannah straightened her back and stretched. "The police want to know all about your adventures, too, Bird. I told them about the scratch on the car. That was very helpful. It's been impounded. They're going over it with a fine-toothed comb at the police station as we speak."

Bird wrote, *Is he OK?*

Hannah nodded. "The police put a guard at his door."

Bird let out her breath in a long sigh. What a relief! Tanbark was so helpless in his present state. *What did the man do 2 him?* she scribbled.

"I was going to ask you. The police will only say he harmed him."

Bird nodded. He'd sure shaken him hard. She wondered if his plan was to smother him with a pillow, or pull out the intravenous lines. Either way, it made her sick.

Hannah stretched her arms again and yawned. "I called my father this morning. Your grandfather. He should at least know. I left a message. I don't really expect an answer." Hannah stood up and ran her fingers nervously through her hair. Bird knew that gesture, and how often it was connected to her grandfather.

Bird thought about the summer before, and how her grandfather, Kenneth Bradley, had tried to sell Sundancer out from under them. The resulting charges against him included insurance fraud, misleading the police and conspiring to thwart justice. But to Bird's mind, the most serious problem with her grandfather could be summed up in a few words: she couldn't trust him.

"Enough of this," Hannah said, suddenly all business. Bird was used to her aunt's sudden shifts away from the subject of Kenneth Bradley. "We've got three others coming with us to the show tomorrow. Liz and Julia will be in the low pony jumper, and Kimberly is doing the metre jumper with Pastor. He's going well for her, now that she's decided she likes him."

Bird was looking forward to seeing Kimberly again. At school, Kimberly was one of Bird's best friends. Spunky, funny and very kind-hearted, Kimberly understood Bird better than almost any other human. Their common love of horses was another bond they shared.

"We'll get you up on Sundancer after the police are gone," Hannah continued. "You haven't had much time in the saddle lately."

Bird felt butterflies in her stomach. She didn't feel at all prepared. She was going to make a fool of herself tomorrow, she just knew it!

Bird didn't have long to fret. After just a few moments, the police cruiser arrived and stopped in front of the house. The same two officers who'd come the night of the town meeting got out of the car and walked up to the front door. Hannah was there to meet them.

"Please come in," she said. "It's Officer Polito and Officer Richardson, if I remember correctly."

Officer Richardson nodded and smiled. "Good memory, Miss Bradley."

"Please call me Hannah. And come on in. Coffee?"

Officer Polito took off his hat. "That would be nice, thank you. Milk and double sugar. Officer Richardson here takes milk."

They got settled in the kitchen, coffee, cookies and notepads at the ready. Bird watched them and wondered if she was in trouble.

Officer Polito spoke first. "Let me review things, if you don't mind."

"Not at all," said Hannah.

"You left a message telling us that Bird found a note in your mailbox at two in the morning. She overheard a one-sided conversation that led her to believe that the man who'd helped her save the horses in the barn fire—a man we now know is Tanbark Wedger—was in danger. She rode her bike to the Orangeville hospital and noticed a car that might have been involved in a hit and run. She also was present when a person was in the process of injuring the patient."

Officer Polito lifted his head from his notes and stared at Bird. "What possessed you to ride your bike to the hospital in the middle of the night?"

Bird could only stare back.

"Bird was trying to help." Hannah came to her defence. "And her throat was scorched in the barn fire, officer. She can't talk."

Officer Polito spoke louder, "Why didn't you contact the police?"

Bird was used to people doing that, as if speaking louder would somehow help her understand. She shrugged and picked up a pen and pad. *It seemed like the right thing 2 do at the time.*

He was not pleased. "It was *not* the right thing to do. You should have walked back into your house and picked up the phone. Period."

Bird noted how quickly he'd forgotten that she could not speak.

Officer Richardson spoke. "Officer Polito is quite correct. But you sure are a brave young woman." She caught her partner's glare. "You really should have alerted us, though. You could have been hurt."

The police had many questions, all of which Bird tried to answer honestly and fully. They wanted descriptions and details and exact recall. Although she listened carefully to their questions, she could not figure out where they were going with the investigation or how all the pieces were connecting. It was still a big mystery.

When the officers were finished, Bird had some questions of her own. She looked at Officer Richardson, who seemed to be the more reasonable of the two. *Is the man I saw in the hospital in jail?*

"He's in custody. We're questioning him now."

What's his name?

"We can't release his name."

Why's he leaving those notes?

"We can't confirm who's leaving the notes," the police-woman answered. "We're still trying to find out who's doing that, and why."

Why did he hit Phil with his car?

Officer Polito interjected. "We don't know that he did, and we're not at liberty to discuss the case."

Why was he hurting Tanbark?

"I was clear before," said Officer Polito. "We can't discuss the case."

Was the barn fire 2 hurt Pierre, or only scare him?

Officer Polito was getting impatient, but Officer Richardson smiled kindly at Bird. "Your questions are all good, but I'm afraid we don't know the answers. Yet. We'll get them, though."

Bird knew there was no point in asking anything more, even though questions kept popping into her head.

Officer Richardson turned to Hannah. "Can we talk about Tanbark Wedger for a moment?"

"Of course."

Bird relaxed. It was Hannah's turn to be questioned.

"You recognized him from the picture in the paper?"

"Yes."

"And contacted us this morning with his name?"

"Yes. I called you as soon as I opened the paper."

"We've been able to locate and speak to his mother. She has positively identified him, and is with him now."

"That's good." Hannah was pleased, and turned to Bird and smiled. Bird felt a weight lift off her shoulders. She realized how much she wanted Tanbark to be okay.

Hannah turned back to the officers. "How is he?"

"Better than yesterday," Officer Polito answered. "Tell us, how do you know him?"

Hannah hesitated. Bird guessed that she wasn't sure how to answer.

"Let me put it this way," he said. "Is he, to your knowledge, related to you in any way? Before you answer, let me advise you that Miss Wedger has already spoken to us."

Hannah looked at her hands. "It is my suspicion that my father is Tanbark's father as well. Please understand, my father has never confirmed this, and will probably deny it."

Officer Polito wrote in his notebook. "And, just to confirm, your father's name is Kenneth Bradley."

"Yes."

"Did you know that Tanbark was in the neighbourhood?"

Hannah shook her head. "No."

"Did you identify him as 'the wild man'?"

"Yes. We referred to him as 'the wild man,' but I never knew that the wild man was Tanbark. He stayed well away from us, and ran whenever anybody was around. I never got a good look at him. I'll admit, I wondered, though. Something nagged at me about him, and then this morning the penny dropped."

"Do you know Tanbark well?" Officer Polito asked.

"Not at all. I met him once when he was about fifteen years old, and haven't seen him since."

"And yet you were able to identify him correctly from the photo?"

Hannah nodded. "Yes. There's a clear family resemblance."

"Is there anything more you can tell us about him?"

"Only that I've heard he has mental health issues."

The meeting wrapped up quickly after that, and the officers rose to leave. After the cruiser disappeared down the driveway, Hannah turned to Bird. "You did very well, honey. I'm proud of you."

Bird nodded her thanks, but she couldn't quite return Hannah's smile. The police were no closer to stopping this nonsense than they were before. Everything was a complete mess—a murder, a new relative and a horse show for which she was completely unprepared. Not to mention the fact that she couldn't speak. When would things get back to normal?

Reading Bird's look, Hannah put a hand on her niece's head. "Cheer up, sweetie. Put this all out of your mind for now. We've got a show tomorrow. Go get your clothes organized in case we need to clean them or sew on a button."

14

NOT ENOUGH PRACTICE

Tan was healing. He knew it—he could feel it. He willed every cell to heal itself, and it was working. This was his full-time job right now. Perhaps when he wrote his book he would instruct people how to do it. He would make a fortune.

HEEDING HANNAH'S INSTRUCTIONS, Bird went upstairs and rummaged around for her show clothes. Her helmet still fit, but her boots were too tight to pull on, and she could barely squeeze into her pants, jacket and shirt. Just another thing that was all messed up. She had no time to practice, let alone go shopping! Maybe she should just cancel.

Dressed in her too-small riding clothes, and carrying her boots, Bird found her aunt in the kitchen.

Hannah burst out laughing at the sight. "You've been busy growing this year."

Bird frowned. It wasn't funny.

"Well, as it happens, I saw this coming. Last week as I was passing Bahr's I noticed a huge sign in their window and stopped in for their big sale. Want to see what I bought?"

Bird watched as Hannah opened the broom closet and reached for a large bag. She pulled out a soft blue, short-sleeved riding shirt with matching rat-catcher collar, then a pair of beige breeches and a well-cut navy coat.

"Try them on! I've been dying to show you. I might have bought them a little roomy, but you've got more growing to do."

Quickly, Bird slipped out of her old clothes and donned the new. They smelled like the saddle shop and felt just perfect. Bird hugged Hannah tightly and tried not to cry. She wanted to thank her, but her voice wasn't working. Bird ran to the phone where the pad and pens were, and scribbled *THANK YOU!!!* as large as she could.

"You're very welcome. They look great on you, and were a really good price." Hannah was obviously pleased. "I love a good sale."

Bird didn't want to be greedy or ungrateful, but there was still the problem of the boots. She looked at them, and tried to figure out how to raise the issue.

Hannah saw her look, and beat her to it. She went back to the broom closet. "Try these on. I think they'll be fine." She handed her a used, but polished, pair of tall black riding boots.

Bird pulled them on over her breeches. They fit just right! Bird looked at Hannah in astonishment.

"They belong to Abby. Before she left for New York she dropped them off. For you. She said they're good luck."

This was too much! Bird dissolved into tears. Abby had lent her these same boots long ago, the first time she'd shown Sunny. Then, they'd been too big for her, but now they fit. Abby Malone, who'd encouraged her and been her mentor and her hero, had actually taken the time to deliver these boots to Hannah. For her.

Hannah hugged her again. "There are a lot of people out there cheering for you, Bird. The Piersons called this morning while you were sleeping. They're coming tomorrow, too."

Bird was overcome. The Piersons had helped her so much the previous year, when Sundancer's future was in jeopardy. What if she made a mess at the show? Her stomach flipped and she plopped down in a chair. She didn't want to disappoint anyone—not Hannah or Abby or the Piersons—but it seemed inevitable that she would. She was so unready!

"Come on, Bird," said Hannah. "It'll be fine. Take these new clothes off and let's go to work."

The steel in Hannah's voice worked wonders. Bird ran upstairs to change into her old things. She folded her new clothes neatly and placed them on top of her dresser, then reached for Abby's boots. She was about to put them safely away in her closet until the show, but then reconsidered. That her saddle and boots felt familiar was an essential part of her confidence heading into a show. Abby had lent her these boots, and Bird wanted to make her proud. She would practice in them.

Hannah and Bird set up a low course in the front paddock, with an in-and-out, an oxer, a water jump and the hedge. Hannah readied another standard to add to the in-and-out to make it a triple. They were ready. There was only one problem. No horse.

Sunny, where are you?

Hiding in the apple trees.

Come on! We have to practice for tomorrow. It's the show!

Show, schmoe. I don't feel like it.

Sunny, you're the one who wanted to do this, remember? To win? You carried the wild man up the Escarpment for this!

I changed my mind.

Why?

I just did. I don't have to give you a reason.

Yes, you do. You owe me that.

Why?

You just do.

Very mature, Bird.

Yeah. You're mature, too.

"Where is that horse? He was here a minute ago, grazing right there beside the fence with Charlie."

Bird shrugged abruptly. She was mad. She wanted to chase him down and beat him up, prove who was boss—even knowing how counterproductive that would be. Even if she did catch him, in his present mood he'd be unrideable. She wanted to scream.

"What's wrong, Bird?" asked Hannah. "You look upset."

Upset? thought Bird. Upset? They desperately needed to practice, and the wretched horse was deliberately hiding from her and ruining everything! Bird had thought they were past all this nonsense. She resisted the urge to stomp off toward the farmhouse. She needed to think. She had a bigger brain, so she should be smarter. Think! The beginnings of a smile crept across her mouth.

Bird climbed the fence. *Do you want to jump a little, Charlie horse?*

Sure, Bird.

Let's get you tacked up.

"Bird?" questioned Hannah, looking at her watch. "What are you doing? We don't have time to work two horses. I have some beginners coming in half an hour."

Bird shrugged. She had something to prove to Sunny. Charlie came to the fence and Bird hopped up on him bareback. She trotted him up to the barn and saddled him. Within five minutes they were ready to jump.

Sundancer had come out of hiding. He glared at them over the fence. *Why are you wasting your time with Charlie?* he asked.

I'm not wasting my time. I'm going to the show tomorrow, with or without you.

Bird and Charlie picked up a nice easy canter and jumped around the course. Charlie was an old pro and caught his leads without effort. He brought his front knees up together and carefully tucked his hind legs over each jump. His tempo never varied.

"Wonderful, Bird!" shouted Hannah. "I haven't seen Charlie jump this well in years. Let me raise the jumps and then I want you to go again." Hannah paused. "Why don't we take Charlie to the show tomorrow? Kimberly can ride him. Up in the barn just now, Cliff told me that Pastor's got an abscess in his hoof and is dead lame."

I'm going to the show? asked Charlie.

If Hannah says so, then you're going. You did that great, Charlie!

Sundancer was mad. *Great? You want to see great?* He sat back on his hind end and leapt over the fence. Hannah, Bird and Charlie watched as the tall chestnut gelding began jumping on his own. He circled in an elegant canter then jumped around the course with a steady tempo, leaving every jump intact. He was perfect.

"Bravo, Sunny!" shouted Hannah. "I've never seen anything like it in my entire life!"

No kidding, thought Bird grumpily. Normal horses don't do crazy things like that.

"Good job! Bird, get Sundancer tacked up and jump him around, since you're showing him tomorrow."

No way.

Sunny, what's wrong?

There's nothing wrong with me. *You're the one with the problem.*

Two cars drove up the driveway—Hannah's students. "I've got to go. Kimberly will have a good time with Charlie tomorrow. Get Sunny around the course, and I'll check back with you, okay?"

Bird nodded and watched her aunt stride up to the barn.

Charlie stood beside her. *Now can I go back to graze?*

Sure, Charlie. Thanks. You were really fun to ride.

Thanks, Bird, but I might not want to go to the show. It's boring. You decide.

She removed his tack and put him in his field next to the grass ring. What a lovely, uncomplicated horse, she thought.

Uncomplicated? telegraphed Sunny. *Are you implying that I'm complicated? Just so you know, the reason I don't want you to ride me is that you're full of turmoil and stress.*

Bird was taken aback. He was right. Totally right. She was stressed after the police interview. She was worried about Tanbark. She wondered if she would ever speak again. She feared making a fool of herself at the show. She was afraid of all the weird things happening around them.

I'm sorry, Sunny.

You can't just assume that I'll be fine if you're not fine.

I didn't think about it like that.

When a person can't drop their garbage, horses can't relax, and if horses are not relaxed, they can't think.

Well said, Sunny.

If you're upset, I'm more upset.

Bird sat on the ground with her saddle and bridle. *I need to put everything else out of my head.*

Charlie is cool. He's able to work when you're stressed, but I can't. I have enough nerves of my own without yours, too.

I hear you, Sunny. Bird put her head in her arms and closed her eyes. She breathed deeply. As she inhaled she thought, "In with the good," and when she exhaled she thought, "Out with the bad." By the third breath, her tension began to leave her.

Sundancer got closer and closer until he was standing over her. He bent his neck and reached down to nuzzle her burnt hair. *I'll be happy to let you ride me now, if you want.*

Bird looked up into the horse's intelligent brown eyes. *I'd appreciate that, Sunny. I want to go into that ring tomorrow and clean up.*

Me, too!

15
THE PALSTON HORSE SHOW

Tan was deeply unhappy. His mother was gone. He hadn't seen her leave and he didn't know where she was. In her place, his father was sitting beside his bed. The man troubled him. He made Tan extremely uncomfortable. Also, his bandages were too tight and the air was too still. Everything smelled like antiseptic. He had to get out. He had to leave this place or he'd smother. The sooner the better. Freedom was everything.

THE NEXT MORNING DAWNED with a clear blue sky. Songbirds chirped and tweeted heartily, and small animals scurried to and fro. Bird woke up feeling much better. She'd slept well. She was ready to take on the world. She jumped out of bed and ran downstairs, still in her pajamas. She hopped the split-rail fence into Sunny's field and gave him an apple.

You're in a good mood. You're jumping around.

I'm really excited about the show. Are you ready to bring home some major ribbons?

Do horses love apples? Yum, that was good.

Bird laughed aloud. *See you in a little while. I'm going to have breakfast and get dressed.*

What about my breakfast?

There's Cliff now. He's bringing you a feast.

I should have known. He never forgets me.

Cliff saw Bird and waved. "Hi there, Smokey!" He'd taken to calling her that since the barn fire. "Did you listen to the news this morning?"

Bird shook her head. She wasn't sure she wanted to know.

"There was an item about Tanbark Wedger. Uncle Tanbark, to you!"

Let it go, she told herself. Put everything except the show out of your mind.

"And you'll never believe this! A group, Justice for the Innocent, admitted to starting the fire. A CBC reporter got an email claiming responsibility. Sort of. I guess they lit a fire in a trash can under Pierre's window to scare him. They say they're shocked and appalled that it spread. Idiots!"

Idiots was right, but the news didn't surprise Bird. She shook her head in dismay to let Cliff know she'd heard, and set her jaw as she watched Sunny eat.

Cliff grinned at her. "Good luck today, Bird. You sure look ready to win!" He waved goodbye and continued to the next field with his buckets of feed.

The Saddle Creek rig nabbed the best parking place at the show, even though they'd pulled in a little later than they'd hoped due to unexpected loading problems. Charlie wouldn't get on the trailer. He'd warned Bird the day before, but Kimberly was understandably upset. Finally, Hannah had to make the difficult decision to leave without him, or they'd be late.

Bird felt bad for her friend. First, she couldn't take Pastor because of the abscess, and now Charlie. Kimberly came with them anyway, because her mother Lavinia had other plans for the day and couldn't come back to get her. Just like always, Bird mused, Lavinia was too absorbed in her own life to give her daughter much thought.

Here, though, was a piece of good luck. The very best

parking spot was being vacated just as they arrived. It was up on the ridge in the shade and close to both the practice and show rings.

Bird couldn't believe how busy the grounds were at seven in the morning. Classes didn't start for over an hour, yet horses were being schooled in every available area. Ponies, jumpers, hunters; kids, teens, adults; even older riders in their fifties and sixties. They came from near and far, but when Bird recognized vans from professional barns, her stomach knotted up.

"Okay, folks." Hannah was using her take-charge teacher voice. "Check your horse first, then let's go get our numbers and riding sequence. Kimberly, you help the younger girls." Hannah opened the drop windows on the trailer to allow in more air, and to let the horses see what was going on.

Bird felt the growing excitement around her. The Saddle Creek horses were standing tall, ears pricked to catch every sound and necks arched with tension. Their nostrils flared in an effort to smell the equine news. The people were no calmer. Julia and Liz and Kimberly were giggling about nothing and shivering with nerves, even in the growing heat of the summer day. Only Hannah was calm and in control, but she'd been taking kids to horse shows for years.

Bird ducked under the trailer partition and stood up beside Sunny as he watched all the action from his window. With so much competition, she wondered briefly why she was there.

No negative thoughts, Bird!

Easy for you to say! Yesterday you were thinking nothing BUT negative thoughts.

Today's a new day. We're gonna win big.

How can you say that? We just got here.

I've looked around. This new fashion is a killer.

What new fashion? Bird looked across the grounds, wondering what he was talking about.

Pulling the draw-reins up tight and see-sawing on our mouths. It's making the horses angry, which makes it easy for you and me.

Bird's eyes settled on the practice ring. Sunny had a point. Everywhere she looked, horses were prancing angrily and riders were picking and pulling and fiddling with their reins.

There must be a reason everybody's doing it, Bird considered. *Does it do any good?*

A little give-and-take might be a good thing to help us drop our heads and use our hind ends, but this is ridiculous.

Hannah uses draw-reins to train horses.

But she doesn't crank them up like that. Look at that one!

Bird noticed a young woman on a pretty bay mare. The reins were so short that the mare's chin almost touched her chest. Her tail swished and her eyes flashed. Her flattened ears warned of an impending problem.

Wait for it!

The thought was barely out of Sunny's head before the mare decided she'd had enough. She couldn't buck with her head held so tight, so she leapt straight up in the air and twisted fast. The rider came off and landed in the dirt, and the trainer came running.

Now for the hard part. Sunny was not at all amused. *She's going to be punished for reacting to cruelty.*

Sure enough, the trainer took the mare by the bridle and backed her up harshly. He shook her mouth hard and yelled.

Bird winced. *I don't even want to know what he'd do if nobody was watching.*

I've been there.

Wait!

What?

Bird stared at the mare. *Did you hear the name he called her? After the swearing part? No, but I know who she is. So do you.*

Bird studied the little bay mare in the ring. She had certainly not expected this. *It's Moonlight Sonata!*

The same.

She's Abby Malone's eventing horse! I didn't know Moonie was showing now. I haven't heard about her for a few years.

She's a good mare, but look at her ears. Bird noted that they lay flat on her head. *She won't stand for bad treatment. Good for her.*

Maybe, but it'll go harder for her than if she accepted it.

Hannah stood in front of Sunny's window and looked up at Bird. "Are you ready to come and get your number?"

Bird nodded.

See you in a few minutes, Sunny. Don't get into any trouble.

Like I can get into trouble standing here in the trailer, tied up.

Others have done it before you.

Hannah and the girls headed to the office to get their paperwork done. On their way past Moonlight Sonata, Bird noticed that the trainer had turned his attention from the mare to the girl on the ground. Bird telegraphed the mare a message.

Don't worry, Moonie. Everything will be fine.

The mare's ears flicked, startled. *Who are you?*

I'm Bird.

Sundancer's Bird?

Yes.

I've heard about you.

I've heard about you, too! You're famous for winning the Caledon Steeplechase the very last year it was run.

With Abby I could do anything. With this girl I can do nothing. It makes me sad.

The trainer held Moonie's reins in one hand. With the other, he was trying to help the girl to her feet. She was crying in pain, and Bird thought her ankle looked odd.

"Can somebody help me here?" the trainer bellowed. "Candace needs a medic!"

Two paramedics ran out to the ring. Hannah and the girls stopped to watch as Candace was strapped to a gurney and carried out. Now the trainer hopped up into the saddle, determined to teach Moonie a lesson. After backing her up across the ring, he raced her around and dragged her to a halt. He repeatedly jammed his heels into her sides and spun her in tight circles.

Let me outta here!

He's only showing off, Moonie.

He's scaring me!

Go with it, Moonie. It'll be over as soon as you give in.

I'll try.

Moonie dropped her head and slowed down, adopting a docile manner. The trainer's face broke into a wide grin. He dropped the reins to wave to the group that had gathered to watch.

I hate to make him so pleased with himself.

Agreed, but at least it's over.

I'll get him back.

Bird laughed out loud.

Hannah turned to her. "What's so funny? I'm so mad right now I could scream! Dexter Pill should know better. I'd take that mare off his hands in a minute! She's a real sweetheart."

An idea crept into Bird's head. *Moonie, buck him off.*

What?

Now. While he's so cocky.

I don't want to get in any more trouble.

Now, Moonie! Do it. I'll help if there's a problem.

Moonie didn't argue. With a mighty lurch, she launched herself into the air with her back rounded and four feet off the ground. Dexter Pill landed in precisely the same place as his student before him. Moonie stood beside him with wide eyes, looking at Bird for directions.

Everything will be fine. Don't worry.

The trainer started shouting. "Someone get in here and help me!"

Hannah rushed into the practice ring, with Dexter yelling as she approached, "Take this horse!" He was covered in dirt and he was furious. Hannah didn't hesitate.

As she led Moonie safely away from the other horses and riders in the ring, a surly, well-dressed woman in her late thirties came up to her. "You can keep her for all I care."

Hannah stopped. "What have you got to do with this mare?"

"I'm Kelsey Woodall, Candace's mother. We leased her from Fiona Malone."

"Of course! Moonlight Sonata." Hannah took another look at the bay mare and rubbed her soft nose. "I thought she looked familiar. She belongs to Abby Malone."

"Thank gawd she doesn't belong to me! You can take her away."

Hannah was puzzled. "*I* can take her? How exactly is this *my* problem?"

"Well, it sure isn't mine. I wash my hands. Oh ..." The woman undid the girth and slipped off the saddle. "It's an Hermès." She turned her back and began to walk away with the saddle braced on her hip. "The bridle's not mine," she called over her shoulder.

Hannah looked toward Dexter Pill, who was up on his feet and brushing himself off.

Bird stepped up to Moonie and took the reins from Hannah. *So far so good.*

Moonie was trembling. *I sure hope so.*

Kimberly had quietly approached and now she stroked Moonie's face. "It's okay, girl," she crooned. To Bird she said, "She's so pretty."

I like this girl, Bird.

Bird smiled. *You see my plan, Moonie?*

Hannah left Moonie with Bird and Kimberly, and approached the angry trainer. "Dexter, two things. First, are you all right?"

"I'm fine, no thanks to that crazy mare."

"Second, Kelsey Woodall told me to take her. I have no idea about your deal with Fiona Malone, but you'd better take Moonlight Sonata back to your trailer and sort this out."

"I'm going to call Fiona to come pick her up. This mare is on trial for a lease. Bucking is a deal-breaker. I don't have time for this." He turned to go.

"Pardon me? I came in the ring to help you, and you treat me like this?" Hannah became even more upset. "Bird! Bring the mare here."

Bird did as she was told. Kimberly followed.

"Hand her over to Mr. Pill."

Bird gave him Moonie's reins. Dexter took them haughtily.

"We'll be on our way." Hannah wiped her hands on her pants, her face flushed with anger.

I don't want to stay with him!

Step on his toe.

"Gosh darned stupid animal!" Dexter Pill hopped on one foot. "She stepped on my toe!" He smacked Moonie hard on her shoulder with his crop and Moonie shied in fear.

Bird looked at Hannah. She put her hand on Moonie's neck, and then motioned to their trailer. She raised her eyebrows in a question and put her hands together as in prayer.

Hannah's mouth tightened as she thought it over. She was a sucker for maltreated animals, and Bird didn't need to be a mind reader to see that her aunt had taken a liking to the mare.

"Take Moonie and put her on our trailer. We'll drop her off at Fiona's on the way home."

Bird nodded happily and patted Moonie's nose. *See? You'll never see that guy's face again.*

"I'm billing you for the transport," Hannah told Dexter as he hobbled away. Her icy tone prevented any argument. "This is totally unprofessional behaviour."

For a moment they stood and watched him go. Kimberly broke the silence. "Is there any way I could ride her today, Hannah? I mean, if nobody else is and she's here and everything?"

Bird waited.

"I have my saddle," Kimberly pleaded. "We put it on the trailer this morning, remember? Before Charlie refused to get on? I'm dressed and everything. My entry fees were prepaid. I even have my hat."

"Let me call Fiona." Hannah pulled her cellphone from her pocket. "I'm sure she'll be delighted."

Kimberly jumped up and down and squealed. "I can't believe it! Finally, some good luck!"

You be nice to Kimberly, Moonie. She's a little green.

I'll get her some ribbons. Thank you, Bird. Thank you so much.

"Bird, take Moonlight Sonata to the trailer and stay with the horses," said Hannah, her phone still pressed to her ear. "I'll get your entry number." Hannah walked off with Liz, Julia and Kimberly. The girls' arms were entwined and they were barely able to contain their shared joy.

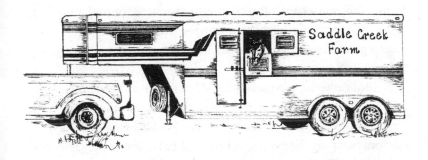

16

GOSSIP

Tan strove to ignore his father's negative energy. His father was smart, but Tan was smarter. He could feel his brain working. Even at half capacity, he was way smarter than most people. Everything was under control. His body was healing and his mind was getting sharper every minute. He was busy devising a plan. He'd be out of here in no time.

BIRD LOADED MOONIE in the spot right beside Sundancer. It would have belonged to Charlie, had he decided to come.

Hey there, Moonie! Welcome aboard! Bird had never seen Sunny so charming to another horse. Was he flirting?

I'm so happy to be here. Those humans really don't care about us. They're in it for the people-money.

That's not good.

Bird listened to the horses chatter as she refilled their hay nets. The ponies introduced themselves to Moonie, and soon they were exchanging horror stories from past experiences. It was a good time to get some buckets of fresh water. It was going to be a hot day.

Bird gathered two green plastic buckets from the tack room at the front of the trailer and carried them across the gravel road to the showers. There were already two horses being bathed, their grooms soaping them up and hosing them down as they gossiped·

loudly over the roar of the water. Bird went to the tap and began filling one of the buckets. She listened idly to the conversation.

"Dex is hopping mad. Lucky for Moonie Hannah took her. Dex might have killed her." The chubby redhead chuckled. Bird knew she didn't mean that literally.

"No kidding! Dex has a temper for sure. None of his horses is doing much. They're all sour." This girl was short with punky, spiked blonde hair.

"Hey, speaking of Hannah, did you hear?" The redhead stopped working. "The creep who whacked that woman? You know, the perv in the woods? He's her brother!"

"No way!" The blonde put down her sponge.

"Everybody's talking about it! You know Kenneth Bradley is Hannah's father, right? The dude who stole Sundancer last year?"

"Yeah."

"Well, Bradley's the father of that creep."

"Seriously?"

"It was on the radio. Which makes Hannah his sister."

"Holy."

Bird stood at the tap, her heart pounding in her chest. This was just what she'd feared. She'd hoped more than anything that the horse people would've been too preoccupied with the show to listen to the news this morning, but clearly that wasn't the case. She put the one full pail aside and began to fill the second, keeping her head down.

"Don't you think it's weird?" Redhead was thinking aloud.

"What?"

"Think about it: Hannah's perv brother is one suspect."

"I think he's the one, by the way," the blonde girl interrupted.

"Hannah's neighbour is one suspect."

"He'll be in the hospital forever. Messed up."

"And Hannah's stable manager is another suspect." Redhead finished her point.

"I see where you're going with this. I don't know about the manager, by the way. Never met him."

"And one of Hannah's students? Her mother's boyfriend is the fourth suspect."

"The ex-cop?"

"Yeah. Isn't it weird?"

"Saddle Creek is right in the middle of it. What do you think that means?"

Redhead shrugged. "Dunno. It's just weird."

Bird had filled the two pails. She turned her back to the grooms and picked them up.

Redhead whispered. "That girl."

"What girl?"

"That one with weird hair, carrying the buckets!"

Bird suppressed the urge to freeze, and continued to put one foot in front of the other.

"So?"

"That's Alberta Simms! Hannah's niece!"

"Bird? Oh no! I bet she heard everything we said!"

"So what if she did? It's all true and everybody's saying it."

"I know, but now I feel bad."

"Get over it. She didn't hear a word. The water's too loud."

Bird didn't put the buckets down until she reached the trailer. Is that what people really thought, that somehow Hannah had something to do with the murder? And what exactly had been in the news about her grandfather? She should've asked Cliff this morning.

Why so glum, Bird?

Nothing, Sunny. Just gossip.

When do we get out there? I'm raring to go.

Hannah will be back soon, and she'll tell us.

Bird sat on the mounting block and waited for Hannah to return, trying to push all thoughts of the overheard conversation out of her mind. To make herself feel better, she willed herself to think of Alec. Bird missed him, and she longed to tell him about all the things that were happening in the neighbourhood. Alec, with his calm reason, would be sure to have good ideas and thoughtful words. He was more than a boyfriend, he was a true friend.

She wished she could call him, but the few phones at the camp were reserved for emergencies and cell reception was awful. Not that it mattered. In her current speechless state, Bird could hardly hold a conversation.

She wondered again about why she couldn't speak. Maybe it *was* the fire and the smoke. She certainly wanted to talk. It wasn't like before, when she'd chosen to stop talking because no one was listening. Now she wanted to speak! She had so many things to say! Maybe she just needed to practice, to get her vocal chords loosened up again.

Bird tried to make a noise, any noise. She took a breath and let it out slowly. She took another breath and tried to hum as she expelled the air. Nothing. She broke off a blade of grass and blew through it. That made a noise. Someone had once told her that vocal chords were similar to a blade of grass. It was the air moving across them that made the noise. She tried to hum again. A squeak! Bird grinned. It was a start.

Bird caught sight of Hannah and the girls walking toward the trailer. Their drooping shoulders told her that they'd heard the gossip, too.

Hannah tried to smile. "We're the talk of the show."

Julia, always looking on the bright side, said, "At least we got good service in the office. Robyn looked after us right away and told us to ignore it all. I like Robyn."

Kim agreed. "Me, too. The radio played the news the whole time. Every ten minutes we heard *again* that Kenneth Bradley, disgraced horseman, is sitting with his illegitimate, crispy son in Orangeville Hospital under guard. It's very dramatic." She shook her head and sat beside Bird on the mounting block.

Bird didn't like hearing this—her grandfather always meant bad news. She hoped Tan was all right, and squeezed over to make room.

Liz was despondent. "Maybe I should g … go home," she said. "We didn't go to my grandparents' because Phil can't leave t … town, but now M … mom thinks maybe we should go without him. I'm not sure I'd remember my c … course anyway, I'm so upset."

Hannah hugged the girl. "Honey, you'll be fine. Your mom told me you're leaving tomorrow. Today, forget the silly stuff and just have fun."

"Yeah," said Julia. "So what if you forget your course?"

"I do it all the time," chuckled Kimberly. "I think I'll win the class if I get it right."

Liz began to smile.

Bird tried her noise again. It came out as a breathy squeal, more like a pig than a person, but she was so happy about it that everybody broke out laughing.

What do you think you're doing, Bird?

Cheering people up. It's working, too.

I have no idea why that horrible noise would cheer anybody up. Let's get out of here and win some ribbons!

Hannah had the same idea. "We've got lots of time, but let's get tacked up and go to the practice ring. Kimberly, you've never ridden Moonie, so you should get to know her." Hannah grinned at them all. "Our only goal today is to have a great time. Enjoy your horse. Enjoy your ride. If we pick up a ribbon, all the better, but our best reward is to ride for the sheer pleasure of riding."

Julia repeated slowly, "Ride for the sheer pleasure of riding. I like it! That's what I'm going to do!"

Liz linked her arm with Julia. "Me, too. That's what I'm going to do, t ... too. Ride for the sheer p ... pleasure of riding!"

Kim joined in. "Me, too! And Bird!"

Bird squeaked as loud as she could, and everybody convulsed with laughter. For the moment, at least, the gloom was pushed back out of sight.

Liz was showing first. She was in a small pony jumper class and Sabrina, the chestnut Welsh Mountain pony, was ready and keen.

Bird put the finishing touches on Sabrina's braided mane and combed out her flaxen tail.

You look divine.

I always do.

But you don't always let kids, especially girls, finish the course.

I do so!

I'm not trying to insult you, but you know what I'm talking about.

Maybe I do. Maybe I don't. Sometimes I like to have a little fun.

Did you know that the winner of this class gets their picture in all the horse magazines?

The winner, as in the kid? Or the winner, as in the pony?

Both together. You'd look beautiful in those magazines, you have to admit it.

You're trying to bribe me, aren't you?

Just a little.

I was going to be excellent today, anyway. Fast but safe. This girl tries hard and she respects me. She's not bad at all for a girl.

Bird patted Sabrina's neck. What a great pony, she thought. And a stern teacher. Sabrina had taught many kids how to ride. She never allowed sloppy treatment, and she demanded complete concentration. Or else. For some reason that Bird had never figured out, Sabrina preferred boy riders to girls.

Bird gave her a kiss on the nose. *Thanks, Sabrina. Not too fast, okay? Take care of Liz. She needs it today.*

I already told you: fast but safe.

Liz was ready to get on, with her helmet snapped up and her number tied around her waist. She was getting more and more nervous as the time grew near, literally twitching as she sat on Sabrina's back. Hannah walked beside Sabrina as they made their way down to the ring, and repeated their new mantra, over and over. "Ride for the sheer pleasure of riding, Liz. Honestly, nothing else matters."

"B ... but everybody thinks we're horrible! They think M ... Mom's boyfriend is guilty—and Cliff, and Pierre, and Tanbark—and we're all somehow p ... part of it!"

Hannah stopped walking and the pony came to a stop. "Listen to me, Liz," Hannah said, her voice serious. "They're wrong. Time will prove it. Believe in your friends, and believe in yourself. Keep your chin up and stop listening to gossip. I mean it."

Liz nodded. "You're right. They d ... don't know what they're talking about."

"Gossips never do. Now, let's review the course."

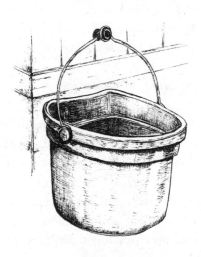

17

MORE GOSSIP

Tan wiggled his fingers, then his toes. Moving each part of his body, one by one, he assured himself that everything worked. The drugs were good to relieve pain, but they dimmed his mind. He was weaning himself off them. He needed to be totally alert for what was ahead.

His father had stepped out of the room for a moment. The nurse came in. He was ready for her. He accepted the pill she put in his mouth, and pretended to swallow. She smiled the fake smile she used to make Tan think she was pleased with him. As soon as she turned, he pushed it out of his mouth with his tongue and let it drop beside the bed. The nurse turned back to him with a thermometer in her hand. Tan opened his mouth obediently.

JULIA AND KIMBERLY were ringside with Hannah, supporting Liz as she trotted into the ring, while Bird stayed with the horses. She stood with Sunny in the trailer. They had a good view of Liz and Sabrina from his open window, and Bird watched as they broke into a canter and began the course.

Sunny missed nothing. *Very nice. But look. Her body bulged around the corner. Liz was pulling her to the wrong jump.*

It's a jumper class, Sunny. That bulge doesn't count.

Her resistance added to the time. Every second matters.

Wow, that in-and-out was perfect! Bird's eyes got round as Sabrina picked up speed. *Is she ever moving now! She's burning up the ground.*

If Liz could let her reins go a little, Sabrina could do her job better.

I know, but that's really hard. When a person thinks their horse is going too fast, we pull the reins to slow you down.

But we fight the reins and go faster!

Holy! She chipped in and flew over that oxer!

She's going to have an excellent time, Bird, if she goes clean.

Only a few more jumps. Watch those little legs fly!

There's the water jump. Perfect! Nothing bothers her.

She's a brave pony, Sunny. Is she going too fast?

I hope Liz can hang on.

She's racing to the last line.

She can do it, Bird. Yeah!

That's it! That's the course! They did it!

Timmy and Moonie joined Bird and Sunny in their celebration. The horses stamped their feet in applause and Bird made her new noise. The show had begun well for Saddle Creek.

Kimberly and Julia raced up to the trailer. "We need Timmy!" Kimberly called, out of breath from her dash. "Did you see Liz go, Bird?"

"I'll never beat that time!" Julia wailed. "Timmy's not nearly as fast, but I love him anyway!"

Bird helped her sister get Timmy down the ramp. She gave him a once-over with a towel to shine him up, then held his bridle while she got on.

Timmy, my friend, are you ready?

Yes, of course. I've done this forever.

Don't try to beat Sabrina's time. Julia hasn't ridden much lately.

I'm not crazy. Sabrina herself couldn't beat that time.

"Thanks, Bird. Wish me luck." Julia looked pale.

Bird squeezed her boot and grinned. She gave her a thumbs-up and patted Timmy on the rump. She watched her little sister and Timmy trot down to the ring to join Hannah.

"What's going on with your voice, Bird?" asked Kimberly.

Bird was startled. She'd forgotten that Kimberly was still in the trailer.

"You talked all year! You talked a week ago when we made plans to show together. Is it the stupid thing about Alec and Pamela?"

Bird felt like all the air had been let out of her body. Alec and Pamela? What stupid thing? At camp? A vision of Pamela's cute face and curvy body came to her mind, and Bird felt dizzy.

"You didn't hear, did you? Ohmygosh. Nobody believes it, Bird! I promise! I didn't mean to upset you!" Kimberly was totally dismayed. "And just before you're about to go in the ring. I'm so *so* sorry! It's just stupid gossip! There's nothing in it! I hate that I even repeated it! Please forget that I said it! You're my very, very best friend. You know that, right?"

Kimberly tried to give Bird a hug, but Bird was limp. She knew her friend hadn't wished to upset her, but she felt ill thinking about Alec with someone else. Especially Pamela Parker. It couldn't be true.

"Bird? Please, Bird? I'm so sorry I said that. It just popped out. And, really, it doesn't matter to me if you can talk or not. We understand each other just fine. I just wondered why you're not talking, that's all!"

Bird looked at her friend. Kim was desperate for Bird's forgiveness. She answered the question by touching her throat, then putting her palms up in a gesture that meant *I don't know.*

"Can you forgive me? For saying anything about ... you know?"

Bird nodded and forced a smile. It wasn't Kimberly's fault that people talked nonsense. Because that's what it was. Nonsense. Stupid gossip. Must be. Had to be ... didn't it? Or could it be true?

"Forget I said it, Bird. Anyway, it's not true! Pamela doesn't hold a candle to you. Anyway, Julia and Timmy just started! Let's watch!" Kimberly put a comforting arm around Bird's shoulders as they left the trailer. They sat side by side on the mounting block to watch, and Bird willed herself to concentrate on the ring.

"Great beginning!" exclaimed Kim. "She's got her head on straight, you can tell from here. Julia means business."

Watch Timmy, Bird, telegraphed Sunny. *He's got it down. He gives her confidence by making her kick him on. It's the oldest trick in the book.*

Good for him, answered Bird. *That was a good corner. Julia's doing just what Hannah told her: eyes looking where she's going, heels down.*

That helps, Bird. But Timmy wants to be second. Clean but not crazy fast.

"Julia's riding great. She's giving Liz a run for her money." Kimberly was excited at the contest.

Timmy could've run out on that jump, Bird, Sunny noted. *But he didn't.*

"Julia lost her reins! Oh, good, she's got them. That was close." Kim let out her breath. "Lucky Timmy didn't catch on or he would've avoided the jump."

Sunny snorted. *What a crock! Of course Timmy knew she lost her reins! Does she think we're stupid?*

Bird laughed her squeaking laugh. It was so much fun listening to her two companions that her thoughts about Alec, for the moment, at least, were pushed aside.

"She took the in-and-out like a pro! They're doing great!" Kimberly was wriggling with excitement.

Timmy's bringing her home! He's on a roll and he's not going to make any mistakes.

"She did it!" Kimberly and Bird jumped up from the block and danced around. "She did it! Hooray!"

He did it! Sunny and Moonie thumped their hooves and whinnied. *He did it!*

Julia proudly trotted Timmy up to the trailer. "That was so

much fun! The class is almost over!" she shouted. "Hannah says that Liz has the best time so far and she went clean, and so far I'm second. We went clean but not as fast." Julia was talking fast and her face was flushed. "Only three more ponies to go!"

Kimberly jumped up from the mounting block. "Right! Stay aboard, Julia! You've gotta be ready to go back in there to get a ribbon."

Bird kept an eye on the competition in the ring. A young boy was desperately trying to beat Liz and Sabrina's time. It would not end well, Bird predicted.

Sunny observed the same thing. *He's headed for a dust bath.*

No sooner was the thought out of Sunny's head than the boy made too tight a turn and yanked his pony's neck right around. The pony wasn't on the correct lead and couldn't keep his balance. He fell on his knees. The boy was pitched forward and flipped over onto his back.

The crowd gasped. The girls watched as the ambulance rolled up to the ring. Paramedics jumped out and ran to the boy, while show staff kept people back.

The dejected pony limped away, led by a young woman. Bird took another look. It was the redheaded groom from the showers. Bird hoped the pony would be okay. He'd tried his best for that boy.

The boy stood up on wobbly legs. A woman hugged him and brushed him off. Likely his mother.

"Holy," said Liz. "Th ... that was awful."

"Scary," agreed Julia. "That could've been any one of us."

Not unless you twist our necks like that. Sunny sniffed. *That boy wants to be an alligator wrestler, not a rider.*

The next pony trotted in. The girl was stiff with anxiety, and when she started her course she kept her reins tight and her pace slow. It was obvious that she didn't want to crash and burn. Bird guessed that her trainer had forced her to go in. Three jumps came down and she had time faults, but she was in one piece when it was over. Her body slumped with relief as she walked her irritated pony out.

It was time for the last rider. Liz and Julia held hands and squeezed them tight. They could be first and second; it all depended on this round.

Bird recognized the plucky white pony. Joey! He must be in his late twenties, Bird guessed. He'd been owned by the Thompsons, then Guy and Bunny, then sold to the Merrills. It was hard to imagine how many kids he'd taught to ride. She watched with interest as he began his round.

The blonde girl sat beautifully. It was either Emily or Jacqueline, Bird wasn't sure. They both rode with confidence, almost like they'd been born in the saddle. No surprise. The Merrills, Bird thought, *were* born in the saddle. The family went back generations in the horse industry—thoroughbred racing, show jumping and fox hunting.

This girl and Joey were a good team, and everybody knew it. This was the competition. Liz and Julia held their breath.

Before they began the course, Sunny made a prediction. *Sabrina's time was too fast for Joey, but if he goes clean, and if he keeps his pace, he'll be second.*

Bird had to agree.

They were right. There were no jumps knocked down, and no time faults.

"I think you and T … Timmy went faster, Julia," said Liz, hopefully.

"We'll know soon enough." Julia was still smiling. "I'm happy with third! I'm happy with *any* ribbon of *any* colour! Timmy's the one who won it, anyway."

She's got that right.

At least she knows it, Sunny.

I'll give her that.

From down at the ring, Hannah waved to the girls. They knew

what that meant. Bird and Kimberly got the younger girls dusted and back up on their ponies. They all came down the hill together. Beside the ring, they waited expectantly for the results to be read.

Seconds later, although it felt like hours, the announcer turned on the microphone. "Please come into the ring, mounted, in this order. Five forty-three. Three sixty-two. Five forty-four. Four seventy-one ..." The announcer continued the list up to eighth place, but the Saddle Creek girls had stopped listening after the first three. Liz and Sabrina were first, and Julia and Timmy were third. Joey and his blonde Merrill rider were second.

Even though it was frowned upon, the girls let out a whoop when they trotted in to get their ribbons.

"What's all the jumping and hooting about?" asked a familiar voice.

Bird spun around. It was Pete Pierson, grinning from ear to ear as he leaned on his cane. Beside him was Laura, dressed in a blue sundress with a matching hat.

"Bird, dear!" she called. "When are you riding? You haven't gone yet, have you?"

Bird shook her head no, and pointed to Hannah.

"Give me one minute!" Hannah called out. "Let's get these girls properly applauded first. They did a super job!"

And applaud they did. The Saddle Creek supporters were proud and appreciative. They cheered for their friends as they completed their victory gallop around the ring, led by Sabrina and Liz. Hannah met the girls, cheeks flushed with pride, as they exited the ring. "Well done, Liz! Great ride! Good for you, Julia! I've got pictures for your mothers!"

While Hannah congratulated the girls, Bird praised the ponies. *Hurray, Sabrina, Queen of Speed! Timmy, my friend, well done! You did everything right.*

Hannah and Kimberly led the ponies and riders up to the trailer, leaving Bird with Pete and Laura. Hannah called to them over her shoulder, "Bird's class begins one hour from now, and she's up second, just after Kimberly rides Moonlight Sonata."

"Moonlight Sonata?" bellowed Pete.

"The same! It's a long story." Hannah continued up the hill. "I'll tell you later, I promise."

"Bird, dear," said Laura. "What's the story about Moonie?"

Bird knew why they were so interested. Years before, Abby Malone and Pete had trained Moonie to win the Caledon Steeplechase. Moonie had been quite a handful until Pete's regular workouts and Abby's devotion and unwavering belief had transformed the mare. Pete had even bought Moonie himself to keep her from being sold before the race. He had a right to know what was happening now.

Bird shook her head and pointed to her throat.

"Oh, my," Laura clucked. "You've lost your speech again?"

Bird nodded.

Pete looked thoughtful. "No wonder."

"What do you mean by that, Pete?" Laura asked.

"Stress, I'd imagine." He put his large hand on Bird's head. "The events of late are taking their toll on everybody. But you, Bird, are more sensitive than most."

Laura was still puzzled. "But Bird spoke perfectly well after the meeting at the General Store!"

"Yes, but things hadn't heated up then, had they?" He looked at Bird closely. "Your hair will grow back quickly. But the memory of the barn fire will stay with you for a long time." He turned to his wife. "The fire, Laura. I'd put my money on that event being the trigger."

Bird stared at Pete, shocked by the obviousness of his theory. Of course he was right! She hadn't been able to speak a word since the fire, but it wasn't because of smoke damage to her throat. It was the stress. Her body was making decisions for her! How strange—and annoying! No wonder Alec was looking around for a normal girl.

All at once Bird felt incredibly angry. She would not let this continue! She would speak, and she would speak when and where she wanted, not just whenever her weird condition allowed her to. Bird opened her mouth and willed her voice to co-operate. Nothing came out, not even the new-found pig noise. Tears sprang into her eyes.

"Now, Pete, you've upset her." Laura threw her arms around Bird, gathering her into a warm hug.

Bird shook her head wildly. The truth had upset her, not Pete. She nodded at him and tried to smile. She wanted him to know that she was grateful.

The redheaded groom passed by just then, still walking the pony that the boy had rolled. "Hey, Bird," she called, her voice heavy with derision. "How's Uncle Tanbark?"

Bird didn't even try to control herself. She twisted herself out of Laura's arms and lunged at the groom. She grabbed her shirt, shaking with rage.

The pony backed up, startled and afraid. *Don't hurt us! Please!*

Bird stopped short, and stared at the pony. She saw herself through the animal's eyes, and it wasn't a pretty sight. She must look like a maniac. She fell on her knees, sobbing, as the redhead hurried away.

Pete knelt beside Bird. "Listen to me. Never, *ever*, let the small-minded people in this world win. Rise above them. Take the high road. Do you understand what I'm saying?"

Bird nodded. She knew he was right, but it was so hard to do.

"Soon enough we'll know the truth about who's to blame for the murder and the barn fire. You know and I know that it has nothing to do with you, so don't let them bring you down." Pete slowly rose to his feet with Laura's help, his jaw set.

Bird tried to take courage from his strength and wisdom. Small-minded people were everywhere. If she let them, they'd erode her confidence until she became one of them herself. She stood up.

She stuck out her hand, and Pete took it. They shook on it.

"Good." Pete smiled at her proudly. "When you get your speech back I want to know the whole story about how Kimberly got to ride Moonie, but now, Laura and I are going to get a bite to eat and find a good spot on the bleachers. We'll be right there when you ride. We're cheering for you, Bird, in every possible way."

As Bird watched them gather their things, she struggled to control a barrage of emotions. Love for Pete and Laura; shame at her attack on the groom; nerves about her imminent ride; a conviction that she would speak again; and, above all, a commitment to herself to rise above gossip and speculation—including the gossip about Alec. She replayed Pete's words. She would assume that small-minded people had started that rumour, and she would not let them win. Her eyes misted over as she watched the Piersons proceed to the stands, arm in arm.

18

Show Time

Tan pretended to sleep. His body was still sore, but his brain was working just fine. In fact, he was in overdrive. His father was still sitting there, watching over him. Tan peeked out of a corner of an eye. Yes. Still watching him. Tan couldn't stay here. He was so agitated that his chest felt like exploding. He was a prisoner in this place, and he knew it wasn't safe to stay. His chance would come. It would. And when it did, he would take it.

AN HOUR LATER, Kimberly and Moonlight Sonata stood beside Bird and Sundancer at the in gate. Kimberly was up first, followed by Bird. To Bird, Kimberly looked pale and limp as she reviewed the course. She reached out and squeezed her friend's arm. Kimberly turned to Bird and stared, then went back to studying the order of the jumps. There was a blankness in her eyes. Bird recognized the look—she was zoning out. Kimberly's worst fear had always been that she'd forget the course. It was perhaps one of the most common fears for riders, and Bird could never figure that out. To her mind, the actual fact of riding a jumper over large hurdles should be far more worrisome.

Hannah walked up and stood beside Moonie. "Ready, Kimberly?" she asked with an encouraging smile. The class had been announced a few minutes before, and Kimberly's number and name had been called twice. People were getting impatient.

Kimberly nodded but didn't move.

What should I do? Moonie asked Bird.

She'll be fine once you begin, so just trot in and start.

She hasn't asked me to.

She's in a daze. Trot in, circle in a canter and start your approach to the first jump. Do you know where that is?

The one just past the starting gate.

Right. The white picket gate. She'll be with you by then. Don't worry.

What if she's still in her daze?

Then go to the next one, the hedge, or come back here.

Moonie shook her mane and trotted in. Bird looked at Kimberly; she was still on auto-pilot.

I hope you know what you're doing, Bird. Sunny clearly didn't like the advice she'd given to Moonie.

I don't.

You just sent Moonie out there with a rag doll on her back and you admit you don't know what you're doing? Even a horse knows it's bad.

Let's just hope she wakes up.

Moonie began her circle at a canter and passed the start-gate as she headed toward the first jump. Kimberly was riding like a robot, but nobody else would know it, thought Bird. Kim's muscle memory was allowing her to move with the horse. With no help at all from Kim, they cleared the gate nicely.

Where do I go now? Moonie was nervous. She cantered slowly, waiting for instructions.

To the hedge! The hedge!

Moonie cantered to the hedge and leaped it easily. *Now where?*

Follow the fenceline and jump the three in a row.

Moonie's ears went back and her tail swished.

Jump the triple with someone sleeping on her back? Sunny snorted.

Sunny was right—it wouldn't be safe for horse or rider. Bird sighed. *Just come on back, Moonie.*

Let me see if I can get her attention. Moonie slowed her pace and did a little buck. Then another.

Suddenly, Kimberly's eyes focused. She sat up and tightened her legs. She was back. Bird relaxed.

Moonie and Kimberly judged the triple perfectly and landed on the correct lead. They increased their speed as they went for the water jump. Clear. A tight turn to the vertical.

Moonie's good, Bird. Kimberly's okay, but Moonie's better than I thought. Maybe we shouldn't have helped her. They could win.

We'll have to be better than them, that's all.

We'll have to be faster.

Sunny and Bird watched as the pair jumped easily around the course. They got their leads, saved time around corners and worked together beautifully. For Bird, it was a pleasure to watch, but Sunny grew more upset with every completed jump.

Sunny, please! Settle down. You're using up all your energy jiggling.

I have lots of energy left. It was better when I thought I was superior. She's so small, that mare, and I didn't know about her form.

Bird patted his neck. *You're my champion, Sunny. Forget about Moonie's round. I want us to go in there and have a good time.*

A good time? I want us to WIN!

Moonie and Kimberly trotted out, with Kimberly all smiles. "That was awesome! I don't even remember going in!"

No manure.

Behave!

It's our turn, Bird. Hang on tight.

Sunny! You are NOT going to do a Sabrina!

To win, I must. Moonie's time was excellent and they had a clear round. Not so much as a toe in the water jump.

Make you a deal. Let's start slow and work up to it if it feels right, okay?

Wimp.

Sundancer and Bird trotted into the ring, both aware that all eyes were on them, and not for the usual reasons, either. Today, their popularity had nothing to do with their skill and everything to do with the strange case that had gripped the community. They were the freak show, Bird mused—the extra entertainment.

While Bird wanted to keep below the radar, Sunny pranced like an Austrian Lipizzaner. He held his head low with his neck arched, and moved with a slow, huge, muscular gait.

No need to show off, Sunny.

Look at their faces! They think I'm awesome!

Let's impress the crowd with your careful jumping.

Another time.

Bird moved him into a canter and they passed the starter. They lined up the first jump, the white picket fence adorned with brightly coloured flowers on both sides and along the ground line. They were airborne when Sunny decided to put on the speed. Bird sensed her loss of control immediately. On the landing, he threw his head and grabbed the bit between his teeth.

Not fair!

Get used to it.

They raced to the hedge. It was wide and tall and made of brambles. Sunny shot over it, landed and was off at a gallop. Around the ring to the left they tore, gathering speed as they rounded the corner. Now they faced the triple: three identical jumps in a row, spaced out with a two-stride and then a three. From where Bird sat, it looked like a mess of red and white bars.

We're going way too fast!

Let me go, Bird, and I'll do this in a one-stride then a two.

You've got to be kidding!

The faster a horse goes, the more ground he covers with fewer strides. Bird knew it was possible, but she'd never attempted it before, and she certainly didn't want to try now. But there was no way to stop Sunny. He jumped the first of the jumps, landed, took one stride and jumped the second. He landed, took two strides, then jumped the third. Sunny made it through.

Who's kidding now, Bird? Whaddaya say? Wanna go faster?

No!

Too bad.

As impossible as it seemed, Sunny galloped even faster as they turned toward the water jump. There was a low yellow and green vertical in front of a pool of water twelve feet wide. They shot over it like a cannon. They were going so fast now that they couldn't turn left where they should have, and had to go the long way around another jump to the fifth hurdle, a purple vertical. Approaching it from a slight angle increased the risk of knocking down a pole, but now they had no choice.

Over they went. Clear. Sunny had his right lead and pulled Bird to the triple bar along the fence to the right. Bird's heart was pounding and her mouth was dry with fear. There were so many ways that this could end in disaster. She stopped trying to control him and merely concentrated on staying on.

I think I hate you, she messaged.

You'll get over it. We need to win!

Sunny continued his reckless race toward the blue in-and-out, then took the multi-coloured optical illusion without reducing his speed.

Things changed as they turned the corner. Sunny looked at all the various angled jumps, and blanked. With Bird no longer steering, he'd lost his bearings.

Where are we, Bird? What jump is next?

It's a little late to ask for my help.

Which one is next? There are too many choices!

Will you behave and slow down?

Probably not. Sunny slowed his pace dramatically to buy some time.

Then I won't tell you.

Even in his hyper state, Sunny sensed that Bird was serious. He cantered a few strides on the spot. *Okay, I'll listen.*

It's the vertical again.

But we've already jumped it.

We jump it again. Let me steer you.

They were over the vertical before Sunny had time to argue. He grabbed the bit again and went left toward the triple bar, which had followed the vertical last time through.

No, Sunny! We make a sharp right. Let me steer!

But that's the hedge. We already jumped it.

From the other side. Turn! Bird yanked right with all her strength.

Okay, already! Now what?

Left to the white picket again, backwards.

Okay!

Now, straight through the gate.

We're through the gate and we're done!

No kidding, we're done. I never want to ride you again!

What?

As Bird and Sundancer trotted out of the ring, Hannah's worried face came into view. "What happened out there? Are you all right?"

Bird didn't even try to answer.

"Cool him out. There are thirty-five riders to go, and there will be a jump-off."

Bird had no intention of following Hannah's instructions. She trotted up to the trailer and slid down. There would be no jump-off for her, that much she knew. She needed a lot more practice time at home before she'd be back in the ring with this horse.

19

THE JUMP-OFF

Tan could see that his father was getting impatient with sitting watch by his bedside. It wouldn't be long now. Kenneth Bradley had never sat this long in his life. Very soon he would not be able to stand it. Tan tried not to smile.

PETE AND LAURA ARRIVED at the Saddle Creek trailer just as Bird was sliding down from Sunny's back, before her feet had even touched the ground. They must have started walking while Bird was still in the ring.

Laura was gushing with excitement over Bird's performance, but Pete knew better. "Win or not, I was sure relieved when you rode out alive."

Bird began to unsaddle Sunny. She loved the Piersons dearly, but right now she just wished they'd go away. She was embarrassed and wanted to be alone. Those people got their freak show all right, she thought, angrily pulling the saddle off Sunny's sweaty back.

Don't take it out on them!

Should I take it out on you, Sunny? Should I beat you with a stick?

Do you want to?

Yes, I do! You showed off, you ran away with me, you didn't listen. We weren't a team out there. It was you against me!

I don't understand.

"Let me untack him and rub him down," offered Pete. "You

get some water and sit for a while. There's lots of time. Cool yourself down."

Bird looked at Pete and nodded her thanks. She didn't want to be anywhere near Sunny. She walked down to the showers and ran cool water over her head, lapping up whatever ran into her open mouth. Then she plunked herself on the ground and leaned against a tree.

Why hadn't she applied for a job at Camp Kowabi? Right now she'd be out on the lake in a canoe. She'd be with Alec, and Pamela would be with somebody else—anybody but Alec. And here was the kicker. She'd chosen to show-jump instead, and she sucked! She'd been an idiot to think she was such a hot-shot rider. She had no business competing on this level. Bird's dreams of glory all came crashing down.

After a few minutes of letting herself wallow in self-pity, she turned to check how the Piersons were coping. She saw that Paul had arrived at the trailer. Hannah and the Piersons were huddled over a sheet of paper.

Kimberly walked down the hill to Bird. "Wow. You were red hot out there!"

Bird knew she was being extra nice to make up for spilling the gossip, but she wasn't ready to feel better. She pointed to the group of adults at the trailer, and looked at Kim.

"Oh. Somebody put flyers on windshields telling us to go to the main food tent for a rally at two o'clock. We're supposed to sign this thing that will go to the mayor and the police chief, and who knows who else."

Bird nodded at Kimberly, wanting her to continue.

"It's put out by Justice for the Innocent. It says the fire was an accident. They didn't mean to burn down the barn, and they didn't want to harm horses or people."

If that was true, Bird wondered why they'd started the fire in the first place.

"They make the point that a bad man is still at large, and the police aren't doing enough. The petition is to get the police to drop the charges against them so they can continue working to catch the murderer."

Bird almost choked. How could anyone imagine that people would agree with that? Pierre Hall and Tanbark were severely injured, a barn was completely destroyed and horses had been put at huge risk. Who on earth would want that kind of "work" continued?

Bird glared at Kimberly to show her dismay.

"You'd never believe it," Kimberly went on, "but I keep hearing that people are going to the meeting to cheer them on! People are fed up with fearing for their safety, and are glad somebody is doing something."

Bird shook her head in wonder. Where would all of this end?

Liz's mother Patty and her boyfriend Philip joined the others at the trailer. Bird saw them shake hands in greeting, then get into a serious discussion. Great, thought Bird. Phil is here just in time to get lynched.

Hannah called down to the girls, "Get ready! There could be a jump-off. There are only seven more horses to go."

A jump-off. There was no way Bird was taking that stubborn, willful, dangerous, crazy horse back in the ring.

"Forget all this Justice for the Innocent stuff until after the jump-off," said Kimberly as they walked up the hill together. "I'm so excited I can't think!"

Bird just squeezed her friend's arm and forced a smile.

Bird? I'm sorry. Really. The transmission came from inside the trailer. *Bird? Can we do the jump-off? Please?*

No. I don't trust you any more, and that makes me sad.

What happened to mad?

I'm past mad and onto sad.

Which is worse?

Sad. Much worse. Now I'm questioning everything about us. I thought we were a team, but now I don't know.

That is worse.

I'll tack you up, Sunny, but we're not going back in there for anything but a ribbon.

I don't get it.

If there is no jump-off, we'll get a ribbon. If there is a jump-off, we don't. Get it?

I don't understand.

Bird was in a grim mood as she stood outside the ring on Sundancer. The last horse and rider had finished the course and were trotting out. They'd had four rails down and two time faults. Bird had no idea where she and Sunny stood in the class, and no interest, either.

Moonie and Kimberly, however, were another thing altogether. Moonie had developed an immediate attachment to Kimberly, and Kimberly was just as smitten. She patted her neck and praised her aloud.

"Good girl, Moonie, my beauty! Good girl."

Get over it. Sunny pinned his ears and snapped at Moonie.

Bird didn't care enough to interfere.

The announcer turned on his microphone and began reading the much-anticipated results. "There will be a jump-off to decide first and second. Coincidentally, our first two entrants had identical times. The third to eighth place winners will be announced after the jump-off. Would five forty-five and five forty-six come to the in-gate."

Kimberly was stunned. "Ohmygosh! I can't believe it! You and I are jumping off to get first? Holy! Moonie, you're awesome!"

Bird! I can't believe it! We went much faster than them!

All your prancing and pulling in the wrong direction added time. Anyway, there will be no jump-off for us. We're not going back in.

No fair!

You heard me, Sunny. I am not taking you into that ring again.

Sundancer's ears flattened and his eyes became slits. He was angry—very angry—but Bird was not about to change her mind.

The jump-off course had been posted, and Kimberly pored over it intently. "I think I know the course, Bird. Do you? It's one, seven, six, nine and finish back over one. Wow, it's difficult." Her entire body was trembling.

Hannah came over with a big smile on her face. "Well done, Kimberly! I'll bet Dexter Pill and his clients wish they hadn't been so hasty."

"I'm so glad they were! I love Moonlight Sonata. I want to ride her all the time!"

"Let's talk about that later," Hannah laughed. "Right now, you've got a job to do. Do you know your course?"

Kimberly nodded. "Yes, I think I do."

"Good," said Hannah. "Remember to sit up after the second jump and keep her steady coming into the vertical. You're up now."

Kimberly and Moonie trotted in confidently, looking around at the jumps in their new order. What a difference from the petrified girl who'd woken up at the third jump, Bird reflected. She admired Kimberly's courage, riding this mare in a jump-off, when she'd only met her today.

They cantered through the electronic starter, and took the picket fence easily. Turning sharp right to the in-and-out, they kept a good clip, but Moonie picked up some speed as she galloped left along the fence to the oxer. Once over safely, they flew left to the vertical.

Sunny was getting quite agitated. He started jiggling with nerves and then hopping up and down.

This is very uncomfortable for me, Sunny.

It's not fair!

Kimberly and Moonie finished up over the white picket, after doing the optical illusion and safely turning a tight corner. Their time would've been hard to beat, anyway, thought Bird.

Hannah came up to Bird and Sunny. "Now it's your turn, Bird. But please, please, please slow it down. It was a mess last time." Hannah reached up and smoothed a stray wisp of Bird's hair back from her face and tucked it under her helmet. She smiled encouragingly. "Do you know your course?"

Bird took her feet out of the stirrups and dismounted. She handed Hannah the reins.

"What are you doing?" Hannah stared at Bird. "Aren't you going in?"

Bird shook her head.

"You know this means you're disqualified?"

Bird nodded. She deserved to be.

Kimberly and Moonie trotted out. Kim glowed with pride and Moonie radiated pleasure.

Bird gave them the thumbs-up and clapped her hands.

"Get up and in there!" yelled Kim. "I've never had so much fun!"

Hannah called out, "Great job in there! Great turns!" She looked back at Bird. "Do you know what you're doing?"

No, she doesn't! But I do! Sundancer reared up on his hind legs and whinnied loudly in rage and frustration. He shook the reins free from Hannah's hands and burst into the ring.

Hannah rushed in after him, just as the announcer's voice came over the speakers. "Loose horse! Loose horse!"

People came from everywhere, hoping to be the hero who caught the wild and dangerous horse.

But Sundancer would not be caught. He had a purpose. He cantered in through the starting gate and sailed over the white picket. Stirrups flapped at his sides and the reins flopped at his neck, but he paid no attention. He took the in-and-out perfectly, picked up speed to the oxer, then galloped on to the vertical.

All around him, people were trying to cut him off. One man brought a bucket of oats, and a woman held out carrots. Others waved their arms in a futile effort to stop him.

The announcer spoke in awe. "Sundancer is jumping the course! Ladies and gentlemen, I've never seen anything like this."

Sundancer ignored it all. He was committed to completing the jump-off. After the vertical, there was a clear run to the optical illusion. Sunny raced. He chipped in at the last minute and gathered himself up and over. He landed lightly, turned left on the spot, and cut the corner so tight it was a miracle he could jump the white picket. Which he did. From a standstill.

The crowd was on its feet. This horse was jumping without a rider—and it was happening right in front of their eyes! Bird and Hannah had seen him do this before, but to everyone else it was unimaginable.

Sunny raced triumphantly through the electronic gate, bucking with joy. He slowed to a canter, then down to a trot, throwing his head jubilantly and waiting for the showers of praise.

But all he saw were panicked people racing toward him. Nobody appreciated what he'd done. Nobody knew that he'd just won the jump-off by three full seconds.

20

THE MEETING IN THE TENT

Tan was alone. Finally. First, his father had started fidgeting, then pacing, then he left the room—for good, Tan hoped, but he couldn't count on it. The nurses were on a shift change. This was his chance. Tan steadied himself. He had no idea how much time he had, but he knew he needed to move quickly. He snorted. He would outsmart everybody.

THE CLASS WAS FINISHED and the ribbons given out. Bird was back at the trailer with Sunny, in a foul mood. She watched from the trailer window as Hannah approached, looking around as if she was trying to find someone. Bird guessed that she herself was the object of Hannah's search, and tuned in just enough to know how worried her aunt was about her. Today, though, Hannah couldn't help her. She couldn't even help herself.

Bird, did we get a ribbon? Sunny asked.

I don't care.

But you always care about ribbons.

I've stopped caring.

I don't understand.

Bird didn't want to continue her conversation with Sunny, and she didn't want to see Hannah, either. It was getting close to two o'clock, and the meeting would be starting in the food tent. She slipped away, heading down the hill with an ominous sense of gloom.

Planning to watch unnoticed, Bird found a hole in the canvas curtain behind the food tent. She peeked in. The tent was crowded with people. It was large enough to feed the competitors, stable hands, trainers, onlookers and families that came to the horse show, but it was not large enough to contain this number.

The backs of three adults, one woman and two men, were a foot or two away from Bird's nose. There was a long table running sideways in front of them, where people had lined up to sign papers, presumably the petition to drop the charges regarding the barn fire.

Bird scanned the crowd. Behind the people signing were groups who looked less pleased and more skeptical. They were likely here to find out what was going on, Bird assessed, as opposed to being supportive. That made her feel slightly better.

And behind the groups of waiting people, at the entrance of the tent, Bird noticed some police uniforms. She felt better still. There was a chance that this event might not get out of control after all.

Bird turned her attention back to the adults behind the table. One of them was Ellen Wells. Bird looked again. Ellen Wells? Was she from Justice for the Innocent? Bird could hardly take in this piece of information. Ellen had always been a positive influence in the area—helpful and engaged in charitable events. She wasn't the type to stir up trouble.

One of the two men with her was Ellen's husband, Jim. The other one looked an awful lot like the man who'd put the threatening letter in the Saddle Creek mailbox: the man who'd gone to Tanbark's bedside. Bird's face flushed and her knees weakened. She thought back to that night. Had he seen her at the hospital? If he had, he'd recognize her now, just days later. And what was he doing here, anyway? Why wasn't he in custody? Suddenly, staying hidden seemed like a very good idea.

Ellen picked up a microphone from the table. "Can everyone settle down, please? The food tent people have generously given us some time, so I'd like to begin. Quiet, please."

A few people at the front stopped talking, but the rest of the room continued to hum with conversation.

Jim Wells took the microphone from his wife. "Please, people! This is important! Quiet!" People paid attention. He handed the mike back to Ellen.

"Thank you all for coming to lend support. My name is Ellen Wells and I'm the one who found poor Sandra Hall beaten and bleeding on the side of the road. God have mercy on her soul."

Some people clapped while others murmured sympathetic "ohs." There were even a few "amens." Ellen let the noise subside before she resumed speaking.

"I'm overwhelmed at your numbers but not surprised. Your concern is our concern. There's a ruthless man at large, a man who fatally assaulted an innocent woman. He will do it again. Yet the police have done nothing except pass around a sketch and question a few people. Justice for the Innocent has done its own detective work and we have actively singled out suspects with the intention of forcing them into the open."

Bird picked out Pete and Laura standing at the back with Hannah, Paul, Patty and Philip. The girls—Kimberly, Liz and Julia—stood together, right beside them. Paul grabbed two folding chairs and set them up for the Piersons.

Ellen continued. "We need your help. Our work is taxing, but we are tireless. We will get our man. We will avenge the death of Sandra Hall!"

A loud cheer rippled through the tent.

"I assure you, we had no intention of burning down the Linwood's barn. We set a small paper fire in a trash can under Pierre Hall's window. The goal was to scare him into confessing, if guilty. Unfortunately, the can must have fallen over, and the fire spread. We are deeply sorry about the outcome, but I promise you, it was unintentional." Ellen put her hand over her heart. She seemed, to Bird at least, genuinely upset.

"The police have laid charges against people in our group, but this was an unfortunate accident! We ask that you sign this petition so the police will drop all charges and let us continue our efforts to find Sandra Hall's killer!" Ellen took a sip of water from a glass on the table as people applauded. "We have no intention of harming anything or anybody. We have one goal and one goal only—to put the guilty behind bars and get justice for the innocent!"

Again, cheers and claps rang out. Bird judged that the group at the front was now larger than before.

"If we have justice for Sandra Hall, we'll have justice for all!"

More applause. Louder cheering.

"If there's no justice for the death of an innocent woman, why fool ourselves into thinking that there'll be justice for any one of us? Please, please, sign the petition! We are doing everything in our power to help. A dangerous man is among us, and we must root him out!"

"We want to hear about the crazy man!" a deep voice called out over the applause.

"What are the police doing about him?" joined another.

"Where's he from?"

Bird listened as more and more people added their thoughts.

"Who is he, anyway?"

"He scares me the most!"

"Bring him in and let him face the music!"

"We can't let someone like that wander around loose!"

Ellen let the panic build for a minute, then called for order. "That's why we're here, folks. To find the killer and bring him to justice! There's another sheet beside the petition. Please sign it with your name and contact numbers. We'll call on you—trust me. You can make a difference."

As Bird watched the crowd shuffle about and cheer, she noticed that Pete had risen from his chair. "Madame Chairman, would you answer a question or two?"

Ellen smiled with tense graciousness. Bird wondered if questions made her uneasy. "Of course. It's Mr. Pierson, isn't it? The cow farmer?"

"The same."

It seemed to Bird that Ellen had tried to belittle him with her description, but Pete appeared not to notice.

"How have you chosen your suspects?" he asked.

"From the witness's composite sketch."

"You mean yourself, of course?"

"Well, yes." Ellen blushed, then spoke again. Her voice took on a defensive tone. "I was the only one there except for the perpetrator."

"How well were you able to see this man from the road, when he was running away from you, up through the trees?"

"I saw his face clearly enough to help the police draw the sketch." She cast a nervous glance at her husband.

"I see." Pete cleared his throat. "Your group has named four men as suspects. All from your sketch?"

"Yes."

"And in our country, people are presumed innocent until proven guilty?"

"Of course! But we can't sit on our hands!"

"I'm sure everyone agrees, but you're targeting all four of these men. What about the three innocent men in that group? Is there no justice for them? Or do you believe that they're all guilty?"

"Of course not." Ellen's neck was beet red. "What are you getting at, Mr. Pierson? We have limited time here."

"I'm getting at this. What is your definition of justice? If you're asking for our help, we have a right to know."

Ellen did not reply.

"Do you feel it's quite all right to burn down a barn?" Pete elaborated. "To severely injure a man before proving his guilt?"

"That was unfortunate. I explained that it was a mistake. But let's not forget, Pierre Hall was abusive to Sandra when they were married!"

"But he's not being accused of that, is he? He was harassed and burned for having the bad luck to resemble a sketch that you created."

Ellen could not find a way to answer. "I'm sorry you feel that way. You can't make an omelet without breaking some eggs. If that's all ..."

"That's not all," said Pete clearly. "If you made a mistake about the barn, however unfortunate, might you not make other mistakes, with equally dire consequences?"

Ellen had gone so rigid that Bird wondered if she might fall over.

"One last thing." Pete looked around the tent. "Is there anyone here who would have lit a fire beside a barn in this dry weather? Are you surprised that it spread? You called it unfortunate. I'd call it plain stupid." He paused. "Let's leave this matter to the police, to be handled in an orderly, legal way." Pete sat down.

A hush had fallen over the entire tent. Jim Wells took the microphone. "This is not the time for accusations, Mr. Pierson. It was an honest mistake. The only time you can be sure of not making mistakes is when you don't do anything, and we're doing something! We need your help, people. We need your support. Sign the petition so we can continue our work on your behalf. On society's behalf. On justice's behalf!"

Bird expected cheers, but now she saw hesitation on the faces in the crowd. Pete's words had changed the atmosphere.

He'd put questions into the minds of people who hadn't taken the time to think for themselves.

The other organizer stepped forward and grabbed the microphone from Jim. "We can't leave this to the police, either! I'll tell you about the police! My brother Les was arrested and man-handled and treated like a common criminal! He should be out on bail, but the po ..."

Jim roughly took the microphone away.

He's not the man from the hospital, Bird thought with relief, he's that man's brother. Looks like his twin.

"Stop it, Hank!" Jim growled away from the mike. "You're not to speak about that."

"I can speak if I want to!"

"Later." Into the microphone, Jim explained. "Hank Crowley's brother, Les, was doing his best for our cause when the police arrested him. The matter will be before the courts, so we can't discuss it." Jim looked at Hank pointedly. "Les's story will be told in due time, but right now we need your help. We have lots of signatures, but keep 'em coming. Thanks so much, folks. We're doing this for you! For us all! For justice!"

With astonishment, Bird watched what transpired next. It happened so fast she would have missed it if she hadn't been looking right at Philip that very second.

At the back of the tent, two men grabbed Philip Butler, one at each arm. One was short and bulky, the other tall and muscular.

Patty let out a scream. The police stepped forward, fully prepared to interfere, and faced the men down without a word spoken.

The men let Phil go, then shoved through the crowd up to the long table at the front of the room. They spun around to face the crowd.

"That's Philip Butler, folks!" shouted the heavy-set man, pointing a finger and shaking it at Phil. "Suspect-at-large."

Bird watched the crowd. Some people appeared confused, some abashed, but a few were enjoying this.

"That man," the taller man stated loudly, "was a policeman. I say was. There were charges against him and he quit the force. Suspicious, you say? He was identified from the sketch."

Several people were nodding. Tension was rapidly building.

The stocky man took over. "Is he a suspect? Yes! What did the police do? Nothing! Are we going to try to get him to admit his crime?" He cupped his ear to the crowd.

"Yes!" a dozen voices chimed.

"If he's guilty, should he go to prison?"

"Yes!"

"Should they throw away the key?"

"Yes!"

The people who engaged in this dialogue got nearer and nearer with each response. The more uncertain people backed away. Bird clearly saw the division growing.

Then, at the back, Paul Daniels stood on a chair and shouted above the crowd. "We're decent law-abiding people, but we're letting these men incite ill will and violence. If we stand by and let this happen, we're no better than vigilantes!"

"What's wrong with that?" a bald man yelled out of the crowd. "Vigilantes stand up for justice! If we do nothing, we're cowards!"

Another male voice added, "I'd rather be a vigilante than a coward!"

Pete stood with Paul. "Democracy allows freedom of speech, like what we have here today. Democracy allows open meetings, like this one. What democracy does not allow is criminal activity, like defamation of character and arson."

Again, people were disconcerted by Pete's remarks. Again, Bird watched expressions change from eager to confused.

Philip squared his jaw. "Thank you, Mr. Pierson, and Dr. Daniels. Yes, I had charges laid against me. But that was many years ago, and those charges were dropped. They were described as frivolous. We are a sorry lot indeed when we allow ourselves to get caught up in things like this, and in organizations like Justice for the Innocent."

There was silence. Philip walked out of the tent into the open air. Patty ran to join him. The Piersons, Hannah, Paul and the girls followed after. The meeting was over.

21

TAN'S ESCAPE

Tan gave himself a pep talk. He was smarter, faster and more creative than anybody else. Nobody would catch him because nobody was as clever. That didn't mean he would take chances. No, he would be very careful and make no mistakes. This was his chance to get out; he might not get another.

HANNAH HAD PACKED UP the trailer by the time Bird returned from the tent. Normally, they would have stayed to watch the Grand Prix class with all the elite show jumpers, but today everyone was tired. Their classes were over and they wanted to go home. Liz had already left with her mother and Philip.

"Where have you been?" asked Hannah, over her shoulder.

Bird looked at her blankly. Did Hannah really expect an answer?

Kimberly gave her a squeeze. "Let's get this out of the way. You know you're a way better rider than me. I just got lucky today." Bird smiled warmly at her friend.

Julia looked at Bird. "You missed the meeting." Her brow was crumpled in confusion. "Some men went to the front of the room and said Philip Butler was guilty and bad. It was awful."

Bird hugged her little sister. She knew exactly how Julia felt.

"Oh, Bird," said Hannah. "I left a bucket and sponge down at the showers. Can you go down and get them for me?"

Bird nodded and walked down the hill. The redheaded groom

was there bathing a horse, but Bird ignored her. She spotted the bucket and sponge, but something else caught her eye.

To her left, in the practice ring, a pony was being disciplined by an angry girl. The girl yanked hard on his nose with a chain, then did it again. The pony backed up and tossed his head while the girl yelled at him. Bird guessed that her pony had bucked her off or kicked someone. But then the girl screamed, "You're useless! I wanted a ribbon!"

Bird was aghast. Nobody should take their frustrations out on a pony! It was pointless, anyway, because when a horse is frightened or alarmed or nervous, he can't think straight. It makes him unable to do anything right.

Bird paused. Something was bothering her. It was Sunny. She was furious with him, and he didn't seem to understand why. He just didn't get it. Wow. She needed to think this out. She watched the girl with her pony, and asked herself some tough questions.

Fact: they rode terribly today.

Why? Because they hadn't practiced enough, and Sunny wouldn't listen. He ran off and almost killed her!

And why did he do that? Because he wanted to win so much that he raced to beat Moonie's time.

But why did he want to win that badly? Bird stood still and thought about it rationally for the first time. Because that's what they always tried to do. To win. Together.

And that's why he did the jump-off without her. He wanted to win, because he thought Bird wanted it.

Bird put it all together. She was doing to Sunny what that girl was doing to her pony. She was punishing him for not being able to understand. He was a horse, after all. Not a human. Even though she treated him like one.

In short, she expected him to reason like a human, and he couldn't.

She looked back to the girl and her pony. She watched as a man took the pony from her. The girl stomped off, still visibly upset, but the pony relaxed as soon as she was gone.

Bird walked quickly past the showers and back up the hill. She had something to say to Sundancer.

"Bird? Did you get the pail and sponge?" Hannah peered around the door of the tack room. "We're ready to go."

Oops. Bird raced back down and grabbed the pail and sponge. Their bottle of Mane 'n Tail was there, so she whisked it up, too.

Redhead was still there. "Say hello to Uncle Tanbark," she said.

Bird smiled at her, nodded her head and indicated that she would do just that. The groom raised her eyebrows and twisted her lip, looking somewhat disappointed. Then Bird realized something—she wasn't faking it. She had let her anger go.

This time Bird returned with the pail, sponge and soap. Hannah put them away and wiped her hands. "We're ready to roll!"

Bird put her hand on Hannah's arm. She raised her index finger, asking for one minute more.

"Okay, but one minute only, Bird. I want to get Moonie back to Fiona on the way home, and it's too hot for the horses. They all want to get back out to their fields."

Bird nodded. Hannah was right, of course, but Bird couldn't put this off one minute longer. She ducked under the bar and stood up beside the chestnut gelding.

I'm sorry I was so upset with you, Sunny.

I don't care.

Bird looked at him. His head hung listlessly, like a broken-down old school horse. *Sunny, listen, please. I didn't see what was happening with us and you didn't know what was wrong.*

I let you down, Bird. We didn't win.

We would've been first or second in a field of forty-five horses, Sunny! That's pretty decent.

I didn't win.

Bird patted his neck. He recoiled from her touch. *Listen, Sunny. I've been too hung up on winning and other stuff. I'll make it better, I promise.*

I don't know what you're talking about.

Bird smiled. *You don't have to. You're a horse. I'm the one who has to know. All you need to know is that I'm sorry.*

Sunny was trying to think. It's very difficult for an animal to think, Bird knew. They react to information, and can't reason the way people can. They are rarely able to make sense of things, and it frustrates them to try.

Don't worry, Sunny. Before we go back into the ring, we're going to practice a lot. And before I get on your back, I'll let go of all my worries.

Sunny took a look at her. *I'll believe it when I see it. Now I want to eat and rest.*

Bird laughed her squeak and rubbed behind his left ear where he liked it. *Thanks.* She climbed out of the trailer and into the truck.

"Ready to go, everybody?" asked Hannah wearily.

The girls in the back seat nodded. Paul had gone off to help an older mare give birth to a foal, and the Piersons had left immediately after the meeting. All who remained were Bird, Kimberly and Julia.

"It was a good day, for the most part," said Hannah, trying to lift their spirits. "Well done."

Julia piped up, "I'll look after Sabrina when we get back. I told Liz I would." Her brow furrowed. "She's got other things on her mind right now."

Bird gave Julia a squeeze. She loved her younger sister's kind heart.

"So," said Hannah, "we'll swing by the Malone's on our way home."

Kimberly sighed. "I don't want Moonie to go. Can I ride her again, maybe, Hannah?"

"Let's talk things over with Fiona. Once we sort out the deal she made with Dexter Pill, we'll have a better idea."

"But Moonie really likes me. I can tell!" exclaimed Kimberly. "Doesn't that count for anything?"

Hannah smiled sadly. "In this business, it doesn't. If horses could choose their riders, I know Moonlight Sonata would say, 'I choose that nice little girl right there.' And you'd live happily ever after. Let's just see what happens."

Julia said, "I know who'd buy Pastor from you."

Kimberly looked at her. "Who?"

"Is he for sale?" Julia rubbed her hands together like a horse trader.

"Depends who's asking," responded Kimberly, equally slyly.

"Liz Brown, that's who. She's been in love with Pastor forever. And Sabrina scared the riding pants off her today." Julia whistled and rolled her eyes.

Kimberly thought for a moment. "I never knew she loved Pastor."

"He's certainly lovable," said Hannah.

"And reliable and handsome and perfectly trained," Julia added.

Kimberly tilted her head. "I want to think a little before making any decisions."

"Very wise," nodded Hannah. "And we don't have any idea if Moonie is for sale, anyway."

The Malone farm came into view as they turned up the gravel side road.

"I'm closing my eyes," said Kimberly dramatically. "I don't want to watch Moonie go!"

"Do whatever you like," answered Hannah, "but we're here. I'll see where Fiona wants us to put the mare." She jumped down from the truck and knocked on Fiona's front door. Nobody came. Hannah knocked again, louder.

From the back seat, Bird saw movement through the living room window. She looked closely but couldn't make anything out through the glare of the glass. She slipped down from the truck and crept nearer. Standing on her tiptoes under the window, she looked in. Somebody was lying on the couch.

The person was partially covered with a throw blanket, head under a cushion. At the sound of another of Hannah's knocks, an arm flew up and removed the cushion. It was a dishevelled Fiona Malone. She blinked in confusion, muttered something, then slammed the cushion down over her head again. She burrowed deeper into the couch.

On the floor beside the couch was an empty bottle. Bird felt a thud of misery in her gut. She had heard that Fiona was an alcoholic, but everybody said she wasn't drinking any more.

Hannah had come up beside Bird. She looked in the window. "Well, I guess we bring Moonie home with us after all. Poor Fiona."

Poor Abby, thought Bird, to have lived with this.

It had been a long, hot day, but now that the horses were bathed, fed and out grazing in the cool evening breeze, everyone was mellow and content. Hannah, Paul and the three girls sat around the kitchen table, drinking tall glasses of iced lemonade and eating tuna melts and tomato salad with vinaigrette. The windows and door were wide open, and the sheer curtains flapped lazily at the screens.

"Mom said she was on her way two hours ago," said Kimberly. "Why can't she just tell me she'll be late so I don't keep expecting her?"

Bird took a drink of lemonade. Lavinia Davis was selfish and demanding. Everyone at Saddle Creek had long ago learned to ignore what she said and accept what she did. Their only concern was for Kimberly, whom they treated like family.

"I want to talk to her about Moonlight Sonata," Kimberly continued. "She was really proud that I won first. I hate to say this, but she was delirious that I beat out Bird and Sunny!"

Bird almost spit out her drink with a laugh.

Hannah smiled kindly. "She'll show up, sweetie. She always does."

"Today or tomorrow," Kimberly added with a sigh. "Or the next day. Anyway, all I can think about is I might never ride Moonie again."

"I'll talk to Fiona tomorrow, Kim."

"It's six o'clock." Paul reached over and turned on the radio. "I wonder if the news will mention the meeting."

"*Good evening. In our top story tonight, Tanbark Wedger, the son of businessman Kenneth Bradley, has gone missing. Hurt in the barn fire in Caledon, he is now being sought by police and medical officials.*"

Bird stopped chewing.

"What did it say?" asked Julia.

"Shh!" Hannah turned up the volume.

"*Sometime around three this afternoon, Mr. Wedger disappeared from Headwaters Hospital in Orangeville. His father, Kenneth Bradley, has put out a reward of ten thousand dollars for any information that leads to his son's safe return. If you see Mr. Wedger, please do not approach him. He has a mental disorder that causes him to be highly unpredictable when confused. Call 1-800-444-TIPS if you think you see him, and again, DO NOT approach him.*"

Poor Tanbark, thought Bird. People will think he's a maniac.

"*In related news, the group calling itself Justice for the Innocent held a rally at the Palston Horse Show today at two o'clock. An estimated one hundred signatures were gathered on a petition to drop charges regarding the barn fire that injured Tanbark Wedger, and is*" *threatening the life of Pierre Hall. Police were standing by, but it was a peaceful gathering."*

"How can they say that?" Julia demanded. "It wasn't peaceful at all! Philip Butler was embarrassed and everybody was yelling!"

Paul explained. "What they mean is that no punches were thrown."

"Then why didn't they say that?" Julia was upset.

"The bigger problem is that Tanbark ran away from the hospital," said Hannah quietly. "He shouldn't be without medical attention."

"He's burned and in pain," said Paul. "I don't know where he'll go."

Bird thought she knew. Right now Tanbark was probably working his way back to Saddle Creek Farm. Where else would he go? He would be stealthy about it, staying away from people and drinking out of creeks and ponds. He'd find cover in the daylight, and travel at night. She guessed that in a day or two he'd be peeking in their windows and causing Lucky and Sunny concern.

"He doesn't like to wear anything but his shorts," said Julia. "They could follow his clothes trail."

"Good idea," said Kimberly. "Let's see. There's his hospital gown. Then his slippers. If he dropped them all in different places the trail would dry up before he'd crossed the parking lot."

Julia grimaced at her. "At least I had an idea. What's yours?"

"Come on, girls," said Hannah. "Clear the table. The pie is ready."

"Pie!" chirped Julia. "Nothing in the world is as delicious as Aunt Hannah's rhubarb and cream cheese pie."

"Is there enough for me?" asked a woman's voice as the door slapped open.

Lucky shot out from under the table and started barking.

"Keep that animal away from me!"

Lucky scooted back under the table with his tail tucked between his legs. Bird understood why. This woman had that effect on every creature.

"Mom!" exclaimed Kimberly. "You scared us! Why didn't you knock?"

Lavinia looked askance at her daughter. "It's a screen door. Who knocks on a screen door?"

"You're always welcome, Lavinia," said Hannah. "And of course there's enough pie. More than enough."

Paul pulled an extra chair to the table. "Have a seat," he said as he swept his arm down like a waiter.

Lavinia sat between Kimberly and Paul. "Thank you, Paul. Do you have coffee, Hannah? Decaf no-fat latte?"

Hannah was bent over the oven taking out the pie. She stopped midway. "Decaf … no-fat … latte?"

"Yes. With artificial sweetener. Half a packet, well stirred. I hate it when all the sweetness comes at the bottom, don't you, Paul?" She almost batted her eyelashes.

Hannah raised her eyebrows at Paul and resisted the impulse to laugh. "I can make a decaffeinated cup of coffee with hot skim milk, but I don't have any artificial sweetener."

"No problem—I carry my own. There's a new product I like, and I refuse to use anything else." She reached into her purse and brandished a small package of stevia.

Kimberly sank her head to the table but not before she rolled her eyes at Bird and Julia.

"Now," said Lavinia. "I want to hear all about this Moonshine Regatta."

Everybody laughed. The mangling of the marc's name gave them all an excuse to get the giggles out of their systems. They couldn't stop for a couple of minutes, because every time the laughter got under control, somebody would start up again.

Lavinia raised her arms dramatically. "I'm not finding anything funny. Tell me what you're laughing about. This minute."

Paul was able to speak first. "It's the mare's name. It's not Moonshine Regatta." He began to laugh again but pretended that he needed to clear his throat. "Excuse me, please."

"It's Moonlight Sonata, Mom," said Kimberly. "Like Beethoven wrote."

"You were laughing at me." Lavinia pouted and crossed her arms.

Bird knew this could get ugly. Lavinia hated anybody laughing at her.

Hannah came to the rescue. "It's a brilliant name, Lavinia. Moonshine Regatta. I'd name a horse that in a flash."

Paul backed her up. "It makes me think of a sailing boat race in Prohibition days. The moon shining on water. Very evocative."

Kimberly mouthed, "They're sucking up," and the girls giggled again.

"That's true," sighed Lavinia poetically. "It is a beautiful name. So, what is her actual name again?"

"Moon ... light So ... na ... ta, Mom," Kimberly groaned. "Moonlight Sonata."

Lavinia waved her fingers in the air. "Okay, already. So tell me, Hannah. Kimberly said she won. First. Over Bird and Sundancer."

Hannah nodded as she scooped vanilla ice cream into a big bowl and set it on the table beside the pie. "She certainly did, Lavinia. Kimberly and Moonie—"

"You cannot call her Moonie," Lavinia interrupted. "That's horrible."

Kimberly looked at her mother directly. "It's a 'stable name,' Mom. And only the greatest horses have one."

"In that case, it's all right. You were saying, Hannah?"

"Kimberly and Moonie were an instant team. They were

right in sync from the beginning." Hannah started passing out plates of pie and ice cream.

"To be totally honest, Mom," Kimberly interrupted, "Moonie jumped two jumps without my help. I was paralyzed with fear and only shook out of it when she bucked."

Lavinia gasped. "She bucked? Is that good?"

"Yes! A little wake-up buck. It was good that she did it, too, or things would've ended very differently."

"You mean you wouldn't have won?"

"Right. We wouldn't have won." Kimberly and Bird exchanged a look. Lavinia cared more about winning than her daughter's safety.

"Well, I want to sell Pastor ASAP and buy Moonie. I don't want two horses on the payroll. Hannah, make that happen, will you?"

"Mom!" exclaimed Kimberly.

"What? Pastor's won third, once. He's never even come close to winning a first. Moonie did today, first time out."

"It's about more than winning, Mom! Pastor's a great horse and I love him." Kim crossed her arms defensively.

"Get over it, Kimberly. I pay good money here, and I pay for firsts. Now, I really don't need pie, so let's get going." Lavinia stood up and smoothed her blouse over her flat belly. "Kimberly? We have to go."

Hannah had seen this coming. It had happened before. She handed Kimberly a big piece of rhubarb pie and ice cream, securely protected in a used plastic yogurt container. "Enjoy your dessert Kimberly." She tousled Kimberly's auburn curls and handed her a fork. "Bring it back tomorrow. Again, congratulations on a really good day."

Kimberly's eyes shone with gratitude, not just for the pie, but for Hannah's praise and understanding.

Bird stood and hugged her best friend goodbye.

"See you tomorrow, Bird?" Kimberly asked. Bird nodded and grinned, licking her lips and glancing at the pie plate. There'd be leftovers to finish off.

Lavinia opened the screen door. "Let's go, Kimberly! Hannah? You heard me about Moonbeam Sonata. Make it happen."

The kitchen door slammed shut. Stifling snickers at the face Kimberly made behind Lavinia's back, they watched as mother and daughter got in a shiny new white BMW coupe and roared down the drive.

22

THE VISIT

Tan waited. He had to be patient. So far, his plan was unfolding exactly as he'd wished. He'd fooled everybody from the people walking down the hall to the old lady at the reception desk. It wasn't all luck, either. It was smarts—and skill.

It felt so good to be free! The fresh night air, the wild energy, the feel of dirt and grass under his feet! But now it was crucial that he reach the girl. He needed her help. He watched the farmhouse. Patience. He had waited this long; he could wait a little longer.

LUCKY'S WHINING WOKE BIRD. She opened one eye. The clock on her bedside table read four-fifteen. It was practically the middle of the night! But then Bird heard something else. It wasn't only Lucky making noise. Through the open window she could hear Sunny racing around outside in his field. Shaking the sleep out of her head, she stumbled to her window. The night was pitch black. No moon or stars were out to light the countryside. She couldn't see a thing.

Sunny! What's happening out there?

No response.

Sunny? Can you hear me?

Still no response. Sunny was panicking, and his mind was closed—he'd switched into his flight reflex. It must be bad.

Bird quickly pulled on jeans and a sweatshirt over her nightgown, and slid her feet into her sneakers. She crept downstairs, careful not to wake anyone else. She had to calm Sunny, or he might colic or twist an intestine.

Lucky? What's going on?

Intruder! Intruder! The dog sounded one shrill, urgent bark.

Shh! Should I let you out?

Yes! Yes!

Will you be in danger?

No! No! Let me out! Let me out!

Bird unlocked and opened the inside door. Lucky shot outside as she reached out to hold open the screen. At the same instant, a man's hand grabbed her arm.

Bird stiffened. She tried to pull back her arm, but his grip was too strong. The hairs all over her body stood up. Where was Lucky? Bird tried to scream, but nothing came out. She held tight to the door frame and refused to be pulled outside.

Terrified, she braced herself with her right leg and walked her fingers along the wall until she found the switch. She flicked on the kitchen lights. In the flood of light, Bird saw who was holding her arm. It was Tanbark Wedger, smiling at her, with a bandage over his forehead.

Lucky sniffed at his leg. *It's the guy who saved you and the horses. No problem.* He picked up a scent in the garden and followed it away.

In a split second, Bird's fear disappeared and was replaced by fury. Tanbark had scared her silly.

The fly swatter hung beside the light switch, and Bird took it in her free hand. She wound up and swatted Tanbark's shoulder with all her strength. He jumped back and dropped her arm. "Ouch!"

She glared at him and brushed herself off. Nobody had the right to manhandle her, mentally ill or not.

"You hurt me! I've got burns! You didn't have to hit me."

Bird glared at him harder and put her hands on her hips.

"That hurt! But forget it. I really need to talk to you. I need to tell you what happened, and I can't tell anybody else."

Bird took a long look at him. This was the first time he'd spoken to her. She saw the urgency in his eyes—and the need. If he'd escaped from the hospital and travelled this far so fast to tell her something, she really wanted to hear what he had to say.

The sound of footsteps interrupted them. Paul was coming down the stairs. Quickly. Bird put her index finger to her lips.

Tanbark dropped back in the shadows beside the door.

Paul was now in the room. "Bird? Is that you? Lucky woke me up. Is someone here? I thought I heard a man's voice."

Bird didn't want Paul to scare Tanbark away. If she could only talk, she could explain it to Paul. She opened her mouth and tried hard. Nothing.

"Bird? Close the door. The bugs'll come in." Paul stepped closer. "Did I hear a voice? Bird?" Paul was beside her now, and Bird could sense his curiosity about why she was acting so strangely. Then he saw the figure outside in the shadows. He stiffened with uncertainty. "Hello there?"

Tanbark backed away. His face caught the light and Paul recognized him.

Bird took a step between them to slow Paul down.

"Stand back, Bird." Paul put his hand out. "Easy now, Tanbark," he said gently, ignoring Bird. "Nobody's going to hurt you." Paul slowly approached. "Why don't you come inside? We have some delicious food left over from dinner."

Tanbark looked wary. With every step that Paul took forward, he stepped back. Bird sensed his growing anxiety.

Paul's face was that of a hunter stalking his game. If Bird could read Paul so easily, Tanbark could, too. Using her eyes and chin she tried to tell Paul to back off or Tanbark would run. Paul didn't pay any heed, and stepped slowly closer and closer.

Sunny messaged her. *Bird.*

Sunny.

He came downwind. I went crazy. I didn't know it was the wild man.

He came to talk to me.

He wants to run and hide.

What should I do?

Nothing. Let him run.

Just then, Tanbark jumped back, spun around and raced amazingly fast across the front field. Paul stood there, watching him go.

Sunny let him run right past. The big chestnut horse nodded his head up and down. *Was I right or was I right?*

You were right.

Paul turned to Bird, concern on his face. "Are you okay?"

Bird nodded.

"I'll call the police. They should know he showed up here. Kenneth Bradley should know, too. He's worried sick."

Bird shook her head. She walked quickly into the kitchen and plucked a pencil out of the cup. She grabbed the pad of paper and wrote: *Don't call police. Not Grandfather, 2. Something's wrong. Tanbark wants 2 talk 2 me. He knows things.*

"He can tell the police. We have to be sensible, here."

He wants 2 tell me, not the police! Wait 'til he tells me, or we'll never know.

Paul thought about it. "I can't promise that, Bird. We don't know when, or even if, he'll come back, do we? But I'll make a compromise. I won't call tonight. They wouldn't be able to find him anyway."

Thanks, she scribbled.

"Understand, Bird, Tanbark needs medical attention. You know that. I'm calling first thing in the morning." He looked at the clock on the kitchen wall. "Which is two hours from now. We can't leave him out there alone in the woods and in need of help."

Bird nodded. She knew Paul was right. But she also had a funny feeling that Tanbark would be safer in the woods. He was strange, but she didn't think he was dangerous. Bird wanted to hear what he'd come to say, and also why he'd left the hospital in such a hurry. She didn't have much time to find out.

Bird waited quietly in her room, listening, until Paul's snuffly snores became steady. Gathering her courage, she slid on her clothes again, crept down the stairs and made her way outside. Dawn had just broken and the early birds chirped as they searched for their worms. She hopped the fence into Sunny's field.

Let's go for a ride, Sunny.

I can tell you're up to something.

You're right.

Say, "As always."

Okay. You're right, as always. I want to find the wild man.

You're crazy.

Probably, but he came here to tell me something and I want to know what.

You won't rest until you do, will you?

No.

Bird and Sunny travelled along the path to the back of the farm. Riding bareback with neither bridle nor reins, they passed the far fields and the wild, rocky area that was only good for cow pasture. Hannah used to have cows, Bird remembered with a snort, but after their last escape, she'd sold them all and vowed never again. That had been the end of Hannah's flirtation with using all the acres of Saddle Creek land. Now they just enjoyed riding through the shrubs and rocks and ledges and drops.

Bird and Sunny came to the lip of the Niagara Escarpment, a rocky deposit left by the glaciers in the Ice Age. Along this same ridge, just a little over a hundred kilometres away, was the famous

Niagara Falls. Bird looked down—way down. On one side of a narrow path was a sheer drop. On the other were thorny, tenacious trees, hanging on to the rocky cliff by their roots.

Last time, when he was burnt in the fire, you went down this way, Bird.

Let's do it again. He probably went back to where he was before.

Nothing to lose—except our lives.

Very funny, Sunny.

Let's go down the way I went. It meets the same path.

Okay.

I'm having a nice time. Maybe horse shows are too much stress. They used to be fun.

They'll be fun again, Sunny. It was my fault. I was preoccupied and inattentive. Sorry.

I was pigheaded and belligerent. Sorry.

Bird smiled broadly as she and Sunny slowly descended into the deep, dark woods at the bottom of the cliff. It was refreshing to have Sunny as her friend and not her enemy. She felt his body stiffen.

Bird, do you smell that?

No. What?

A storm's coming.

Now?

No, but very soon. It makes me nervous.

Don't worry, Sunny. We'll be home before the storm.

Promise?

Promise. The sky is blue. Red even, over there on the horizon.

That colour red is the storm coming. I'm very nervous.

They descended farther. The trees obscured the light, and, step by step, they became more engulfed in darkness. Sunny startled at a sound.

What was that, Bird?

I didn't hear anything.

Humans have very poor ears. There! It happened again!

Sunny, I can't hear a thing.

I can! This is scary, Bird. Let's go back.

But we're having a lovely time!

Speak for yourself. There it is! A hissing sound. Let's go!

I don't want to go back yet! I want to find the wild man. That's what we're doing down here, remember?

If it's a huge snake, I'm outta here.

The snakes here are harmless.

They're ugly and they wriggle. I want to go home.

Sunny, stop jiggling. I don't have a saddle!

I jiggle when I'm nervous. Can we turn around?

Just then, out of the trees, came the thunderous crashing noise of an animal charging through the woods.

Sunny reared up, spun around and shot off like a rocket, leaving Bird in a heap on the ground. With one eye she glimpsed the terrified horse scale the Escarpment like a deer.

With the other, she looked up at the blurry figure of Tanbark Wedger, still garbed in his filthy hospital gown. Bird tried to smile; then she passed out.

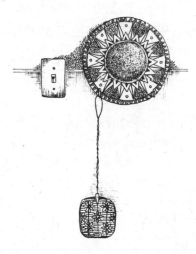

23

THE STORM

Tan congratulated himself. He'd accomplished everything so easily! First his escape from the hospital, and now the girl had literally fallen into his hands! He would be patient a little longer. Once she regained consciousness, he could tell her the entire story—at long last.

BIRD DREAMT ABOUT ROCKS and a tent made of old horse blankets. The green one belonged to old Sir Galahad—Saul was his barn name.

But was it really a dream? It was hard to tell.

Bird thought she heard a rustling near the tent, but she wasn't sure. Noises echoed hollowly and made no sense. Everything was a little fuzzy. Her eyes couldn't focus properly. Her arms and legs wouldn't co-operate, so she lay slack.

The rustle again. Maybe it was real.

Bird girl. I'm here.

Cody?

Yes. You're tied up. Don't try to move.

Oh. That's the problem.

I've been watching. If you are in danger, I'll kill him.

I'll be okay. He has something he wants to tell me.

He's not right in his brain. He might make a mistake.

Bird felt a chill run up her spine.

Sunny's reappearance at Saddle Creek caused a stir. The frantic, sweaty horse galloped the entire way home, stopping in front of Cliff in a flurry of sparks on the barn's cement floor. Cliff put a halter on the quivering animal and walked him down to the farmhouse. He knocked loudly and waited.

It was still early and Hannah hadn't yet come downstairs for coffee. When she opened her curtains and looked down at Cliff, holding a lathered and jumpy Sundancer, she threw on her housecoat. She ran down the stairs and opened the door.

"What's going on? Why's Sunny all upset?"

"Is Bird here?" Cliff asked grimly.

Hannah ran back up the stairs, two at a time. She looked in Bird's room. Empty.

"Paul!" she yelled. "Bird's gone and Sunny's lathered!"

Paul appeared immediately, tying the belt of his dressing gown. "Call the police, Hannah. Tanbark Wedger was here last night."

"What?"

"Just call the police. Ask for the chief, Mack Jones."

"What are you going to do?"

"Start looking for Bird." Paul went downstairs to the door, where Cliff was trying to deal with Sunny. He was rearing up on his hind legs and pulling on the lead.

"When did Sunny show up?"

"Just now. I came right over. He's never done anything like this before. I'm thinking Bird might've taken him out for an early ride and something happened." Sunny lurched, causing Cliff to swing away.

Paul nodded. "I'm thinking the same thing. Was he tacked up?"

"No." Cliff jerked the shank and tried to make Sundancer behave. "He was just like this. No saddle, no bridle."

"We can't put him in his field like this."

"No, he'd jump out. I'm going to walk him until he's cooled, then put him in a stall until we find Bird."

"Thanks, Cliff. I'll let you know what's happening."

"I'd appreciate that."

Wasting no time, Paul got dressed and started following Sunny's trail of hoofprints. Julia and Hannah stayed by the phone, waiting for Mack Jones to return their call.

Hannah knew that Paul's quest would be fruitless—the ground was too dry for tracking—but she also knew he needed to try. He was worried, but he also felt guilty that he hadn't called the police the night before. Several times before he left he'd told Hannah that this would never have happened if he had.

Hannah turned on the radio.

"*There's a storm watch for the area northwest of Toronto. Close your doors and windows, folks. It's going to be a bad one. Look for hail and strong winds up to eighty kilometres an hour.*"

Julia looked out the window at the darkening skies. She hoped they'd find Bird before the storm hit.

The phone rang. Hannah jumped, and grabbed the receiver. "Hello?"

"Hannah, it's Patty. Sorry to call so early, but I knew you'd be up. Phil got another note."

"Oh, Patty. What does it say?"

"I'll read it." Hannah heard the rustle of paper. "*The madness stops when you admit your guilt. Do it now before somebody else gets hurt.*"

"Did you call the police?"

"Yes. I'm waiting by the phone now."

"So am I. Bird's missing."

"Oh my gosh! What can I do?"

"Nothing. Just hope for the best. Call me later, okay?"

"Okay."

"Oh—Patty? How's Phil doing with this?"

"I don't know. He went out as soon as he saw the note, and he hasn't come back."

Hannah sent Julia up to the barn to get Cliff. Within minutes, the tall farm manager and the small blonde girl approached the house.

"Come on in, Cliff," Hannah said warmly. "Thanks, Julia."

Cliff stood by the door.

"Cliff, sit down. I want to ask you something." Hannah pulled back a chair.

Cliff remained standing. "The answer to your question is yes."

"Yes? What question do you think I was about to ask?"

"If I got another note. I did." He reached into his pocket, and pulled out a crumpled piece of paper. He slapped it on the table.

Hannah read aloud.

"*The madness stops when you admit your guilt. Do it now before somebody else gets hurt.*"

Cliff hung his head. His hands kneaded each other in helpless anxiety. "That somebody else is Bird, Hannah. She's getting hurt because I won't admit my guilt!"

"*Are* you guilty?" Hannah's voice contained a note of alarm.

"No! But maybe they'll release Bird if I confess."

"You'd confess to something you didn't do?"

"Yes. And then after they release her, I'll tell the truth."

"Cliff." Hannah sank into the chair she'd offered him. "First, Bird's disappearance has nothing to do with anything you've done or not done. Second, we don't know who the 'somebody else' in the note refers to. Third, never make a false confession—it's against the law. Fourth, Patty Brown just called to tell me that Phil got a note, too. It's identical to yours. That's why I sent Julia to get you."

Now Cliff needed a chair. Julia pulled one out as his knees buckled, and got it under him before he fell to the floor.

"I thought when Sunny came racing home that Bird was kidnapped and it was because I should confess." Cliff was babbling now. "This whole thing is making me crazy! I wondered if I should make a fake confession just to stop it all, but then I worried they might believe that I really did it and put me in jail even after I told them I didn't, but I'd do that for Bird, if it would help. I can't think about what she might be going through right now."

Hannah reached out and put her hand on his shoulder. "I repeat, never make a false confession, Cliff. It would only confuse things further and make the truth harder to find."

Julia spoke. "That's really, really nice of you, Cliff. You'd get in trouble for Bird. I would, too, if it would help."

The phone trilled. Everyone stiffened. Hannah picked it up before the second ring.

"Hello?"

"Hannah, it's Fiona Malone." Her tone was cool.

"Fiona! I forgot to call you! I have Moonlight Sonata here."

"So I hear. Dexter called. They don't want to lease her."

"Fiona, I know you're upset. We brought her to your farm around four yesterday, after the show. You were ... not home. I didn't want to leave her with nobody around."

"Dexter also said that one of your students rode her."

"Fiona, I talked to you about that, remember? You said it was all right."

"Oh. Well, no hard feelings. Just get Moonie back to me today. I need to figure out what to do with her."

"It could be a while. A suspicious person was outside the farm early this morning, and Bird's gone missing. I'm worried sick."

"Hannah! I'm sorry! You should've said something. I understand. Good luck finding Bird. Don't worry about Moonie—if she's no trouble, that is. Otherwise I'll hire old Smythe to come get her."

"She's no trouble. In fact, I have a student who'd love to ride her."

"The one who got first place yesterday?"

"Yes."

"Go ahead. Let's talk when Bird is found."

"You bet."

"Hannah? Please call if there's anything I can do."

"Thanks, Fiona."

Hannah hung up the phone and let out her breath. "I completely forgot about Moonie."

"Understandable," said Cliff.

The phone rang again. Hannah swept it up.

"Hello?"

"Hello, Hannah—it's Mack. I got your message. Bird is missing and Tanbark Wedger was sighted at your house this morning?"

"That's right. Paul's gone looking for her, but it's dry out there."

"Do you have any idea where she is?"

"Not really, but Sundancer, her horse, came up from the direction of the Escarpment."

"I've sent a team with dogs. They'll arrive soon, and will stop by to get something with her scent on it. If Paul comes back tell him to stay put."

"I will."

"Tell me about Tanbark."

"I didn't see him. I was sleeping. Paul told me that the dog woke him up around four-thirty. He went downstairs and Bird was already at the door. When he got closer he saw that Tanbark was there, too. Paul tried to get him to come inside, but he ran off."

"Did Paul tell you why he didn't call us?"

"Bird asked him not to. She said Tanbark came to tell her something important."

"I see. I'll talk to Paul later."

"Mack? There's something else. Cliff is sitting in my kitchen. He got another note."

"You're not kidding."

"No. Philip did, too. Patty Brown called me a minute ago. The notes are exactly the same."

"What do they say?"

Hannah read from Cliff's note. When she was finished, Mack was silent. "Mack? Are you still there?"

"Yes, Hannah. I'm thinking." There was another pause. "Something's not right. I'm beginning to smell a rat."

"A rat? What do you mean?"

"It's just a feeling. After that meeting at Palston, and Justice for the Innocent accepting responsibility for the fire, I didn't expect more notes." He breathed sharply. "I'm going to bring in Ellen and Jim again for questioning. Tell Cliff not to worry, and tell Paul to hang tight. We'll do everything in our power to get Bird safely home."

24

THE CANINE UNIT

Tan felt so much better outside, where he belonged. The burns were already starting to heal, and the scrapes were scabbing nicely, but it was the freedom that thrilled his heart and made everything seem possible.

Bird would soon wake up, and Tan was feeling more and more anxious. He didn't know how to tell her. Would she help him? He'd let her sleep this long, but his time was limited. They'd be searching for him, high and low.

Tan took a big breath of air. His lungs still hurt. He coughed a few times and tried again.

PAUL WALKED THROUGH THE KITCHEN door and took off his boots. He was grimy and sweaty. "No sign of her. The trails are so well used I can't make heads or tails of anything."

"Mack's search team is on the way and they're bringing dogs. He says to stay where you are."

"I went as far as the Escarpment, then turned back." He sat down heavily in a kitchen chair and rubbed his face. "It's all my fault."

"Hush! It's not your fault. Cliff thinks it's his fault, too." Hannah told him about the note and relayed her conversations with Mack Jones and Patty Brown.

Paul listened, then paused in thought. "Remember the night of the Inglewood General Store meeting?"

"Yes, I do."

"The moon was bright that night, and Bird and I stood outside with Lucky before we turned in."

"She told me. If I remember correctly, you said something very poetic about how the brightness of the moon obscures the stars, but they're still up there, nevertheless."

Paul stood, and held Hannah in a warm embrace. "You remember correctly. I'm more and more sure that the answer is right in front of us, but we can't see it because the moon is too bright."

"And in your metaphor, what does the moon symbolize?"

"Justice for the Innocent, the threatening notes, the commotion. All these things take our attention from the truth."

"Mack is wondering the same thing."

Just then the phone rang. They both tensed.

Hannah answered.

"It's your father, Kenneth Bradley." How many fathers used their full names when calling their children, Hannah wondered as she braced herself.

"Hello, Dad."

"I heard that Tanbark was seen at your farm. True or untrue?"

"True."

"Then why the blazes didn't you call me?" His voice was filled with anger.

"I didn't know until this morning, and we called the police immediately."

"Why call the police when you can call me? I'm the one who posted the reward."

Hannah took a deep breath. "It's not about the money, Dad."

"You're trying to tell me you don't want the money? You turn your nose up at ten thousand dollars? With the problems you have balancing your books each month?"

202

"Dad, stop. I don't want the reward money. I have more on my mind at this moment. Bird's missing."

"Where is she?"

"If I knew where she was, Dad, she wouldn't be missing." Hannah had used up all of her patience.

"Don't be snippy with me!"

"The police are coming with dogs. My guess is when they find Bird, they'll find Tanbark, too."

"Good. I'm coming over."

"What for?" Hannah caught Paul's eye and grimaced. Kenneth Bradley in her kitchen was the last thing she needed.

"To help look. My son is missing."

He hung up, leaving Hannah with the phone in her hand. The line was dead.

Paul reached over and took the receiver. He replaced it on its hook on the wall. "What's he going to do? Head up a search team?"

Hannah nodded. "Why does it feel like things are getting worse?"

Sunny began to wake up in his stall. The drugs that Cliff had given him when he'd arrived back at Saddle Creek were wearing off, and the peaceful stupor was replaced by urgency. He needed to get Bird. He needed to bring her back, out of the woods where frightening things lived. He neighed and paced, working himself into a complete lather.

Cliff heard all the noise and came to investigate. He took one look at Sunny's dripping sides over the open Dutch door, and made a decision. "I'm giving you another shot of Atravet. A little stronger this time." Cliff had the syringe in his hand. "I hate doping you, son, but I can't let you out and you're killing yourself in here." Cliff was quick. The needle found its place, and, against his wishes, Sunny gave in to another wave of medicated slumber.

The police department's canine unit arrived at Saddle Creek just before ten. Julia, Hannah and Paul watched the two athletic bloodhounds leap out the back of the black and white SUV. They were big, handsome dogs, each with a harness and Red Cross kit. Four officers wearing black caps and hiking boots huddled on the driveway with Mack Jones, listening to their orders.

A moment later, Kenneth Bradley's glossy black Cadillac screeched to a halt in a cloud of dust. He got out of the car and straightened his jacket. Hannah noted his shiny shoes and crisply pressed pants and tie—he was not dressed to go searching. He stormed over to Mack and the officers. Hannah knew he'd try to take over, but she had faith that Mack would ignore him. Kenneth's altered demeanour told her that she was right.

Now her scowling father turned for the house.

"Paul, please handle him. I just can't." Hannah turned and went upstairs. "I'm sorry. I really am. Julia, come with me."

That left Paul alone. He stood straight and prepared himself for an unpleasant conversation.

Kenneth Bradley walked straight into the Saddle Creek kitchen and confronted Paul. "What kind of Mickey Mouse operation are you running here, Daniels?"

"Please come in, Mr. Bradley," said Paul pleasantly. He hadn't been addressed as Daniels since his school days. "Have a seat. Can I get you a coffee?"

"The police out there don't know what they're doing! I'm a colonel in the Armed Forces. I've been trained to handle search-and-rescue missions! They should avail themselves of my expertise." He sat in a chair and pointed to the coffee pot. Then he motioned for the coffee to appear on the table beside him.

Paul smiled to himself. "Cream and sugar?"

"Not on your life," barked Kenneth. "I take it strong and black."

"It's good of you to stop by, Mr. Bradley."

"Nonsense! I have a missing son somewhere out there. I won't rest until he's been found."

"And Bird, too."

"I expect she'll show up. Bit of a wild one, that girl."

Paul noted his lack of interest. "I'm glad she hasn't caused you any concern." He placed the coffee on the spot that had been indicated.

"Tanbark has been missing quite a bit longer. He's got a problem, you know."

"I hear. Tell me, why do you think Tanbark came to Caledon?"

"I can guess. I wanted to see him again. I'm a loving father, and I try to help. So, a few weeks ago I left a message for him. Through Alison, of course. He's been on the street for years, but once in a while he calls his mother. I expect she gave him my message and he came looking for me."

"He'd come all this way for a visit?" Paul appeared skeptical.

"Why not!" Kenneth barked. "I'm his father! But I also told him I'd help him financially. That might have been a motivation."

"Might have been." Paul nodded. "He didn't find you, though. You found him."

"Yes, yes. In the hospital. He got close, though."

"He's been around here for a week or so. Spooked us, actually."

"Why the blazes didn't you call me?" the older man sputtered, spitting out a spray of coffee.

Paul never got used to Kenneth Bradley's instant temper. "We didn't know who he was, or what his problems were."

"He's got more problems now. He killed that woman, Sandra Hall, whoever she is. I'd stake my life on it. But he'll get off because of insanity."

Paul was stunned, baffled by Kenneth's sudden switch. He'd said that he was a loving father trying to help, but in the next breath he'd accused his son of murder.

Bird felt a little better. Her head had cleared. She opened her eyes. Things were jumbled so she shut them again. The image of Tanbark Wedger, sitting with his back to her, stayed behind her eyelids.

Cody? You still there.

Yes.

Bird relaxed under his watchful presence. Now she smelled what Sunny had predicted earlier: a storm was coming. The woods had darkened and an eerie quiet descended.

She opened her eyes again, and studied the makeshift tent. Tan had secured the horse blankets in a crevice created by two huge vertically sheered rocks. The tent was approximately six feet high and six feet deep. Bird admired how stable it was. It was protected by the Escarpment itself, and ingeniously undetectable.

Hannah and Paul and Sundancer would be looking for her. They'd likely be coming soon, so she needed to do what she'd set out to do—hear Tanbark's story. She must get his attention, but her arms and legs were tied up and she still couldn't speak.

Bird tried to sit up. Her head started to spin again. Just as she was about to give up and rest a bit longer, Tanbark turned to her with a questioning look. She waited for him to speak.

"Your name is Bird. Mine is Tan. Pleased to meet you." He smiled.

He's handsome, thought Bird. Dirty and wild-looking, but handsome. He'd draped another horse blanket, a wool cooler belonging to Charlie, over his back.

"You know we're related. My father is your grandfather, although I was surprised that he admitted it." Tanbark sat cross-legged under the horse cooler as he leaned back on one of the rocks that supported his makeshift tent. His fingers drummed the dirt floor.

Bird tried again to sit up.

"If I untie you, will you make a run for it?" he asked.

Bird shook her head.

"Then let's get you comfortable." Tan hastily began to loosen the knots. "I have a story to tell."

25

TANBARK'S STORY

Tan's chance was finally here. Now he could tell her his story. But now that everything was exactly how he'd wanted it—exactly how he'd dreamt it would be—he found he couldn't begin! He felt anxious, overly excited. He strained to get himself under control.

BIRD WAITED PATIENTLY for Tanbark to begin his story. The rain had begun in earnest, and it pounded on the horse blankets overhead. She wondered if they would collapse. They were weatherproof, but even the best horse blankets get soaked through. And they were old. It was only a matter of time before the dripping began.

After several minutes, Tanbark began to speak. "People don't understand me. I am not like other people, and I don't want to be, but I'm not crazy." His words came out in a rush. "No, I am not crazy. I want to live like people used to live long ago. Off the land."

He scratched at a scab on his foot until it bled—was it from when he dragged himself away from the fire? "Your grandfather, who is my father, phoned my mother. He wants to give me money. A lot of money. I don't trust him, but I want the money. I came here to get the money, but then all this … stuff … happened."

Bird wondered what he'd use the money for, living off the land.

"Soon people will recognize me as a leader. Soon everyone will want what I have. I have found the truth about life, and that is what everyone is searching for. They will line up to hear my wisdom."

Bird nodded her encouragement, but a prickle of fear began to snake up her spine. He wasn't making a lot of sense.

"Communication is the way of the future! With my father's money I will make a CD. In a month, maybe two, I'll be an international superstar. That will be the path!" Tan rose from the ground with unexpected energy. "That will be how they'll find me. People will flock to me and I'll share with them the secret of life." Tan rocked back and forth on his feet, his head almost touching the roof of the tent.

Bird's heart sank. Hannah had told her that he had a mental illness, but she hadn't known what to expect. After all the trouble it had taken to find him, was it possible that he'd have nothing useful to say? Was it also possible that he might harm her?

"I have a plan!" Tan bellowed to the skies. He stepped out into the rain and threw up his arms. "Rain all you want! Rain on my head! Rain! Rain! Rain! Nothing will stop me!"

This wasn't going well. Tan had untied her arms and legs, and her hands moved well, but she was having trouble getting the feeling back in her feet. That might be a problem if she had to run. She wiggled her toes in an effort to get some circulation.

Tan ducked back under the tent and sat. The shouting was over. "Let me tell you what I saw," he said in a conversational tone. His voice had become reasonable, and his expression had changed. His eyes had become focused and alert.

He was suddenly sane-looking, Bird thought. She adjusted to the mood swing, and wondered at the complexity of the man.

"I was minding my business," Tan said. "I was down the hill in a ditch beside the road where there are rabbit holes. A car was coming. It blew a tire, POP!" His eyes opened wide and his fingers flew up.

Bird jerked with fright.

"The car stopped. I flattened myself in the ditch so they wouldn't see me. Right close by, a man and a woman got out. The woman had been driving. I guess it was her car because she opened the trunk and knew where stuff was." He faltered.

Bird waited.

"This is where it gets secret."

Bird nodded, indicating that he could trust her. She tried to look sure of herself, but she was nervous. She had no idea of what she was about to hear, or whether she could believe it.

"They argued. I heard most of it. She was mad because he wanted to stop seeing her. Something like that. She wanted him to marry her. She was broke and needed money. He said he'd give her money but didn't want anybody to know about them, let alone marry her. Et cetera, et cetera, et cetera. Boring. I wanted them to change the stupid tire and leave. Let me get up out of the ditch and find breakfast."

Tan's eyes began to dart, and his fingers twitched. He scratched his head rapidly and jiggled his knees. Bird nodded quickly to catch his attention and keep him focused.

"Why don't you talk, Bird? Are you crazy?"

Bird just stared, totally unsure of how to respond.

Luckily, she didn't have to. Tan immediately forgot his question and continued his story. "So, now comes the weird part. Can I trust you? Can I?"

He peered into Bird's eyes. He moved his face closer and closer, looking, Bird guessed, for the answer. He got so close that Bird was scared again. She was completely blocked in the tent with no place to go.

Finally, Tan sat back. "The man starts to walk away. Leaves the woman with the flat tire. She's yelling at him to come back, that he can't leave her like this, that she doesn't know how to change a tire, she loves him, et cetera, but he keeps walking. He's an old bugger, too." Tan licked his lips. "He just walks away. She picks up the tire iron and keeps yelling. She yells out that he'll regret leaving her, and she waves the thing around in the air, but he keeps walking. She screams again. Calls him names. Bad names. He keeps walking. Then …" Tan stopped.

"I hear dogs." He jumped up and ran out of the tent.

Great, thought Bird, just when he gets to the good part. She strained her ears to hear what Tan had heard, but the rain was too loud. If Tan had truly heard dogs, a search party was likely in the area. They were running out of time.

A minute later, he was back. "I'm going to tell you this fast, Bird, and then I'm going to run away. They're going to pin this on me. They always pin things on me. I know that, because I know." He looked over his shoulder anxiously. "I know things. Spidey-sense." He tapped his head.

"Listen to me, Bird. That woman smashed herself with the tire iron. She didn't mean to. She hauled it up over her head, it slipped out of her hand, and it smashed her. The blood poured out. It was everywhere—just came gushing out. She looked so surprised. Her eyes went big and she fell right down and her head hit a rock. Thunk. I can't get that out of my mind." He shook his head, as if he could shake it free of the image. "Still can't."

Now Bird heard the dogs, too. They sounded close.

Tan was up on his haunches, ready to run. "Look, the dogs are coming and they'll blame me, so listen." He talked so quickly that Bird had to lean forward to hear. "The man, well, he kept walking. He looked back at her. He saw the blood and he saw her on the road and he kept walking until he got in a black car and took off. Another car was coming and I was so freaked that I jumped up and ran away into the woods. I'm scared about being blamed. I know they'll blame me. They always do."

Tan was on his feet, quivering. He stepped from one foot to the other. "I gotta go. But one more thing, Bird. This is important!

The man? In the car? Who walked away? It was my father. I recognized him when he came to the hospital. And Bird? On the road that day? He saw me, too. He knows I know, he just doesn't know how much."

And with that, Tanbark Wedger took off running. Bird lost sight of him as he ducked and wove through the trees and disappeared into the pounding rain.

Sunny awoke to lightning and thunder. He tossed his head to shake out the drugs. Apart from the noise outside, the barn was quiet. He was alone. He pushed on his stall door. Solid. He tried the hardware and latch with his lips. Too tricky. He looked down at the hall floor. Slippery. He looked up at the height of the ceiling. It was his only choice.

Sunny backed up as far as he could. Keeping his head low to avoid the rafters and bunching all his weight over his rump, he neatly leapt over his stall door without touching a hair. He landed lightly, but the sparks flew as his steel-shod hooves hit the cement. The smell of sulphur rose to his nostrils. Sundancer trotted out of the barn and bolted into a gallop the second he touched dirt. He raced full out, along the trail, through the rocky crags and all the way to the top of the Escarpment.

The rain was hardening and turning to hail. It pelted his coat. A flash of lightning lit up the sky, followed by the mighty roar and crack of thunder. He was terrified, but Bird needed him.

Stay alive, he messaged. *I will find you.*

In the tent, Bird heard Sunny's words and was comforted by them. *I'm safe,* she answered.

The storm was worsening. Bird stayed under the horse blankets, thinking hard about what Tan had said. Sandra Hall had hit herself with a tire iron—hard. Hard enough to knock herself to the ground. Hard enough to kill herself. It was horrible. Bird couldn't even imagine it! Was it even true?

And her grandfather saw Sandra on the ground, bleeding, but didn't call for help. Why?

Bird struggled to put the pieces together. Tan was clearly ill, but he had no reason to make this up. A man who would save horses—and another human—from a barn fire wasn't likely to kill a woman on the side of the road. Was he? And besides, it all kind of fit. Even Kenneth Bradley watching over Tanbark on his sickbed. Tanbark had been right to leave the hospital when he did, thought Bird. He was the only witness. And if Kenneth didn't want the truth to come out—and he obviously didn't—he would want to keep Tan quiet. Bird shivered.

Cody crept into the tent and shook himself off.

Cody! I'm glad to see you, but you're getting me all wet!

I need to be dry for a small time.

Bird smiled. *Okay.* Cody's presence made things much better.

Sunny is coming. The dogs are leaving and so are the humans.

That's good. The wild man is gone, too.

Yes. Maybe he will return. Maybe he will not.

I'll stay here until the lightning stops.

And until the bad man leaves.

The bad man?

I saw him. He's in your den. Waiting for the wild man to be captured.

Bird knew who Cody meant. He called her grandfather the "bad man," and her "den" was the farmhouse. Now that she'd heard Tan's story, the last thing Bird wanted was to run into Kenneth.

Bird girl, I will go now to show Sunny the way.

How are you going to find him in this hail?

He'll get to the place where he lost you, then he'll look around.

Cody slid out of the tent and melted into the wild weather. Bird loved the mysterious ways of the coyote. She admired how he knew so many things and kept track of where everybody was, up at the house and down in the woods. He was a very smart and honourable animal, she thought.

Three minutes later Cody reappeared, followed by a drenched and huffing horse. Bird got to her feet and went out to greet them.

Sunny!

I'm sorry I left you down here, Bird. I'm ashamed.

You were frightened, Sunny! You did what horses do. I'm not mad.

I've come to carry you back to safety.

We're safe here. Come out of the storm. Bird had been outside for less than a minute, and she was already drenched. She tried to steer the horse under the tent.

Where's the wild man? asked Sunny.

He ran away a minute ago.

The sky became electrified with a bolt of lightning. A deep rumble followed instantly behind.

Sunny trembled. *Let's go!*

But Bird was firm. *We'll stay here until the storm passes. I'm not arguing with you about this. We don't want to be struck by lightning.* She reached up and patted his nose. *Come under the tent with Cody and me. And here's a blanket for you. We don't need anything more.*

Once under cover and out of the elements, Sunny relaxed. *It's nice in here, with you and Cody.*

Bird smiled as she adjusted the wool cooler on his back. They were cozy and dry under this makeshift tent, and she could think of no better company. They would wait out the storm together.

26

THE PLOT THICKENS

Tan felt so good. He had told the girl—finally!—his story. The hail and the lightning didn't bother him one bit; in fact, he enjoyed it. He stretched up to embrace the forces of nature as a crash of thunder rattled the trees. The rain cleansed his body and the electricity around him cleared his brain. Now he needed to find a place to stay for the night. At least the dogs were far away. There was no hurry now. Something would come along. It always did.

PAUL AND KENNETH WATCHED the tracking dogs and policemen trudge back to their truck in the teeming downpour, empty handed. Kenneth Bradley became more and more outraged as he watched them load up.

"Mickey Mouse, Daniels! It's Mickey Mouse and Donald Duck time! In my day we never gave up until we had our man. Give me an umbrella. I'll give them a piece of my mind."

Paul rummaged around in the broom closet and found a big black umbrella. He handed it to Kenneth. Grabbing it, the older man slammed the kitchen door and stomped through the mud and rain to the police truck. Paul chuckled at the scene before him. Kenneth waved and gestured while the men went about their jobs. Casually and efficiently they got the dogs, equipment and men into the truck, while Kenneth grew angrier by the minute. Finally, he threw the umbrella on the ground and raised his fists in a challenge.

The leader of the unit quietly got behind the wheel and drove off, leaving Kenneth alone in the driveway. He turned toward the house and prepared to storm in.

Paul was trying to sort out how to handle the situation when Kenneth had a change of mind. He got in his new car soaking wet, and drove away with his wheels spinning in the wet gravel. The car lurched suddenly when it found traction, and with a mighty roar from the high-powered engine, Kenneth Bradley was gone.

Paul let out a loud sigh.

Hannah and Julia came running downstairs and threw open the kitchen door.

"Thanks!" Hannah put her arms around Paul and hugged him. She kissed him full on the mouth. "I sure owe you one."

"Anytime," said Paul good-naturedly, "if you pay me in kisses."

"Deal." Hannah's smile faded into a more serious expression. "I saw the canine unit leave. Did they call it off?"

"They did. I expect Mack'll call and tell us what's happening. He said from the outset that the dogs would have a tough time in this weather."

Hannah nodded. "I know. The dryness, then the downpour." Her face dropped. "I'm having a tough time myself. I'm worried about Bird out there alone with Tanbark. He's not a sane man."

Julia gave her aunt a hug. "She'll have Cody watching over her. That's what cheers me up."

Hannah's eyes welled up. Her mouth twisted as she made an effort to hold back the tears. "That's so sweet, Julia. And of course you're right."

A soft knock sounded on the screen door. It was Cliff.

Hannah ushered him in.

Cliff stepped in and stood on the mat. "I overheard what you said, Julia. About Cody. Well, she has Sundancer watching over her, too."

"What?" Everybody spoke at once.

"He's gone. He jumped out of his stall. You can see the marks his hooves made in the hall."

Paul stood up. "The storm's getting worse with that hail, but I hate sitting here. Should we go out looking?"

"I'm ready, but Hannah and Julia should stay here in case there's any news."

"I should come, too," Hannah said. "I know the trails better than either of you."

"And leave me alone? No way!" Julia gasped. "I'll be so scared!"

"Somebody has to be here in case they come home, Hannah," said Paul. "And Mack will be calling. It's best that you and Julia stay here, and Cliff and I go search."

The phone rang. Hannah sprang out of her chair and grabbed the receiver.

"It's Kenneth Bradley. Any sign of Tanbark yet?"

"Dad, no. And we haven't found Bird yet, either." She looked at Paul. "Do you want to come help Paul and Cliff search? They're just leaving."

Paul and Cliff both grimaced.

"No," barked Kenneth, loud enough for the men to hear. "I certainly do not! Call me when you find him. Where have you been, Hannah? I was just over there."

"Too bad I missed you. I'll call with any news."

"You do that." He hung up.

Less than a second later the phone rang again. It was Mack Jones. "We called off the search for now, but don't worry, we'll find her." His voice was as calm and reassuring as always. "I'm sending the dogs back the minute the lightning stops."

Hannah closed her eyes and rubbed her forehead. She wondered how good an idea it was for Paul and Cliff to go out, if the professionals would not. "But what about Bird?" she asked Mack.

"Knowing her, she's found shelter. The problem is getting down there. Someone's going to get hit with lightning."

"I totally understand. Can they follow the scent later, though? After this storm?"

"They won't even try to track them," Mack explained. "They'll be scenting for humans. They'll go through every thicket and swamp and they'll find her."

Hannah dared not ask if that meant dead or alive.

"Call me immediately if she comes home, or if there's anything at all that concerns you."

"I will."

"Oh, Hannah. A head's up. Philip Butler hasn't been seen all day. Call me if he shows up there?"

"Yes, of course." Hannah's head spun as she hung up the phone.

Paul sensed something wrong. "Hannah?"

"Philip hasn't been seen all day."

"Is that a problem?"

"He's not under arrest," added Cliff. "He can come and go as he pleases."

Paul agreed. "Why don't I call Patty? See what's up."

Hannah nodded. She sat at the table, hands clasped in front of her. With Bird gone and Tanbark on the loose, she didn't want to think of anything else that could go wrong.

Paul punched in the numbers. After a brief conversation, he hung up. "Patty hasn't seen him all day—not since he got the note."

Hannah shook her head. No matter how bad it got, it always seemed to get worse. She wandered to the freezer and absent-mindedly took out a frozen chicken pot pie.

She turned to Cliff, who still stood dripping on the mat. "Please stay for dinner, Cliff."

He shook his head. "No thanks. I've still got things to do after we go looking for Bird."

Hannah's mouth set in a determined line. "Mack called his men off for safety reasons. No matter how much I want Bird back, you cannot go looking in this weather. We have to trust her ingenuity, and believe that she's found a dry place."

A crash of thunder underlined her words.

Paul put down his coat. "I hate to admit it, Hannah, but you're right."

Cliff wasn't so sure. "What if that guy's got her scared? We can't wimp out on her. She wouldn't wimp out on any of us!"

Bird was very hungry. She hadn't had breakfast before she'd jumped on Sunny's back that morning, and she calculated that it must now be close to six in the evening. It was difficult to be accurate since she'd been unconscious for part of that time, and the stormy skies and dense treetops made it impossible to see the sky. The only thing she knew for sure was that her stomach was completely empty. She'd missed breakfast and lunch, and now dinner.

Sunny stood in the middle of the tent with his head down, slowly turning. He nibbled on the grass in and around the tent.

If I could digest it, I'd eat that grass, too.

I'm glad you can't. There wouldn't be enough for me.

Nice that you're so generous.

Bird's stomach grumbled loudly. The hail and strong winds howled above them, bending treetops and flattening undergrowth. The sound of ice pellets hitting the blankets overhead was deafening. There was no way they could leave. Bird looked through Tan's garbage for anything that might be edible. All she found were empty cans and a banana skin.

Cody stood up and stretched. *I'll catch you a rabbit or a gopher. Maybe a rat.*

Really? That sounds oddly tempting, if a little creepy.

Better than starving.

We'll cook it over Tanbark's fire. Bird studied the charred remains in the firepit that Tanbark had used the night before.

Get it started and I'll go hunting.

Cody slunk around the farmhouse in search of food for Bird. The wind was blowing from the northwest, so he stayed in the lee on the southeast side of the house. The kitchen door faced south, and he peeked his nose around the corner. The cooking smells were unbearably enticing.

The screen door opened, and Cody pulled back. A second later, Lucky trotted out and started sniffing around for a bush.

Lucky!

Cody?

Yes.

It's raining ice cubes. I'm going back in.

Wait. Bird needs food. Get some.

They'll punish me!

I don't care. Get food. Now.

I'm afraid!

Cody crept out of hiding and growled at the young dog. *Are you more afraid of them or me?*

Lucky stood awkwardly in the driving rain, staring at the soaked, snarling coyote. His decision was immediate. *Wait here.*

He pawed at the door to be let in. The door opened, then closed.

Cody waited.

Suddenly, inside the house he heard surprised shouting and the clattering of objects dropping to the ground. The screen in the door ripped apart with a long, soft zipping sound, and Lucky raced out with his tail between his legs. His mouth was clamped on an entire loaf of fresh bread in a plastic bag.

I'm coming with you, Cody. No way I'm going back in there.

Good work, Lucky. Come this way.

Mack Jones sat in his office at the Caledon police station. The constant hail and high winds rattled the window behind him as a flash of lightning momentarily lit up the skies.

Across from him sat Jim and Ellen Wells.

"Thanks for coming in." Mack leaned forward in his chair. "I asked you here because we need to talk—honestly. The way I see it, you're lucky we don't have enough proof to pin on you for the moment, but believe me when I say we're looking." Mack's eyes squinted sternly. He continued. "First, you've sent out more notes threatening people. That's got to stop."

"At least we're doing something." Ellen stuck out her chin as she spoke. "You don't know how worried people are! Until we catch the man who killed Sandra, there will be no peace around here."

"Have you considered that you're adding to their worry? That you're obstructing the police with this harassment?"

Jim added, "You police are holding an innocent man in custody while the guilty one runs free."

Mack raised his eyebrow. "If you're referring to your friend Les Crowley, his innocence will be tested by the courts. I think you'll agree that a hit and run, coupled with an assault on a hospitalized man, should not be overlooked."

Jim pursed his lips. "He got carried away."

"For good reason!" Ellen's face reddened with emotion. "Sandra's death must be avenged."

"Avenged?" asked Mack quietly.

Jim answered quickly. "Ellen means that we must help solve this crime, and do our civic duty."

Mack nodded slowly. "Explain."

Ellen answered, her voice quivering. "I saw her covered with her own blood, Mr. Jones, lying on the hard road. I feel a personal obligation to find that, that ... monster! I couldn't live with myself if I didn't try."

"And you, Jim? What makes you so involved that you'd take part in criminal activities?"

Jim licked his lips nervously and his eyes darted around the room. Ellen spoke in his stead. "My husband is a noble man who is doing the right thing. It's not illegal to try to flush out a culprit."

"It is illegal to burn down buildings. It is illegal to deliberately hit someone with a car. It is illegal to write notes threatening bodily harm. A man is fighting for his life, and another was hospitalized." Mack waited for this to sink in. "You are both in serious trouble. If Pierre Hall dies, you'll be in more trouble than the man who killed Sandra Hall."

The desk phone rang. Mack picked it up reluctantly, unwilling to break the tension of the moment. "Mack Jones."

Ellen and Jim watched as the chief of police's face darkened. He uttered brief, serious acknowledgements to the caller, and jotted notes on his pad. Then he abruptly placed the receiver in the cradle.

"Do you have your cellphone on you, Jim?"

Jim blanched. He patted his pockets nervously.

"It is also illegal to forcibly detain somebody." Mack rose to his full height. "You'll both be spending a little time with Les Crowley." He pressed a buzzer on his desk, and looked impassively at their stricken faces. "You might be interested in who called just now. Philip Butler. He found your cell, Jim, in your jacket pocket. It was in the laundry room of your locked basement."

Cliff left Hannah and Paul in the farmhouse, and headed home. He bent against the howling wind as he pushed through the mud and pounding hail, and pulled his collar up as high as it would go to protect his neck. Hannah had said she'd phone if there were any further developments, but he was still mad that she'd refused to let Paul help him search for Bird. He would look for her alone.

Lightning flashed, and the thunder was simultaneous. Cliff knew it had struck close by. He stopped, and stared in astonishment as the old maple in the front field burst into flames. The lightning had spared the farmhouse by metres! Maybe Hannah was right, Cliff thought. Head down, he hurried on.

He wasn't expecting company.

A large man jumped out at him as Cliff ran up the steps to his porch. He took hold of Cliff's upper arm and shoved him hard. Reflexively, Cliff spun and elbowed him hard in the jaw. He watched the man tumble into the muddy garden below. Boss barked frantically from inside the house.

Cliff stood firmly in the rain, keeping the man in sight as he flailed and stumbled to his feet. It was Hank Crowley, Les's brother. Cliff had gone to school with Les, but he knew Hank by sight.

"Hank," said Cliff. "Fancy meeting you like this." Cliff grabbed the man's arm and pulled him up, twisting it behind his back as Hank squealed in pain. "I wondered when one of you would try something like this. We're going to see Hannah and Paul. They'll want to know why you dropped in."

Bird and Sunny both heard Lucky coming. The big pup thrashed and crashed through the brush and arrived under the tent with great fanfare. He proudly dropped the squished loaf of bread at Bird's feet, then shook himself from head to toe.

Lucky! Good boy! How did you find me? Bird rubbed his head and scratched behind his ears.

Cody showed me. I'm a good boy, aren't I?

Yes, Lucky. Good boy!

Cody quietly snuck into a far corner. *Bird girl.*

Cody. Thank you so much.

Sundancer snorted. *Where's the dead meat you promised?*

People food is much easier to obtain in a storm. Eat, Bird girl.

I'm so glad to have this, Cody. Tan's matches are wet. I couldn't start a fire and I'm not hungry enough to eat raw things.

The animals watched Bird devour the bread. She offered to share, but Cody refused, and with a stern glance ordered Lucky to refuse as well.

Despite the continuing storm, it was very cozy in the horse-blanket tent. The wind raged around them and the rain and hail continued to fall, but they were together and safe. Sundancer lay down in the middle, and Cody and Lucky snuggled up to his belly. After eating as much of the loaf as her stomach could handle, Bird rested her head on Sunny's neck and promptly fell asleep.

Cliff and the unwilling Hank approached the farmhouse just as Patty and Liz were dashing through the rain from their car. Hannah held open the screen door and strained to hear Patty's words over the storm.

Patty was saying, "I hope you don't mind, Hannah. We were getting so edgy we thought we should just come over."

Hannah ushered them in, then caught sight of Cliff on the walkway with Hank slightly in front of him. "Cliff? Who's that with you?"

Paul quickly joined her at the door. "Is that Hank Crowley?"

"Sure is."

Paul caught on quickly. "Bring him inside."

Hannah knew exactly what to do. "I'll call Mack."

Cliff and Paul each took an arm and hauled Hank into the house.

"Julia!" ordered Paul. "Get the clothesline from the closet!"

Julia jumped into action as Liz covered her mouth with her hands. "W … what's going on?" she wailed.

"Don't worry about anything," Cliff answered. "This guy's not going anywhere."

"This should do until the police come," said Paul, tightening the knots in the clothesline that held Hank to a chair. "Hannah? Did you get through?"

"Sure did," she said, hanging up. "Right to Mack." She turned from the phone in a daze. "Wow. Things are happening fast. He's just arrested Jim and Ellen."

Paul reacted with a jolt. "Pardon me?"

Hannah nodded, then turned to Patty. "Patty, sit down. Mack tried to call you. I told him you were here."

Expecting the worst, Patty dropped into a kitchen chair. Liz sat down on her knee trembling.

All eyes were on Hannah as she began to speak.

"Philip's fine, but he was locked in the Wells's basement all day. He's on his way here with the officers."

Paul spoke. "Locked in the Wells's basement?"

Patty mumbled, "All day?"

"Why?" whispered Liz. "Why would they l ... lock him in their b ... basement?"

Cliff spoke thoughtfully. "They're ramping it up, that's why. Pierre and Tanbark were hurt already, so today it was Phil's turn—and mine."

Paul slowly turned to face Hank. "Do you have anything to say for yourself?"

Hank refused to open his mouth.

"Fine." Paul reached over and tightened the last knot. "You can talk this over with the authorities."

There was another knock on the door.

Hannah opened it to find Pete and Laura Pierson huddled under a small pink umbrella. "Heavens! Please come in!"

"We won't disturb you," said Pete, his eyes taking in the whole scene, "unless we can help. You have more than enough going on."

Laura hugged Hannah tightly. "Fiona told us that Bird was missing. You poor dear! You must be beside yourself!"

Hannah tried to answer, but the tears she'd been holding back all day filled her eyes and her throat constricted.

"We've been trying to get through, dear, but your line has been busy," Laura continued. "We couldn't wait another moment. What can we do?"

"Julia! Liz!" called Hannah, brushing away the unwanted tears. "Pull some chairs by the fire for Mr. and Mrs. Pierson." She faced the elderly couple with a smile. "Come in now before you catch pneumonia, or we'll have to tie you up like Hank, here!"

Pete and Laura stepped inside and stood on the mat with rain dripping off their coats. Hannah hung their umbrella and coats on hooks, as chairs were readied.

Pete looked hard at Hank, who blinked and squirmed under his gaze. "I've known you since you were a boy, Hank. I knew your father and grandfather, too. You've made trouble for yourself and for your family. You've made trouble for the whole community. I hope you think it's worth it."

Hank's eyes wavered for a second then hardened. He kept silent. Only the nervous movement of his fingers suggested that he'd heard what Pete had said.

As the Piersons sat down by the fire, a crunching of tires on the gravel driveway outside signalled another arrival.

Paul and Hannah looked at each other and spoke at the same time. "The police."

27

BIRD'S VOICE RETURNS

Tan had found the perfect hiding place—an old deserted cave that was dry and quiet inside. Best of all, it was on the path to a fresh water hole where animals of all kinds came to drink. That would make scenting him very difficult. Tracking dogs just weren't that smart. He crawled in and made himself as comfortable as possible on the hard ground surrounded by rocks. He grinned and fidgeted. Things were turning out just fine.

BIRD SLEPT SOUNDLY through the storm. The hail slowly turned to rain and the winds began to weaken, imperceptibly at first, until the storm was finally over.

Cody was the first to awaken. He wiggled silently out of the tent on his belly and crept away.

Sunny woke next, and stayed still for as long as he could stand it.

Bird, I need to stand up.

No answer.

Bird! Seriously. Horses are not meant to be off their feet for too long.

Bird stirred slightly, then rolled over. As soon as she was clear of him, Sunny stood. He shook himself, then stretched. The scent of fresh wet grass drew him outside, and soon he was busy filling his empty belly.

Lucky snored deeply, and Bird turned over to find a more comfortable position.

When the cruiser stopped in front of Saddle Creek, Paul opened the ripped screen door, wondering briefly what had possessed Lucky. The officers got out of the patrol car, followed by Phil. Patty ran outside and embraced him. "What happened?" she asked.

"I'll tell you all about it," said Phil, "after the officers have removed our friend Hank." They walked into the house with arms entwined.

Paul and Cliff untied Hank and the two policemen snapped on the handcuffs. One officer spoke to Hannah as he worked. "The chief has put another search team together, and they're on their way now."

Hannah nodded eagerly. "I'm so glad."

A moment later, they were gone.

"Well," said Hannah as she watched the cruiser's tail lights disappear down the lane. "Hank's gone. I'm glad."

"The rain's stopped, too," said Paul, looking at the sky.

"I just wish we knew where Bird was," Julia said quietly, her voice cracking with emotion.

"They're starting the search again, honey," said Hannah, giving Julia's shoulder a warm squeeze. "Mack told us that as soon as the lightning stopped, the dogs and men would go down and find her, and that's what they'll do."

Julia burst into tears. "I hope they find her," she whispered, "but I really hope she's still alive."

Liz hugged her friend and began to cry, too. "Don't c ... cry, Julia," she croaked. "When you c ... cry, I c ... cry."

Cliff was the first to voice what they were all thinking. "I'm going to get a flashlight. Who's coming with me?"

Julia jumped up. "I am!"

"Me, t ... too!" cried Liz.

"You can't hold me back!" said Hannah.

"I'll take my cell," Paul said as he grabbed a flashlight. "We can form our own team. Never too many hands."

"Pete and I will stay here to answer the phone," said Laura. "I'll put the chicken pie in the oven, and we can all eat when Bird comes home."

Just as she spoke, the phone rang. Paul put it on speaker so he could grab his jacket.

"Hello?"

"Kenneth Bradley here. Have you found Tanbark?"

Everyone stopped what they were doing.

"No, Mr. Bradley. Mack's sending some dogs down soon, though."

"Soon, you say? What incompetence!" Kenneth sputtered. "I'll do it myself. I've got my own search team and I'll find him myself." He slammed the phone down with considerable energy.

"He didn't even ask about Bird," said Julia.

From the corner of the kitchen, Pete's quiet voice interrupted their thoughts. "Why is he so eager to find Tanbark that he would forget his granddaughter?"

No one could answer.

Cody slunk back into the tent and pulled at Bird's shirt.

Wake up, Bird girl. Wake up.

Bird opened an eye and looked at the coyote, whose nose was touching hers. *What?*

Wake up. It's time to go back to your den. They worry.

Bird sat up straight, knocking Lucky by accident. The dog jumped up in alarm. *I'm ready! I'm ready!*

The storm was over and it was getting dark. Bird was so tired that she had trouble thinking. What had Cody said? They worry? Suddenly it hit her. Hannah and Julia didn't know where she was.

Cody, how long have I been sleeping?

No matter. Go now.

Sunny! Let's go!

I've been ready for ages.

Bird scrambled up on the chestnut gelding's back. *Can you find your way home in this light?*

Can birds fly?

Bird patted his neck affectionately and wound her fingers through his mane to help stay on. Lucky followed at Sunny's heels and Cody wove in and out behind them and in front, through the trees and around the rocks, all the way up the Escarpment.

Once they were up the slippery, rain-soaked trails and past the rocky outcrop, Bird urged Sunny into a canter. He was eager to get home, too, and they sailed along freely. Sunny sure-footedly galloped along the well-known paths as darkness fell, eating up the distance easily.

As they arrived in the back field, Bird saw what looked like stars sparkling in front of the house. She blinked hard and looked again. What the heck was that?

Julia was the first to see them coming. "Bird?" she hollered.

Hannah turned to look, aiming her flashlight into the darkness. "Julia, what do you see? Where are you looking?"

"There, Aunt Hannah. There! Way past the barn. I swear it's Sunny with Bird on his back." She started running. "Bird! Bird!"

"I can't see anything," said Cliff, "but I hear hooves."

"Something's coming," Paul said as he strained to see. "There, behind the barn. Do you see it, or am I imagining things?"

Slowly the shapes of a horse and rider followed by a dog began to solidify in the mist.

"She's coming home!" yelled Hannah. "Bird's coming home!"

Julia ran toward Bird as fast as she could, gasping for air.

Lucky could no longer contain himself. He barked and wiggled with excitement, then he shot toward home. He raced past Sunny and bumped into Julia, who patted him as he passed. He dashed to Hannah, then to Paul. Lucky whined and sang, wagging his whole body.

Slowing Sunny to a trot, Bird saw the outline of a small figure barrelling toward her.

"Bird!" called out Julia as loud as she could. "Bird!"

"Julia!" Bird yelled.

Sunny's ears spun back. *Bird! You spoke!*

In a rush of energy and excitement, Bird realized that he was right—a word had passed her lips. "Julia!" she cried again, louder this time. "It's me! I'm home!"

Julia and Sunny almost collided in the dark. Bird slipped off her horse's back and hugged her little sister tightly.

Breathless and sobbing, Julia pulled back. "Bird, you talked! You said my name."

Bird laughed and cried at the same time. "I did, didn't I?" she said. "I can talk again, Julia! I can talk!"

Hannah stumbled on some tufts of grass but found her feet in time to catch herself. As soon as she reached her niece, she hugged her so tightly that Bird began to hurt.

"Aunt Hannah! Let go," she laughed. "I'm in greater danger now than I was all day!"

The others were right behind, exuberant with joy and relief. Bird was fawned over and Sunny was praised and patted. Slowly, the elated procession made its way to the farmhouse.

"Where were you?" asked Paul. "What happened today?"

"I'll tell you the whole story."

"Did Tanbark kidnap you?" he persisted. "I can't believe I didn't call the police right away."

"Well, he tied me up, but only to keep me with him until he could tell me his story." Even to Bird's ears, it sounded weak.

"I thought you might be dead," Cliff blurted.

"I'm sorry, Cliff. I was knocked out when I fell off Sunny, then tied up and I couldn't get away. Then the storm hit and I fell asleep. Cody woke me up and we raced home as fast as we could."

"Cody woke you up?" Julia asked. "So he was watching over you the whole time?" She turned to Hannah. "Like I said, right?"

"Yes, the whole time." Bird scanned the shrubs that lined the path to the house, but she could not see the coyote anywhere. A great gratitude swelled up in her chest. *Thank you, Cody.*

It was my duty. His reply came from the bushes.

Sunny tossed his head. *I helped, too, after I escaped the barn.*

"And Sunny helped, too. He came to rescue me and bring me home."

Lucky pawed Bird's leg. *Me, too! Me, too!*

"And Lucky brought me a loaf of bread so I didn't starve to death. Good boy!" Bird rubbed his ears and Lucky wiggled happily.

"So that's what was going on!" Hannah said with a laugh.

"We couldn't figure it out," added Paul. "We didn't know what had gotten into him! But how did he know where you were?"

"Cody brought him down," answered Bird. "Then we all slept until the storm passed."

"A nap in the storm?" Julia shook her head, puzzled.

"Tanbark had made a tent out of stolen, or borrowed, horse blankets. It was actually quite protected and dry."

"That's another mystery solved," said Cliff. "The green one that old Saul wore and the red waterproof?"

Bird nodded. "And Charlie's wool cooler."

"Bird, darling! Darling Bird!" Laura came running out. "There's chicken pot pie and I've made some hot cocoa and cookies for you."

"That sounds too good to believe," Bird said. "I'm so hungry I could eat a …"

Don't say it.

Bird laughed at Sunny's warning. "I'm so hungry I could eat out the entire refrigerator!"

Just then, the canine unit truck pulled up at the house. Mack Jones got out of the passenger door and walked up to the group. "Do I see who I think I see?" he asked, smiling broadly.

"You do, indeed," answered Paul. "Bird just got home, and she can talk again! You can call off the search. For her, at least."

"Welcome home, young lady." Mack examined Bird carefully. "Are you all right?"

"I'm fine. Tanbark saw what happened to Sandra Hall. That's what he's been wanting to do all along—to tell someone."

Mack nodded eagerly. "We'll want a complete statement of course. Where is Tanbark now?"

"I don't know. He ran away when the dogs got close. I have no idea how long ago that was, or where he went."

"Did he hold you against your will?"

"Yes, but he only wanted to make sure I'd stay and listen to his story."

"Did you feel in danger at any time?"

Bird paused and thought carefully. This was a more difficult question to answer. "He's weird, and has some crazy ideas, but I never really thought he'd hurt me."

"Where did you last see Tanbark and when?"

"In his tent at the bottom of the trail and off to the south, but I can't tell when because I fell asleep after he ran away."

Mack checked his watch. "It's ten o'clock. We called off the search at seven. He could be anywhere by now." Mack turned to signal the driver of the van. "Start the search for Tanbark Wedger!"

When Mack turned back, Paul spoke. "Kenneth Bradley has sent down a search team, too. Perhaps you can co-ordinate with him."

"No!" Bird shouted. "Don't let him!"

Mack peered at her with a raised eyebrow. "Explain, Bird."

"My grandfather should not find Tan. It's very, very important."

"Why is that?"

But Bird wasn't listening. She grabbed Sunny's mane and leapt up onto his back with one fluid motion. She dug in her heels and urged him to retrace their steps.

Sunny, we're going back down.

Sunny balked. *You're whacked!*

Maybe so, but we have to find Tan. Now.

How are we going to do that?

Cody!

Yes.

Can you find the wild man?

Yes.

We'll follow.

All at once, a doubt began to grow in Bird's mind. Even if she found Tan, how would she convince him to come back and tell everybody what had happened? He might be too nervous. But his version of the events was crucial. Somehow, someway, she needed the others to hear it. She had an idea. "Julia! Get me your recorder!"

"My digital recorder? My new one? Why?"

"Just get it! I'll explain later!"

Julia ran into the house.

"Bird!" Hannah's voice was hollow with worry. "You're not going back down there. I will not allow it."

"Sorry, Aunt Hannah," Bird steeled herself, "but Cody will find Tan the fastest. Grandfather cannot get to him first! He might try to kill him! I'll be fine!"

Hannah spoke to Mack earnestly. "Mack, stop her. This is dangerous work."

Mack looked at Bird sternly. "Listen to your aunt, Bird. I need to hear what Tanbark said. You must get down and tell me now. My team will find him. This is not a job for an inexperienced child."

"Trust me!" cried Bird. "There's no time! I'll tell you later! I have to warn him! He knows too much and my grandfather wants to shut him up."

Paul tried a more gentle approach. "Get down, Bird. Sunny needs some feed and rest. So do you. You've had a very long day."

"Julia!" Bird yelled. "Hurry!" She turned to Mack, Paul and Hannah. "You don't understand, and it's a long story. Keep my grandfather away from Tan! I'll tell you everything when I get back." She had just decided to leave without the recorder when Julia reappeared with a small device in her hand. She reached up to Bird and gave it to her.

Bird slid it securely into her pocket, and, without another word, Sunny and Bird shot off at a gallop toward the back of the farm. Cody was waiting at the top of the Escarpment, sniffing the air with intense concentration.

The race was on.

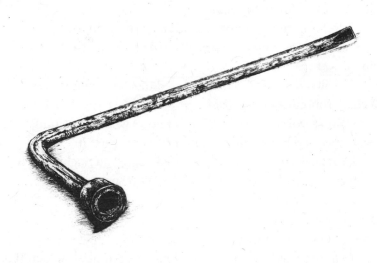

28

THE SEARCH FOR TAN

Tan listened to the baying of the hounds. They were far away, but he thought they were getting closer. He prided himself on having ears as sharp as a dog. He would have lots of warning. He wasn't worried in the least.

MACK IMMEDIATELY LEFT with the search team, and Hannah, Julia and Paul resigned themselves to waiting in the farmhouse. Cliff went up to the barn to check on the horses, and Pete and Laura settled in the armchairs by the fire. Phil, Patty and Liz decided to go home to get some rest.

"Call any time day or night, Hannah," said Patty as they headed out the door. "Especially if there's anything we can do."

"I will. I promise." Hannah closed the door then slumped in a chair, rubbing her forehead.

"Don't worry," said Pete. "Bird knows what she's doing. She has a special relationship with nature. Let her use it."

Hannah looked at the insightful old man. "You might be right."

Pete smiled. "Of course I'm right. With Sunny's strength and speed, and Cody's nose and tracking skills, Bird has the best chance out there of finding Tanbark."

"If he's still out there," said Paul.

Pete stretched his arms and rubbed his aching shoulder. "I'll bet he's close by. At least until his mission is accomplished."

"What mission?" asked Julia.

"Whatever it was that brought him here in the first place."

Bird and Sunny were back down below the Escarpment at the tent, exactly where they'd started. Cody crossed and double-crossed the deer trails and hiking paths. Bird watched as he systematically checked under every leaf that had a trace of Tan's scent.

The tracking dogs were close enough to hear, but there was no way to tell if they were Mack's or her grandfather's.

Cody, can we find him first?

Yes, Bird girl. He went this way. Follow.

Bird and Sunny kept as close as possible to Cody. Nose to the ground, he followed the scent. As they picked through dense underbrush and walked flat-footed across slippery rocks, the baying and crying of the hunting dogs never let up.

Can you hear two teams, Cody?

The dogs have split into groups. I know not which team is which.

Do any of them have the scent?

No. Soon, though.

Bird struggled to calm herself. She knew she couldn't rush the coyote, but they had to find Tan before Kenneth Bradley.

Cody stopped and raised his head. *The wild man is hiding in a hole where coyotes were before.*

Where?

Look where I look.

All Bird saw was a group of large rocks and a steep cliff. *I don't see anything.*

Get down to the ground, and follow me.

Bird did as she was told. *Stay here, Sunny. I'll be back. Hopefully with Tan.*

Don't be long, Bird. It's dark.

Sunny stood by the edge of the drop while Cody led Bird down.

There was no path, and the descent was slippery and rocky. Eventually, a small cave was revealed in the side of the hill.

He's in there.

Cody and Bird heard the dogs at the same time—closer now. They'd found the scent and were coming fast.

Hurry, Bird. I'll distract them.

Be careful, Cody! Bird was alarmed at the thought of her coyote friend putting himself at the mercy of packs of hunting dogs.

Never fear. I will be safe. In an instant, the coyote was gone.

Bird was alone in the dark. She took a deep breath and concentrated on her job. She crawled onto her knees and looked into the black mouth of the cave. Bugs buzzed around her.

"Tan? Are you in there? It's Bird." Her voice echoed lightly against the earthen walls.

There was no reply.

"Tan, I know you're in there. Listen to me. Your father is looking for you with dogs. He's got a search team down here."

Still no sound. Not a breath or a rustle. The cave smelled dank and uninhabited, and Bird didn't want to imagine what kind of biting things and slithery creatures were there with her. She shivered with nerves, ready to bolt. She filled her lungs with fresh air and put her head inside.

"Tan, come home with me. It's very important. Tell your story to the police. Tan? Are you in there?"

Deep in the cave, Bird heard the sound of movement. It was a scratching sound, like claws on earth. Could coyotes still be in there? Was this the right cave?

"Tan? Look, if you don't want to come back with me, at least get your story recorded so the truth can come out. I have a digital recorder. Then I'll go away. I'll leave you alone to be caught by your father. Your choice."

No reply. Just those scratching sounds. Try as she might, Bird could not get a read on whatever was within. The little hairs on the back of her neck were standing straight. One more try and then it would be time to leave. "Say something, Tan! I'm scared."

"Nothing to fear, Bird."

Bird went limp with relief. "Why didn't you answer me?"

"I didn't want to be found, stupid."

In the distance, Bird heard the dogs change directions. Their cries grew fainter until she could barely hear them. Good old Cody.

"You brought a recorder?" asked Tan. "Can I sing you my newest song? It's cool."

Bird hesitated. There was no time to waste. "Come home with me now, and you can sing it on the way."

"No way, on the way. I'm not going with you. I'll stay here where I'm safe. Are you crazy? I'll sing it now, and you will record it."

Time was running out, but if singing would get Tan to tell his story, she didn't see why not. "Sure, but then you have to tell what you told me. About your father and Sandra Hall and what happened that day."

"You said you'd leave me alone after that. That's my deal, or no deal at all."

"Deal. Come out of the cave and talk to me."

"No. You come in."

"It's creepy in there. And smelly."

"Do you want my story or not?"

"I'm doing this for you, Tan! I have nothing to gain for myself."

"So why are you here?"

"I guess for nothing!" Bird's voice was rising in frustration. She forced herself to calm down; she didn't want Tan to clam up, not when she was this close. "Look, Tan, you're the one who's running. You're the one who's going to be blamed. You're the one who needs the story told."

Tan considered this for a moment. "I'll meet you halfway."

"Halfway?"

"Halfway or no way. You can't pretend that you don't care if you came all this way to find me."

Bird forced her irritation aside and leaned out to take another huge gulp of the clean night air. Then she crawled in. Tan's outline appeared in the gloom of the cave. She sat facing him, bent into a pretzel to avoid touching the sides of the cave.

Tan waited until she was settled. "How did you find me?"

"It wasn't me, it was Cody."

"The coyote?"

"Yes."

"I wonder about him. Did he pull me away from the barn fire?"

"Yes. He saved my life, too."

Tan pondered the idea. "I thought he hated me. I guess I owe him."

"We both do. He's distracting the hunting dogs now, and keeping them away." Bird listened hard for sounds of their return. Nothing. So far, so good. "Can we do this now?" she asked. "Record your story? If you're not coming back?"

"Start the machine." He cleared his throat. "I'll sing first."

Bird pressed the start button and the machine whirred into action.

"It's all a hoax," sang Tan in a soft, tuneless monotone. "It's all a joke. We live and toil, and then we croak."

"Cool," Bird mumbled.

"Did you like it, really?"

Bird chose her words carefully. "It's, well, not exactly uplifting, but it's … real."

Tan nodded enthusiastically. "You get it. That's wild, man."

"Wild … man," Bird repeated with a chuckle.

"What's so funny?"

"That's what we called you, before we knew your name."

"What?"

"The wild man."

"Anyway, there's a lot more, but you'll have to buy the CD. No free lunches!"

Bird nodded. "I don't expect any. Now, can we do this other thing? What you saw the day Sandra Hall died?"

"Sure." Tan got himself comfortable, and Bird waited as patiently as possible. She did not want to spook him before his story was safely recorded. She listened again for the tracking dogs and heard them, faintly, on the other side of the deep ravine.

Tan began his story. "I was minding my business, hunting for rabbits on the edge of a field. A car came ..." He repeated, almost exactly, what he had told Bird earlier in the day. Minutes later, the entire story was recorded.

Bird said, "That's great," and pressed the stop button. She tucked the recorder safely into her pocket and prepared to leave. "People won't believe it when they hear this."

"Then why did we record it?"

Bird smiled. "I just meant that people will be amazed by the truth, not that they literally won't believe it."

"Then why didn't you say that in the first place?"

"Gosh, Tan, I'll be more clear in the future. Anyway, see you. I hope I'll bump into you someday." She crawled toward the exit.

"Where are you going?" Tan asked.

"Home. We're finished. I'll leave you alone, like I promised."

"But what about me?" Tan's face twisted. "You're going home, but where am I going? Did you think of that?" He started to twitch with agitation. "You came to me. How can you leave me and ruin my life?"

Bird had not seen this coming. He didn't seem to know what he wanted. For the second time in the same day, Bird was reminded just how ill Tan was. "You told me you wanted me to leave you alone. That was our deal. Remember?"

"Do you think it's fun living in horrible caves all the time?"

"Well, no. I wouldn't do it."

"Would you like to hide from people all the time?"

"No."

"And how would you like to eat garbage and catch animals for food?"

"I wouldn't."

"I don't want to be wet and dirty all the time. I want dry clothes."

"Then it's simple." Bird didn't know how Tan would react, but it was worth a try. "Come home with me."

Tan smiled broadly. Bird saw the whiteness of his teeth in the gloomy cave. "Okay. We have a new deal. I'll come home with you. And why can you talk all of a sudden? I thought you were crazy."

Bird laughed. "We're all crazy, Tan. Some of us are just a little crazier than others."

She felt his eyes squarely on hers. "Do you think I'm crazy?"

Bird nodded and smiled warmly. "Yup."

Tan thought hard, his face working with the effort. "Do you think I can stop needing to run and run?"

"Yes, I do, Tan. You can do this."

Bird! Sunny was impatient. *Are we going to live down here or what? The bugs are killing me.*

I'm coming now, Sunny. With Tan.

The wild man?

The same.

Don't expect me to put him on my back again.

No. He'll walk.

29

THE HOMECOMING

Tan figured that he could handle anything that came his way. He was ready to spring into action if need be. He didn't think this was a set-up or a trap—Bird wouldn't do that to him. But he would be ever alert.

BY THE TIME THEY CLIMBED back up the rocky ridge and got to the barn, the night had turned cool. Bird was totally exhausted, but she had something to do before going to the house. She let Sunny into his freshly bedded stall and gave him an extra flake of hay, making sure the water bucket was filled right to the top. When he'd drunk his fill, she topped it up again. In the feed room she mixed a warm bran mash with molasses and hunks of carrots and apples.

"Can I have some, too?" asked Tan as he sat slumped over on a bale of hay. "I'm hungry."

"Just wait. Aunt Hannah will feed you something even better."

Sunny dug in eagerly, then looked at Bird. *Are you going to stare at me all night?*

We're leaving, you grouchy thing. Thanks for coming down and saving me today.

Anytime.

Tan and Bird left Sunny to his dinner and walked down the Saddle Creek lane in the dark. The stars were bright, and a sliver of moon arced in the sky. The smell of the damp earth and green grass filled their nostrils. Fresh, cool air swept the scent of sweet flowers over them. Bird was happy to be out of the dank cave.

She looked around. *Cody. Thank you. I'll leave a ham bone on the back porch.*

Much appreciated, Bird girl.

Good night, my friend.

Good night. The coyote ran off into the night.

"Where does he go?" asked Tan.

"I don't know. He has his ways."

"I like that. His ways. I have my ways, too."

Bird agreed. "You and Cody have a lot in common."

"Like a soulmate."

Bird smiled at him and nodded as she opened the kitchen door.

Hannah was the first to jump up from her chair. "Bird! Thank god! We were so worried ..."

Then she saw Tanbark. She stopped in mid-stride. Bird watched the emotions flit across her face: fear, curiosity, wonder, shock. Hannah hadn't seen her half-brother for many years, and he had been sane and clean when last they'd met. He must seem utterly alien to her now, covered in dirt, skinny, unwashed and wild.

"Aunt Hannah, this is Tanbark," Bird said. "He's hungry and cold."

Laura Pierson pulled the fleece blanket off her legs and thrust it at Tan. "Poor dear!" she crooned. "Let me wrap you up."

Tan stepped back quickly, trembling. Bird looked at the room from his perspective. There were a lot of people. Laura, Pete, Hannah, Paul and Julia were all staring at him with concern; pity, even. It must all be overwhelming for him, she realized, especially considering how little he'd had to do with humans in the last few weeks. She stepped behind him and secured the screen door, just in case he decided to bolt.

Like Bird, Pete seemed to understand. "Come sit with me by the fire, my boy. There's no need to talk." He smiled warmly at Tan and motioned to the chair just vacated by Laura. "Come, son, sit."

Tan took a hesitant step forward, then looked at Bird. She nodded encouragement. He took a shallow breath and plunged into the chair. His eyes were shut tight, and his entire body shook with nerves. No one moved.

"He needs some space," said Pete in his gravelly voice. "We can't crowd him."

Laura crept up with a cup of tomato soup. "Tan? Are you hungry?"

Pete was about to chastise her when Tan opened an eye and held out his hands. Everybody watched as he gulped down the soup.

Julia picked up the fleece blanket from the floor and tucked it in around Tan's legs. "Welcome, Uncle Tan," she said with a smile.

Tan looked quizzically at Bird.

"I think that's right," Bird said. "You are Aunt Hannah's half-brother, so you're our mother Eva's half-brother, too. That makes you our uncle."

"Your half-uncle, dear," said Laura.

"But we would never call him that," said Julia. "It would sound funny to say, 'Half-Uncle Tan, would you take me to the zoo?'"

"Call me anything," said Tan with a shrug. "It doesn't matter. I'm not taking you to the zoo and your half-uncle is still fully hungry."

His words broke the tension in the room. Everyone laughed as Hannah brought Tan and Bird steaming plates of chicken pot pie, and watched contentedly while they ate every last bite.

Moments after Tan was finished eating, his head began to nod. It fell to the headrest, and his eyes closed. He was asleep.

"I called Mack at home to tell him Tan's here," said Paul quietly. "I convinced him to let the man get a good night's sleep before any questioning. Bird, he said to tell you that you're quite the girl."

"Can you tell us now what Tanbark saw that day?" asked Hannah.

Bird nodded. Very quietly, so as not to disturb his sleep, she told them everything Tan had said. There was complete silence in the room as the story was digested.

"Remarkable," whispered Pete. "Remarkable."

"Do you think it's true?" asked Paul.

Bird nodded. "I do. But I don't know if anybody else will."

That night, Bird slept more soundly than she ever had before. It was a deep, dreamless, untroubled slumber. She awoke, refreshed and smiling, as the sun spilled through the slit between her curtains. Songbirds trilled outside her window, informing her that the storm was indeed over. In the corner, Julia's futon was already empty.

Finally, the problems in Caledon were over! Once Mack heard Tan's story, things would get back to normal, and she'd be able to concentrate on Sunny and their next show. Tanbark would testify that Sandra Hall had accidently bludgeoned herself, fallen on a rock and died. There would be a collective sigh of relief when everyone realized that the bogeyman wasn't real. They would go on with their lives knowing that there was no predator on the loose ready to attack innocent victims with a tire iron. Kenneth Bradley would have some questions to answer—like why he walked away from a bleeding woman and didn't call for help—and the Wells and their accomplices would be punished. Best of all, Tanbark would get the help he needed.

Tanbark. Bird wondered, for the umpteenth time, how mental illness affects people. How does it work? Where does it come from? Why do some people get it? Can anybody get it? Can people get cured? Bird was confident that Tanbark would get better. There was so much about him that was good and positive, and he had so many people around him who cared. She felt sure that once Tan made the decision to see a good doctor, he would get better.

Bird smiled again and closed her eyes. Her daydreams floated in another direction. Now she was receiving an award from the Town of Caledon and the police department for her excellent sleuthing. She would wear a hat to cover her stubby burnt hair when she humbly and eloquently delivered her thank-you speech. People would clap and cheer as she accepted a huge bouquet of flowers.

Bird stretched from head to toe. She thought about the horse show. The Palston Classic was in just two days! She and Sunny had been working together much better since the show the week before, but there was still so much more to do.

She desperately wanted to make a good impression this time. Eva and Stuart were coming home the same day as the show. Imagine how proud her mother would be when she learned the whole story! Bird the hero. Alberta the hero. Perhaps it was time to graduate to her given name—like when Hilary James became Hilary instead of Mousie.

The daydreams continued. Alberta Simms, receiving the silver trophy at the Classic after jumping a perfect round on Sunny. The trophy this year would be presented by the elderly Donshell sisters, Matilda and Maudie. Alec would appear just as she accepted the trophy. His eyes would shine with pride as he made sure that everyone knew he belonged to her. He would publicly declare, over the loud speaker, that the rumours about him and Pamela were false and that there was only one girl in the world for him. Then, he would sweep her up in his arms and deliver a delicious kiss, right on her lips. Bird smiled with delight. This daydream could go on forever …

A loud yell brought her back into real time. "Paul!" In the room next to hers, Hannah hollered again. Bird sat up straight, and all the rosy thoughts tumbled from her head. She jumped out of bed.

"Paul! Tanbark's bed is empty and the window's wide open!"

Bird ran to the hall. "He's gone?"

Hannah pointed. The filmy curtains flapped in and out of the screenless, gaping window, and the covers of the bed lay rumpled on the floor. Bird walked in and looked out the window to the flower beds below.

"Aunt Hannah, come look."

Together, Bird and Hannah studied the two deep footprints in the dirt where Tan had landed. The window screen lay beside them.

Paul and Julia arrived after a search of the ground floor. The four of them looked at the prints in wonder. It was a long way down.

"What do we do now?" asked Bird.

Paul pursed his lips. "Mack Jones isn't going to be happy."

"I never imagined that he'd jump out the window!" said Hannah. "He seemed so happy to be here, and to be fed and warm."

Bird nodded. "He was happy, but right now he's kind of like one of the barn cats. Once they're fed they need to be out roaming again."

"Maybe he knew he'd have to go back to the hospital," reasoned Julia, "and he didn't want to go."

Bird nodded. "Exactly. I bet he just doesn't want to be fenced in, or feel trapped, especially when his father is out there looking for him."

The sound of gravel crunching under tires drifted through the window. A familiar car was driving down the lane from the road. Hannah and Paul hustled downstairs while Bird hurried to get dressed.

Paul opened the door to welcome Mack. "Come in, Mack. Hannah's got the coffee on. Bacon and eggs?"

Mack shook Paul's hand and walked in. "No thanks, Paul. Just ate. But I'd love a coffee. Milk and sugar. Thanks. And good morning to you all."

"Coming right up," smiled Hannah, a little too brightly. "Good morning to you, too, Mack."

Bird stepped into the kitchen.

"Morning, Bird," Mack said. He looked at her with sparkling eyes. "Well, you're the little hero, aren't you? You brought back the man the whole county was searching for."

Bird decided to plunge right in. "I brought him back, but he escaped in the night."

Mack's eyebrows shot up and his smile vanished. He looked at Paul, then Hannah, then back to Bird. "Tell me you're joking."

"No," said Bird calmly. "He jumped out the bedroom window. His footprints are there for you to see."

Mack marched outside and examined the site. He returned with a furrowed brow. "No doubt about it; he jumped out."

Paul spoke up. "I'm sorry, Mack. You wanted to interview him last night."

Mack shook his head. "I have to take the blame, Paul. I thought he'd be a better witness after a rest. I should get back to the station. Hannah, cancel that coffee." He took out his cellphone and pressed a speed-dial number. "Tanbark Wedger is at large. Put out an APB."

"Mr. Jones," said Bird as Mack slipped the cell back into its holder. "I have a recording of what Tan saw."

Mack looked at her with astonishment. "You got it?"

Bird pulled the tiny recorder from her pocket and held it out on the palm of her hand. "I recorded the whole thing last night in the cave, before Tan decided to come back with me."

"Let's hear it," said Mack. He sat down at the kitchen table and motioned for Bird to do the same. Bird placed the device on the table and pressed play.

The sound was uneven and hollow as Tan's voice sang. "*It's all a hoax. It's all a joke. We live and toil, and then we croak …*"

"What's this?" asked Mack.

"He wanted to record his new song, so we did," answered Bird. "His story is next."

They leaned in to listen as Tan began. "*… I was minding my business, hunting for rabbits on the edge of a field. A car came …*"

Everybody was spellbound. Nobody spoke. Finally, Tan's story ended and Bird's voice could be heard on the tape: "*That's great.*" Then there was the click of the stop button, and silence.

Julia spoke first. "It's like Tan's song!" she exclaimed. "It's all a hoax! It's all a joke!"

"It's not a joke." Mack was not amused. "If we can believe Tanbark's recital here—and that's a big *if*—countless hours of police work and unimaginable fear for personal safety have been for nothing. Not to mention the barn fire and injury." He stood. "Although this does solve one puzzle."

"What's that?" asked Paul.

"There was only one set of fingerprints on the tire iron, and they belonged to Sandra Hall."

Bird tilted her head. "So Tanbark is telling the truth!"

"Maybe. We'll look at the facts again with his story in mind." Mack walked to the door. "Bird, I'll need that recorder."

Bird nodded, then glanced at Julia. Julia shrugged her shoulders. "It was a birthday present, but you're welcome to it."

"Thank you, Julia." Mack started for the door. "I'll bring it back."

The telephone shrilled, and Hannah answered.

"Hello?… Yes, Lavinia, Kimberly's got a lesson at nine … She'll go to the show if you want … I'm busy right now, can I call you back about Moonlight Sonata?… Yes, Lavinia, I really am busy … I'll call you back." Hannah hung up and sighed.

"Sorry, Mack," she said. "We'll call you if Tan shows up."

"He might get hungry for more of Hannah's food," said Bird.

Julia nodded. "Food might be the only reason he'd come back."

The phone rang again.

"I'll leave you now, folks," Mack said as he made his way to the door. "Call my cell if he shows up."

Hannah picked up the receiver as the screen door closed behind Mack. "Hello?... Oh, Dad!" She covered the mouthpiece and whispered to Paul. "It's my father. Get Mack back in here."

"What were you saying?" Hannah pressed speakerphone so everyone could hear.

"You heard what I said, Hannah. I asked if you'd heard from Tanbark." Kenneth Bradley's voice filled the kitchen.

"Not today," answered Hannah, searching Mack's face for the right way to handle this. Mack scribbled quickly and handed her a note.

"What do you mean, not today?"

Hannah quickly read Mack's note. "He was picked up yester-day, but he got away. Mack's people are out looking for him now." She looked to Mack for approval, and he nodded.

"He got away?"

"Yes, Dad. He got away."

"Did they question him? Hannah, this is important."

Hannah watched as Mack nodded. "Yes, I think they did."

"You *think* they did? Not that they can believe anything he says. He's mentally ill! He has no contact with reality. Delusional." There was a slight pause, and when he spoke again, his voice had taken on a suspicious edge. "What else do you know, Hannah? Tell me!"

"I don't know anything, Dad. Why don't you call Mack Jones directly and ask him?"

"Mack's nothing but a useless bureaucrat! He couldn't catch a blind cat in a sack! Look, Hannah, you're lying to me and I want to know why. I monitor the police dispatches, so I know what's going on. Tanbark spent the night at your house. Why didn't you call me?"

Hannah was stunned. She stared at Mack, uncertain of how to proceed. Mack was taken off guard, too.

Seeing her aunt hesitate, Bird decided to act. She threw caution to the wind and jumped in. "Hello, Gramps. It's Bird here. Don't blame Aunt Hannah. She's protecting me."

"Explain yourself." Kenneth's voice was smooth again.

"Well," said Bird carefully, ignoring all the flapping hands and warning looks. "I told her not to call you."

"You're lying."

"I'm not. I told her not to call you."

"And she listened? To you?"

"She did. She didn't call you, did she?"

"Look here! I don't care who did what and what happened when! I want to know where Tanbark is, and what he said to the police—and I want to know NOW!" Bird cringed at the anger in Kenneth's voice. He had given up all pretense of civility.

"There's no reason for you to yell at Bird, Dad." Hannah jumped in. "Call the police about this, not us."

"You called the cops, but you didn't call me!" Kenneth's voice was threatening and low. "You had him and you let him go! Now I'll have to find Tanbark myself. I'm not happy about this, Hannah."

A chill ran down Bird's spine. He's a sick man, she thought. Far more dangerous than Tan. She watched as Mack passed Hannah another note.

"I'm sorry Tan got away. It didn't work out like we'd hoped. I'll call you if I see or hear from him again, okay? Are you home today?"

"Yes. And Hannah? If you think you can fool me ... Hannah? I'll be watching you." With that, Kenneth Bradley hung up.

A second later, Mack stood up. "That doesn't sound good. And he's monitoring the police frequencies. Interesting. I'll have to bring your father in for questioning, Hannah. I'll keep you in the loop."

"I have no idea what just happened here," said Hannah, as Mack left for the second time.

Bird stated, "If mental illness is hereditary, we know exactly where Tan gets it."

Hannah stared at her. "Out of the mouths of babes."

"Your father is certainly good at turning people upside down," agreed Paul. "And inside out."

Bird nodded. "Gramps has got himself into a real mess, and he'll have to deal with it." She stood up from the table.

"That's the right attitude." Hannah looked at her niece with approval. "The police will take it from here."

Julia piped up. "Bird, you were so smart getting Tan's story recorded, but if it's true what they say on *Law & Order*, it might not be admissible in court."

Paul laughed. "You did a great job, Bird. This whole thing is almost wrapped up."

30

TAN EXPLAINS

Back in the cave, Tan had slept well. He knew he couldn't stay there, though—his father would eventually find him with the dogs. But at least his sleep was much less fitful, now that he wasn't worried about the coyote. Cody. Tan grinned. His soulmate. The thought of Cody saving his life in the fire flashed in his brain. He owed him big time.

But he'd think about that later. Now, he had to worry about remaining free. Bird was protecting him—and that gave him comfort—but he had to remain alert if he was to stay alive.

AN HOUR AFTER MACK LEFT Saddle Creek, Kimberly, Liz, Bird and Julia were all tacked up and on their horses. Hannah put them through their paces. It felt good to be thinking about something other than murder or Tan.

Sunny was showing off for Moonie. He stretched out long and low at a trot with his head tucked nicely and his neck perfectly arched.

Nice, Sunny.

I'm not doing this for you.

It's still nice.

We're going to win this time.

Don't worry about winning. That's what got us in trouble last time.

You can pretend, Bird, but you don't fool me.

Bird laughed aloud.

"What's so funny?" asked Julia, trotting by on Sabrina.

"I'm just happy to be riding," answered Bird.

"Me, too!" yelled Kimberly from across the ring. "I love Moonie! She's so light on her feet and collected. I feel like a good rider when I ride her. I hope Mom lets me buy her."

I hope Kimby can become my person, messaged Moonie.

Liz sighed. "I feel so safe on Pastor. He wants to do the r ... right thing all the time."

Liz can ride me anytime, Pastor told Bird.

Bird smiled. It was nice when horses and people agreed. It didn't happen nearly enough.

Hannah called out to Julia, "Do you want to take Sabrina to the show, or Timmy?"

"Can I decide later?"

"I need to know soon. Sabrina has a better chance of winning, if she behaves, but Timmy is more predictable and safer. It's up to you."

"It's so hard to choose!" answered Julia. "Now that I have the choice, I'm not sure which one I want to take."

Bird looked at Sabrina closely. She was an exceptionally pretty pony, with her flaxen mane and tail and chestnut coat. Her face was beautifully dished with a lovely white blaze, and her legs were delicate and long for a Welsh pony. The judges always loved her.

Sabrina, do you want to go to the show with Julia?

Yes, I do. She's just right for me, even though I prefer boy riders.

Why is that? I've always wanted to know.

Because of Keghan, Dillon, Evan and Michael. They're my boys. I taught them well and they treated me like a princess.

As you deserve!

That goes without saying.

Will you be nice to Julia?

Yes. And we'll win the best ribbons.

"Let me decide for you, Julia." Bird rode up to them. "Take Sabrina. She'll do the job for you. And it's good to challenge yourself."

"If you say so." Julia grinned. "Timmy has been so wonderful for me. Now he can teach some other kid to ride."

That's what I like to do best! Timmy messaged from his stall.

"Okay, Sabrina it is." Hannah clapped her hands. "Now, is everybody warmed up? Let's jump!"

She had set up a course of low jumps, including a water hazard. The kids had a great time counting their strides and finding the right spots from which to jump. Bird knew that Hannah was doing her best to make everyone forget the troubles of the past week. And she was succeeding.

One field over, Tan watched the girls' riding lesson from the cover of bushes. Cody watched Tan from another clump, deliberately positioning himself between the wild man and the people. He raised his head to signal Bird.

I see you, Cody. Any news?

The wild man is here. Look farther to the treeline.

I don't see him.

He feels uncertain.

Bird thought for a moment. *Keep an eye on him. I'll speak to him when I'm finished here.*

Good.

Sunny threw his head up in frustration. *Leave it alone! It's over!*

Sunny was wrong. It wasn't over. Bird felt sure that the mystery of Sandra Hall's murder had been solved, but Tan was still out there on his own, without medical attention or a place to call home. And Kenneth Bradley was eager to find him. For Tan, nothing was over. Bird wondered if it ever would be. She ran her fingers through Sunny's mane. *I have to do this.*

You make me worry. I thought this was over and that you could settle down and ride the way you used to.

Don't worry, please, Sunny. I just need to speak to him.

The rest of the lesson went without a hitch. Hannah was pleased with the girls' work, and Bird soaked up the confidence and camaraderie around her with a deep sense of pleasure.

Paul arrived home for lunch. He'd been worming and giving shots to several barns full of horses. "I've got ice cream!" he called from the driveway. Bird smiled. Paul was trying to help them forget, too.

"Lunch break!" called Hannah. "You were all fabulous. Tomorrow, the horses will be perfect."

"Aunt Hannah, is it okay if I come down in a few minutes?" asked Bird. "I'd like to get a few things done."

Hannah rubbed her niece's burnt hair and smiled. "Sure thing. I promise we'll save some food for you."

"Ice cream, too?"

"Ice cream, too."

Bird listened to the chatter and jokes as everyone walked to the house in high spirits, leaving her in the barn. If Tan was watching, he'd know she was alone. He would come to her.

She soaped Sunny and walked him dry. She pulled his mane just a little to make braiding for the show easier. She organized and cleaned his show tack, and put a clean cooling blanket, saddle pads and leg wraps aside for quick packing.

As she worked, the excitement of the impending show built in her chest. Also, for the first time in her life, she was happy that her mother was coming home. Eva. Bird smiled. She'd called just once while they were away, to make sure the girls were fine. Hannah had not told her about all the chaos; she'd decided there was no point in ruining their honeymoon. Bird was happy for her mother. Finally, Eva had found what she was looking for in her life—though she hadn't even known what that was until it found her.

Maybe life's like that, Bird mused. Maybe it takes a lot of luck.

She'd been thinking about Alec, too. Why shouldn't he have a flirtation or two? They weren't married or anything, not even really going out. If the rumour was true, so be it! Let him go! He wasn't worth another minute of moping. There was always another train coming down the track, as Pete sometimes said. Or lots more fish in the sea. Bird squared her shoulders and began to hum a funny song from a musical her class had seen. "I'm gonna wash that man right out of my hair ..."

A little later, Bird finished all her chores, and Tanbark still had not come. It was time to go find him.

Cody?

Here, Bird.

Can you take me to Tanbark?

Tanbark has come to you.

Bird spun around.

"Boo!" Tanbark was standing right behind her, eyes glistening a little too brightly. His body quivered with glee.

Bird was catching on—Tan was always either too sad or too happy. Too happy meant she needed to be very direct or he wouldn't pay attention.

"Don't do that!" Bird snapped. "You scared me!"

"So, what's the word, Bird? Do you like that rhyme?" He grinned.

"The word is that we're in big trouble with the police because, after all the trouble I went to finding you in that cave and bringing you home, you jumped out the window before they could even talk to you!"

"That's not my problem."

Bird stared at him. Could he really be that selfish? "What is your problem?"

"The way I see it, my only problem is how to stay alive until my father's put in jail."

Bird waited for him to continue.

"I saw what happened at the road that day. I saw who walked away. And I'm homeless, which equals insane."

Bird nodded. He was making sense. "Go on."

"Put it all together, Bird. I get locked up either way. Prison or the funny farm. Or far worse."

Bird stared. "Let me understand. He wants you found," she said slowly, "and if he can't discredit you, he'll possibly want to permanently silence you. Is that what you're saying?"

Tanbark shrugged. "Yeah, that's what I'm saying."

"Do you think he'd really do that?"

Tanbark shrugged his shoulders. "I don't know. I'm staying out of sight, just in case."

Now Bird understood why Tan had jumped out the window. It wasn't his need to be free, or even a fear of other people. He was literally afraid for his life.

"I'll help however I can," said Bird. "And there's the recording. I gave it to the police."

"Good. It will speak for me."

"I'll bring you food and dry clothes. Cody will be our go-between."

"Cody?"

"Yes. He'll be watching you. When you want food, come around the house and he'll let me know. Then I'll send him to you with something to eat. You never have to tell anybody where you're hiding, that way."

Tan tilted his head. "And people think I'm crazy."

31
THE PALSTON CLASSIC

Tan felt pretty good. Bird would look after him. She thought of every-thing—even his food. Simple! Whenever he was hungry, all he had to do was come around the house. Cody would see him, tell Bird to fetch food, and presto! This was the life!

THE NEXT MORNING, Bird awoke with a start. The horse show! Bird jumped out of bed. Today! She threw off her nightgown and nervously dressed in her still-new show clothes. She was glad she'd carefully laid them out the night before. She was in no condition to make decisions.

Outside Bird's window, Sunny calmly grazed. Aunt Hannah believed that a little dirt was far better than a jangled horse. Bird completely agreed. The horses liked their routines. They spent all their summer nights out in the fresh air, so why coop them up the night before a show, just to keep them clean?

Bird found Hannah and Julia downstairs in the kitchen.

"Morning!" Hannah chirped brightly. "Show time!"

Julia rolled her eyes. "She's been like this all morning."

Bird grinned. She took the glass of orange juice that Hannah offered, drank it down and sighed with contentment. "Here's to a great day."

"Paul's already at work. The Petersons' young draft cross got caught in wire overnight. He'll be fine. Just a few stitches."

"He must have stood still until someone found him," Bird said.

"Exactly. When he didn't run up with the others for breakfast, they went looking. There he was, quiet as can be, waiting for help."

Bird was already wolfing down her scrambled eggs on toast. "Cool horse." Most horses got so frightened that they would tear their leg to bits trying to get away from the wire. Especially when the others went running off.

"I'm taking Sabrina for sure, Aunt Hannah. Final decision." Julia tapped the table decisively.

"That's good, because that's who's ready." Hannah began clearing up. "Put your lab coats on over your show clothes, girls. And rubber boots to keep your riding boots clean. Let's get the show on the road."

Within minutes, they were up in the barn. Cliff had the big rig gassed up and ready with hay nets and water. The tack trunks were stocked with coolers, leg wraps and extra equipment. "Just in case" was a serious part of their packing.

By then, Cliff had brought in the horses that were going. Sundancer, Moonlight Sonata, Pastor and Sabrina had eaten their oats and were ready for Bird and Julia to start grooming them.

A few minutes later, Lavinia showed up with Kimberly and Liz, whom she'd picked up on her way to Saddle Creek. "Gotta run!" she sang out. "Hair appointment! Should I bleach or colour? Big decisions today! See you later at the show, sweetie!" With a backwards wave, she was gone.

Kimberly completely ignored her mother. "What a beautiful day!"

"Easy for you to s … say," worried Liz. "I'm riding P … Pastor. I've never showed a h … horse before. P … Ponies are closer to the ground if you fall off!"

"But ponies are far more likely to throw you," Kimberly reassured her. "Tell her, Bird."

"I'm not listening to this!" exclaimed Julia. "Sabrina isn't either. Are you, Sabrina?"

People say the stupidest things. Sabrina was indeed listening. Bird couldn't help but laugh.

With everybody working together as a team, the horses were soon ready. The girls walked them onto the trailer, and they were on their way.

They arrived at Palston early and got the parking spot they wanted. Bird climbed out of the truck, and surveyed the grounds. Everywhere she looked people were unloading horses, running for water, hauling feed nets, gulping down coffee—organizing themselves for the day ahead. Things were certainly getting busy.

Julia stepped out of the trailer. "Are you feeling ready?" Bird asked her sister.

"No! Yes ... well, almost. I'm nervous! Can you help with my hair?"

"I'd love to." Bird patted her own dry, singed locks. "Unburnt hair will be nice to work with for a change."

Minutes later, Hannah was back. "No lineups. It's so much better to be early." She was pleased. "Bird, I've put you in the meter-thirty class, and Kimberly, you're staying in the meter. This way we can bring home all the firsts."

Kimberly smiled. "Great. I like that class. Has my mother talked to you about us buying Moonie, Hannah?"

Hannah nodded. "She's waiting to see how you do today. Fiona Malone is ready to talk about it, and I talked to Abby, too. Abby needs the money for school, and wants what's best for Moonie. She knows that her mare wants to keep working, and she'd love to have Moonie at Saddle Creek."

Kimberly nodded. "I guess that answers all my questions." She rubbed Moonie's face. "Moonie, let's rock our class."

Bird finished braiding Julia's hair and firmly placed the riding helmet on her head. "Gorgeous!" she pronounced. She helped her sister into the saddle and wiped off her boots.

"You have tons of time, Julia," Hannah said. "Go stroll around and get used to everything."

"When should I be back?"

Hannah checked her watch. "Your class is at nine, and you're the third one in. Be back in fifteen minutes and I'll put you over some warm-up jumps."

Julia waved as she trotted away.

"Now," said Hannah. "Let's get Pastor ready!"

Sabrina and Julia did extremely well in the jumper class. Julia was totally focused and Sabrina was a little machine. She got over the jumps with economy and left them all up. Her time was four full seconds faster than the next best, and they got the first-place ribbon that Julia had dared to hope for.

Liz and Pastor fared well, too. They had a smooth, clear round and got all their leads. Pastor was perfect, and Liz rode flawlessly, but in a hunter class where the results are subjective, the judges decide between equal performances, depending on their own preferences. They gave the first-place ribbon to an elegant thoroughbred, and the second to a fancy dappled grey Swedish warmblood. Liz and Pastor were presented with third.

Lavinia's white BMW arrived in a cloud of dust, mere minutes before her daughter's class. She drove right up to the Saddle Creek horse trailer, scattering ponies and riders in her wake.

"Am I too late?" she hollered through her window, scaring a tall young horse. He skittered sideways and up before his rider could contain him. "Control your horse!" Lavinia scolded.

Hannah appeared around the side of the trailer in time to catch the rider giving Lavinia the finger. "Lavinia, are you done creating havoc?"

"Am I too late?" she repeated, oblivious to Hannah's reprimand. "Has Kimberly gone yet? My hairdresser was late. Do you like what he did?"

Bird jabbed Hannah in the ribs. "It looks like she goes to my hairdresser," she whispered. Lavinia's hair had been bleached and cut in chunks. It was stylish in a punky sort of way, but Bird's words weren't far from the truth. Hannah snorted in spite of herself.

"Excuse me!" she said, trying to recover. "A blackfly flew up my nose." She made a show of using a tissue to blow her nose. "Kimberly is up in ten minutes."

"Whew! I thought I'd missed it. Fiona Malone is meeting me at the ring. Which one is it?"

"Ring three. Just over there." Bird pointed helpfully. The loud revving of Lavinia's motor again startled all the horses.

Hannah stood firmly in front of the car, with her arms out and her palms up. "No, Lavinia! You can't drive there. You'll have to walk down."

Bird watched Lavinia's face as it went from pouty to resigned. She jumped out and dropped her keys in Hannah's palm. "I've got to find Fiona and work her price down."

Bird and Hannah restrained their laughs until Lavinia was out of earshot. "That woman will never change!" gasped Hannah.

"She didn't even say good luck to Kimberly," agreed Bird.

Kimberly spoke from inside the trailer. "Is she gone?"

"Yes," answered Bird. "Did you see her new hairdo?"

"Sure did. You've set a trend, Bird. Don't wait for me to follow it."

"At least I didn't pay to get it done."

"Make fun all you like, girls," said Hannah. She'd resumed her voice of authority. "Your mother is here to buy you a horse, so have some respect. She wants the best for you, Kimberly."

"Actually, she wants to say that her daughter is winning at all the shows. But that's cool. It works for me!"

Kimberly backed Moonie down the ramp. Hannah and Bird

inspected them both. "Good to go, Kimby!" declared Bird. "I like your new all-brown theme."

"My mother bought me everything new to match Moonie. I sure hope we buy her or it will all go to waste."

"Looks are one thing, remember, but performance is everything," Hannah said. "Kimberly, get your mind on the job ahead."

Bird could feel the energy coming off of Kimberly's body. Her friend was overly excited, and adrenaline was making her brain fuzzy. "Take a deep breath, Kimby. Do you know your course?"

"Backwards."

"Then put everything else out of your mind. Shake your head. Now your hands. Now your legs. Fill your lungs completely. As you empty your lungs, empty your mind."

Kimberly followed Bird's instructions, and gradually began to relax. "That's better," she smiled. "Thanks, Bird."

Are you ready, Moonie?

Now that Kimby's ready, I'm ready.

Good girl. Don't worry. Just get it done.

I always do.

That's what makes you so special.

Bird patted the mare's face.

Hannah said, "Let's get you up, Kim. I'll see you down at the gate."

Kimberly rode Moonie down to the action below. As Bird watched them go, she saw by her friend's posture and the mare's calmness that they were in fine shape. Kim's catatonic state had been a one-time thing.

When do I get to go? Bird? It's me. The one left behind all alone in the trailer?

Don't feel too sorry for yourself, Sunny. We're up soon.

A horse could get upset all alone like this.

Sabrina will be back after her shower. So will Pastor. You won't be alone for long.

Good. I'll start my stretching in here.

Bird was walking down the hill to join the others when she noticed a red-haired groom at the showers. It was the same girl who had given her a hard time the week before. Bird paused. It was as good a time as ever, she thought. "Hi, my name is Bird," she said, as friendly as possible. "We met last week."

The groom stared, wide-eyed and open-mouthed. "I thought you couldn't talk."

Bird shrugged. "It's a problem I have. It comes and goes. Sorry I lost my temper."

"No kidding! You pulled two buttons off my shirt."

"I didn't deck you, though, for making fun of me and my family. I wanted to." Bird watched the girl's eyes widen even further.

"Are you still mad?"

"A little. You were rude and an apology would be nice."

"You grabbed me and roughed me up!"

"And I just apologized."

The girl didn't respond right away. Bird noticed her chin working and her eyes flitting around. Finally, she spoke. "Yeah ... okay ... I'm sorry."

Bird smiled. "Thanks. I feel better."

The other girl smiled back. "Yeah! I feel better, too. I've never apologized before. It's not so bad!" She chuckled a little and shuffled her feet in the dust. "My name is Wanda. No hard feelings?"

"No hard feelings, Wanda. See you around. I've got to watch my friend ride."

Bird arrived at the ring just in time to watch the final few jumps of the rider before Kimberly—a young woman on a dark grey mare with black legs, mane and tail. Bird liked the look of the horse, and thought she might have seen her before. Then she remembered. It was Ruby Tuesday, born close by and sold to a woman in Ottawa. Bird admired the way she'd matured, and was happy that they'd had such a good round.

"Bird! Come here!" Kimberly was in a panic.

"I'm here already. What's wrong?"

"Do that thing again."

"What thing?"

"That thing you did before to make me relax. My mother's over there pointing at me and everybody's looking and smiling!"

The girl's gone all nervous. I don't want her to turn into a zombie again.

Bird patted the mare while she spoke to Kimberly.

"Take a deep breath, Kimby. In. Out. Deeper than that. In. Out." Kim began to breathe. "Good. Now, drop your chin to your chest. Breathe. Good. Now shake out your hands. I've got Moonie, don't worry. Good. Now take your feet out of the stirrups and shake your legs."

Kimberly was trying her best, but nothing helped. "It's no good!"

"Clear your mind, Kimby."

"I'll forget my course!"

"No you won't. You've memorized it. All you have to think of is the first jump. They'll all follow after that. Breathe."

"I'm trying! I can't do this! My mother is telling those people that I'm going to win. I know it!"

"Once you're in there you'll be fine. You'll know what to do. Trust me, Kimby. Trust Moonie. Clear your mind. Don't think."

"I can't stop thinking!"

Bird stared into her friend's worried face. This was serious. She had to think of something, and fast. An idea popped into her head. "Okay, then," she said, keeping her voice light. "Go in there and make a mess of it. See how many jumps you can knock down. See how many times you can go off-course. Have fun! Wreck the place! Ruin your mother's day!"

Kimberly stared at Bird, then burst out laughing. When she regained her composure, all the tension had left her body. "Why not?"

The announcer called her in. "Number six-oh-three, Kimberly Davis on Moonlight Sonata, owned by Abby Malone."

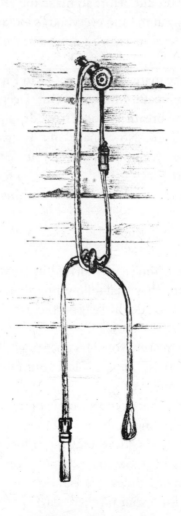

32

KENNETH BRADLEY

Tan was hungry. He thought of all the delicious food at the farm-house—chicken pot pie, fresh milk, rhubarb cream pie, ripe bananas—and his mouth watered. All he had to do was go to the farmhouse and find Cody. He started up the hill.

KIMBERLY ENTERED THE RING, relaxed and confident, a big grin on her face. She and Moonlight Sonata trotted around the jumps, checking them out and getting a good look. The whistle blew. Kimberly asked the mare for a canter.

As they rode through the starting gate, Kimberly gave Bird a broad wink and a wicked grin. Oh no, Bird thought in horror. She's going to take my advice literally! Bird forced herself to watch.

They headed for the first jump, lifted off perfectly, landed lightly and sailed on to the next. Bird relaxed. Moonie was quick but accurate, and Kimberly had never ridden better. She smiled as she made her way around the course. It was clear that she was having a wonderful time.

Bird glanced at Lavinia. Kimberly's mother was spellbound. Beside her on the front-row bench sat Fiona Malone. Bird smiled as Fiona clutched Lavinia's arm, and Lavinia put her hand over Fiona's. For the moment at least, two opposites were united by a common goal—a first-place finish for horse and rider.

Bird turned her attention back to the ring, where Kimberly had completed the in-and-out, and the rails were still up. Things were looking good. Bird cast her eye to the timer. Kimberly and Moonie were moving fast.

The water jump was next, and Moonie was flying. Up and over. They landed on the correct lead for a tight turn to the optical illusion. Bird held her breath. Perfect.

Seconds later, Moonlight Sonata and Kimberly were finished the course. They were clear and had the best time so far, with twenty-eight riders to go.

"Thanks so much, Bird!" Kimberly was laughing and patting Moonie's neck as they left the ring. "I couldn't have done it without you!"

"I told you to make a big mess of things. You failed miserably!"

"I had the best time of my entire life. I love Moonie so much!"

"You remind me of Abby up there," said Fiona, as she and Lavinia hurried over. "Moonie hasn't gone as well since Abby left for New York."

"Moonbeam Promenade is utterly adorable," crooned Lavinia. "Utterly adorable."

Kimberly slid down and hugged Moonie's head. "Thank you, girl. You did a super job."

"But did she win?" asked Lavinia.

Bird left the group smiling, while everyone showered Moonie with attention. She slipped into the trailer with Sundancer.

Is it time?

Yes, Sunny. I'll give you all my attention now.

Good. I've been standing here all day. My ankles will swell up.

It's only been a few hours. Your ankles are fine.

Easy for you to say! You've been running all over the place while I've been watching people. Take a look at that man there.

Bird looked out his trailer window. *What man, Sunny?*

The man wearing the hat that looks like dinner. He's hiding from something.

Bird snorted. A man about fifty yards from the trailer was

wearing a big straw hat—Sunny would think it looked like dinner! She examined the man more closely. With his dark glasses, scarf, hat and furtive demeanour, he might well be hiding from something. Bird narrowed her eyes and stared harder. Even with all that camouflage, he looked very familiar. But there was no time to think about it. *Let's get ready.*

You bet!

Bird had Sunny brushed and tacked within a few minutes. She backed him down the ramp and walked him over to the mounting block where she stepped up and put her left foot in the stirrup. As intent as she was on the task ahead, the man with the straw hat and dark glasses still bothered her. Who did he remind her of? It was something about the way he moved. From her new vantage point on the mounting block, she let her eyes drift over the crowd. She looked down the hill and searched for the straw hat.

There it was. And suddenly, she knew who he was. Her grandfather, Kenneth Bradley.

What on earth was he doing here? Yesterday, Mack Jones had been all set to bring him in for questioning. Was he hiding from the police? She needed to find out.

What are you waiting for?

Be patient, Sunny. That man with the straw hat is my grandfather.

What has that got to do with anything?

I can't concentrate unless I know what he's up to!

What if he's here because it's a nice day? Get on! Let's go!

I have to talk to him. Let's get back on the trailer.

You've got to be kidding!

It'll take just a minute.

That's what you always say.

Bird put the grumbling horse back in the trailer and walked down the hill. What am I doing? she asked herself. He hates me, and he's in disguise. I'm the last person he wants to see. And what the heck am I going to do when I get there? She breathed deeply. She'd just have to figure that out.

Kenneth Bradley saw her coming. Bird watched as he looked around furtively, then checked from the corner of his eye to see if she had recognized him. She kept walking. He had nowhere to go.

"Grandfather!" called Bird gaily as she approached. "You came to watch me ride! How wonderful you could make it!"

Several ladies standing in a group nearby smiled at the scene. Bird watched his expression change several times until he decided to play along.

"Bird, my dear!" He held out his arms for a big hug. "I wanted to surprise you!"

"You did! You did surprise me!" Bird embraced him and held him tight.

"Let me go, you awful child," Kenneth hissed in her ear.

"Pardon me, Grandfather?" said Bird loudly.

"I said, let's go somewhere quiet so we can get caught up!" Kenneth shouted.

"Why not come to the trailer and help me get ready! We're up soon!"

"Good idea!" Kenneth took her by the arm and bowed to the ladies, who were all a-twitter. What a nice a man he was, to come to the show to watch his granddaughter ride!

"You can stop talking like an idiot," he muttered to Bird as soon as they were out of earshot.

"So can you," responded Bird. "And you can stop squeezing me. You're bruising my arm."

"What the hell are you doing anyway, coming over to me like that?"

Bird put on her most innocent expression and kept walking. "I was glad to see you. You did come to see me ride, didn't you?"

"Of course not! Why would I do that? I'm hiding from the police. Damn idiots think I'm guilty of something."

"Well, if you're not guilty, you have nothing to worry about. Anyway, you can't hide forever. They'll find you sometime. Isn't it better if you go to them?"

"That's ridiculous! Ridiculous and ignorant!"

Bird shook her head. He really was the rudest man.

"Look, Bird, this is serious. I'm in trouble here, and I just thought of how you can help."

"Me? How?"

"Let's go inside." Kenneth gestured at the trailer. "I don't want anybody to see me."

"Sure, but I don't have a lot of time before my class."

"This is more important!" he snapped as they walked up the ramp.

Bird, girl. Sunny pawed the floor. *The old man's desperate. He smells of fear.*

I can smell it with my human nose.

Don't make him mad.

Kenneth stood in a shadow. "You can find Tanbark for me," he whispered in a raspy voice. "If I can find him, all my troubles will be over."

"Why's that?"

"You don't need to know that! Where is he?"

"Why do you think I know?"

"Because he's never far from you! That's why I'm here. I thought he might show up. Still might." Kenneth peered out a window. "If you wanted to, you could find him pretty darn quick!"

"I don't know about that."

"You sure as hell could!"

You're making him mad, Bird. Don't do it!

I'm not going to give up Tanbark.

But you could trick this man.

Good thinking.

Do it fast. We're going to be late.

Stop pawing and snorting. I need to think.

Sorry! I'll just shut up and stop giving you good advice!

Bird smiled.

"What are you smirking about, young lady?"

"I just had a wonderful idea."

"Tell me! And *I'll* decide if it's wonderful or not."

"First, tell me why you want to find Tanbark."

Kenneth was annoyed. His eyes darted back and forth as if searching for a way to avoid answering her question. After a couple of seconds, he said, "To help him, of course! Why else? The man needs psychiatric assistance."

Bird nodded thoughtfully. "That's what I thought. That's why I'll tell you where he is."

"You will?"

She nodded again. "He's being questioned right now by Mack Jones."

Kenneth stood stock still, mulling over this bit of information. "I don't believe you."

"Then why ask? You won't get any more help from me!"

Easy there, Bird.

"If he'd been picked up I would've heard it. I hear it all."

"They're on to you. They don't talk about anything concerning this case on their frequencies."

Kenneth's cheeks puffed up and his eyes narrowed into slits. "Horse shit!"

"You asked, I told you. Now, I really have to get Sundancer out."

"Okay, okay." Kenneth's head jerked and his mouth worked as he thought it out. "They'll find me anyway. It's better that I go to them. And I can poke holes in what he says. He's lying, you know!"

Bird nodded. "Right." She didn't know what else to say.

"Whatever he's telling the police right now, he's making it up."

274

"Right."

"So now I need a way to get there. I came in a taxi so no one could follow me. I need to take this truck, Bird! Unhitch this thing and give me the keys."

Bird blinked. "Aunt Hannah has the keys. She's waiting for me down at the practice ring."

"Then go get them! On the double! There's no time to waste!"

Someone's here, Bird. The colour lady.

Bird looked outside. Laura Pierson was walking toward the trailer. She wore her bright orange pantsuit with matching scarf and shoes. Her handbag and belt were white. The colour lady, indeed.

Perfect! thought Bird. The Piersons. Who could be better?

"Bird dear?" Laura's voice trilled from the rear of the trailer. "Wasn't Moonlight Sonata brilliant? Kimberly gets along with her so well. I just wanted to let you know we're here, dear. Pete and I came to cheer you on."

"Mrs. Pierson? Can you come in? I need some help."

"What are you doing?" Kenneth was shaking with anger. "Get rid of them!" he hissed.

"They're your ride to the station." Bird stood firm.

Kenneth stopped arguing.

Laura answered, "What help do you need, dear? I'm not much good with horses."

"It's nothing to do with horses. Can you and Mr. Pierson drive my grandfather to see Mack Jones? He wants to help Tanbark, and he needs a ride to the police station."

Laura's eyes adjusted to the shade inside the trailer, and she took in the sight of Kenneth Bradley, standing a few feet away. She looked at Bird calmly. It was a look that told Bird that she trusted her enough to ask no questions.

"Certainly, dear. Pete and I would be pleased to help." Laura reached out and took Kenneth's arm. "Come this way, Kenneth. Our car isn't far."

Kenneth glared at Bird as he walked down the ramp, but Laura just winked. "Good luck with your show, dear! Tell us all about it later!"

Bird watched as they made their way through the parking lot. Kenneth's big straw hat and Laura's filmy orange outfit were easy to follow as they wove through the crowd. Pete joined them, and the trio got into his vehicle.

Bird knew that the Piersons would do the right thing. Now she just needed to warn Mack.

Okay, boy. Are you ready?

Does clover taste good? Of course I'm ready!

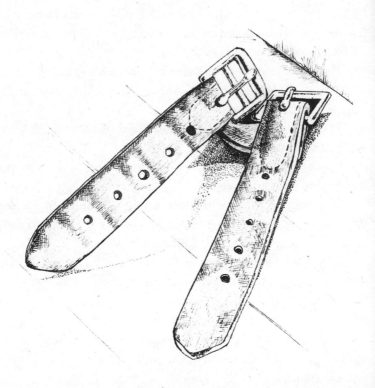

33

BIRD AND SUNNY

Tan caught another glimpse of Cody. This wasn't the plan! He was to come to him with food, not follow him around and peek at him from behind trees! What was this? Tan's stomach growled. He was getting very angry.

HANNAH WAS WAITING for Bird at the warm-up ring. "Where were you?" she asked, hands on hips. "You're late."

Bird leaned down from Sunny's back and whispered, "I need your help."

Hannah looked up, startled.

"Grandfather was here, hiding from the police and looking for Tan," Bird said quietly. "I told him Tan was with Mack Jones. He's gone there now with the Piersons. Can you reach Mack right away and let him know?"

Hannah nodded slowly. "For sure. Right away. But how … never mind—we'll talk later. For now, put it out of your mind." She shook Bird's ankle affectionately. "Can you do that?"

"I can."

"Warm up, then we'll do some practice jumps." She took her cell from her pocket and pressed Mack's numbers.

Bird and Sunny began their routine. Walk for five minutes, trot for five minutes, then walk again. Pick up a collected canter for five minutes, half on each lead, then walk for five minutes. Sunny was responsive and limber and eager to go.

Hannah had commandeered one of the four jumps set up in the middle. She waved Bird over. "I talked to Mack. It's all under control, so don't worry about a thing. Now, let's get jumping! Trot in, and canter away."

Bird felt her anxiety drain away. With calm assurance, she trotted Sunny up to the vertical and popped over it, cantering away.

"Great. Now, wait until I make it an oxer." Hannah quickly dragged two more standards up beside the existing ones, and doubled up the jump. "Okay, canter in."

They cleared it and quietly landed.

Hannah was pleased. "Come again from the other direction, then we're done. Your class is being called. You're up in ten."

"Right you are!" Bird called back as she came at the jump. Sunny cleared it with ease. Bird looked at Hannah and smiled. "We're ready."

"Do you know your course?"

"I sure do."

"Looking good, Bird!" Hannah waved at her as she walked to the Grand Prix ring, where Bird would be showing.

Sunny, let's not worry about anything today. Even winning.

We can't lose, Bird. We're the best.

Bird patted his neck. *Remember last time? We stank.*

Yeah, okay. We stank. But today's a new day!

We could stink again if we try too hard.

Nice confidence builder!

Let's go in and have a wonderful time. Let's enjoy the moment. Jump for the joy of jumping. Remember?

I can do that. If you can.

I can. I really can. And she meant it.

Bird and Sundancer watched the competition as they waited their turn. Bird was relaxed, and was actually pleased when one of her fellow riders had a good round. This was the way to do it, she thought. So much less stress.

Lots of good horses here, Bird.

You're right.

You really don't care if we win?

Nope. I'm here to have fun.

You're serious?

I'm serious about having fun. I want to have a good time out there.

Sunny lowered his head. He became calm. Bird reflected, one more time, on how much animals are affected by people's attitudes. Now, the announcer called them in. "Number one-oh-seven. Sundancer, owned and ridden by Alberta Simms."

A hush went through the crowd as Sundancer trotted in. The sight of the tall, handsome chestnut with the glossy coat and intelligent eyes turned people's heads. His light, springy action and supple, proud bearing told anyone who knew horses that this animal was capable of great things. And he was cool. Gone was the maniac of the previous show.

They moved into a canter as the whistle blew. They gathered speed through the starting gate, and cleared the first hurdle comfortably. Bird gave Sunny his head as they landed and took a stride before turning left to a line of blue verticals.

Are you having fun yet, Bird?

I'm having fun.

So am I.

Bird could hear Sunny breathing in time with the rhythmic beat of his hooves. The whole world was her and her horse—nobody else. This wasn't ordinary fun, it was big-time fun.

The ring was huge, which allowed Sunny to open his stride and keep a good pace.

I like this ring!

I do, too. It's wide open.

Like the big field at home.

They turned left again across the diagonal to face a multi-coloured oxer and then a green and orange vertical with out-landish wings. Sunny's big stride ate up the distance and he lifted his knees effortlessly. He cleared them both by inches, judging their height and width flawlessly.

Did you like the way I did that, Bird?

I liked the way you did that.

Now they turned to the right and headed to the triple. Bird watched through Sunny's ears as the animal executed the difficult series with ease. She merely held on with her legs, gave him his head and let him do it all. They landed the third hurdle and continued along the fenceline to the water jump. Up and over without a splash.

Nice release, Bird. I would've been in the drink otherwise.

I'm here to please.

A hard left and they were moving on to the skinny, which was half the width of the other jumps, designed to test the navigational skills of the rider and the bravery of the horse. Sunny didn't flinch.

Now they were headed for home with one jump to go.

I want to race this one, Bird. Let me go for it!

Why not? Let's mess it up. The reverse psychology trick had worked on Kimberly; would it get Sunny's attention, too?

Mess it up?

Yeah, mess it up. We're not here to win, right? We're here to have fun.

Sunny slowed and became careful. *Okay. Spoil my fun.*

Spoil your fun, but win the trophy.

Sunny and Bird flew over the last big oxer and landed clean.

Now can I race?

Go for it!

Sundancer and Alberta Simms finished their round with a standing ovation. Trainers for years to come would refer to it as the perfect trip, but Bird had no way of knowing that. All she knew was that the roar of the crowd was almost deafening. She leaned forward and stroked Sunny's neck, enjoying the moment. This was what riding should be like. This was perfect.

Hannah greeted them at the gate with tears in her eye. "I have one word to say, Bird, and that is WOW."

Bird laughed. "Thanks! A little different from last time, wasn't it?"

Hannah laughed with her. "Last time does not exist! You were fabulous, Bird. Totally together and controlled, but you had speed and accuracy. I have nothing to say but bravo." She patted Sunny's neck. "Good boy, Sunny. Well done, both of you."

In a matter of seconds, Bird was surrounded by friends and family. Liz and Patty were there with Phil; Julia and Paul and Hannah were, too; even Kimberly and her mother and Fiona Malone. And ... Bird could hardly believe her eyes.

Bird blinked. Her mother! Eva and Stuart had arrived home from their honeymoon just in time for the horse show. Eva looked rested and beautiful, dressed in white pants and a trimly cut pink jacket with matching flat shoes. "Mom!" Bird yelled. She slid down from Sunny's back and hugged her mother with all her strength. "I'm so happy to see you!"

"I'm so happy to see you, too!" Mother and daughter held each other tight. "I'm so happy to be home!"

Bird felt hot tears on her cheeks. Through blurry eyes, she looked at her mother's smiling face and saw tears rolling down hers, too.

"We're a real pair," said Eva. "The Blubber twins!"

Stuart came up behind them. "Bird, you did a super job out there. What a gorgeous horse!"

"Welcome home, Stuart!" Bird included her new stepfather in the family hug. Julia ducked under her arm, and they all held each other close.

"I didn't think you'd be back in time to see us ride," said Bird as she took off her helmet. "Did you see Julia go?"

"We certainly did!" enthused Eva. "Julia was incredible! We're so proud of you both."

"Why didn't you tell us you'd be here?" demanded Julia.

"We didn't want to put you girls off your game, so we kept low." Stuart grinned and rubbed Bird's stubbly hair. "Looks like you've been chopping off your hair again."

"It's a long, long story," answered Bird. "I'll tell you everything later."

"You certainly didn't keep us up to speed!" Eva sounded slightly annoyed, and Paul quickly intervened.

"We didn't want you to worry," he said. "There was absolutely nothing you could have done from Ireland."

"We wanted you to enjoy your holiday," added Hannah.

"You've filled us in a little, but we want to hear it all," Stuart said to Hannah. He could not keep the concern out of his voice. "A lot has happened since we left."

Bird nodded. "It was only ten days, but it sure seemed longer."

Julia interrupted. "Wait! The announcer is talking!"

They listened. "Attention, please. Would these horses come back into the ring, in this order. One-oh-seven, one-two-nine, one-three-five ..."

Bird threw her arms around Sunny's neck and launched herself up onto his back. She quickly replaced her helmet and snapped up the chinstrap. *We did it, Sunny. You are the best horse in the entire world.*

You're not half-bad yourself.

After receiving their ribbon, it was time for the victory lap. All eyes were on Sunny and Bird. Sunny sprang into action. He picked up his left lead and galloped away from a dead halt.

The wind whistled in Bird's ears as they flew around the

ring, followed by all the other winners. Sunny's strides were enormous and free, his fiery coat glistening in the summer sun. Bird felt peaceful. And totally happy.

34

CODY

Tan was now irritated beyond control. First he couldn't find Cody, and now that he'd found him, the coyote wouldn't bring him food! The stupid animal was playing games with him! Rage consumed him. Bird had promised! He was hungry! Really hungry! That was the deal! It wasn't fair! Stupid idiots! He'd show them!

MACK JONES WAS WAITING for them back at the trailer. "Congratulations, Bird! You're the talk of the show."

"Thank you, Mr. Jones."

"You look puzzled."

"Well, yes. I thought you might be busy with my grandfather."

"You always get right to the point." Mack shaded his eyes from the sun. "There's news."

Bird slid down and rubbed Sunny's right ear. She looked at Mack earnestly. "Tell me."

Mack's face told her that the news wasn't entirely good. "I don't want to tell it more than once, so let's wait for the others to catch up."

Bird looked behind her. They were taking their time, chatting away. "Hurry up, everybody!"

Hannah and Eva were the first to respond. Then, when Stuart and Paul noticed Mack, they hurried as well. Soon, the entire small crowd had gathered around.

"Hannah, Eva—I'm sorry to have to tell you that your father has been charged with mischief and conspiracy to mislead the course of justice."

Mack's words were met with dead silence.

He continued. "Kenneth was apprehended today, thanks to Bird and the Piersons. And finally, we've been able to piece the whole story together." Mack leaned on the trailer. "Kenneth and Sandra were having a secret affair. They had an argument on the side of the road, just like Tanbark recorded. Sandra hit herself with the tire iron and fell, cracking her head open on a rock. Kenneth left her in distress and said nothing. When she died, he devised a scenario to keep his part in this whole mess a secret; one that involved the Wells."

"The Wells!" said Bird. It all made perfect sense! "They were right in the middle of everything!"

"Turns out that Jim Wells was paid to form a committee to divert attention. Muddy the waters, so to speak."

"Paid by whom?" Stuart asked.

"Paid by Kenneth." Mack was solemn. "Jim needed the money to pay off a bad debt."

"All this to keep Kenneth's part in this quiet?" Hannah asked. "Wow."

"Yes, wow. It's quite elaborate, isn't it," agreed Mack. "But poor Ellen truly believed in the cause. She was played for a fool."

"Ellen was the one who found Sandra Hall by the side of the road?" Eva was still struggling to put it all together.

Mack nodded. "It became her mission to out the guy who did it. It's just sad that her husband led her on."

"But there were others involved in Justice for the Innocent," observed Paul. "What about Les and Hank Crowley?"

"We've interviewed them all. Jim was the ringleader and the only one being paid. Everyone else thought they were doing their civic duty in trying to bring an evil man to justice."

Paul added, "There was a lot of fear out there to tap into."

Bird was thoughtful. "Aside from Jim, I bet they wish they'd got the facts straight before jumping on the bandwagon."

"You got that right," agreed Paul.

"There's no penalty for airing your views," Bird continued, "but they went way farther than that. What about the barn fire?"

"The fire was set by Hank Crowley, in a trash can under Pierre's window," Mack answered. "Jim Wells admitted that he and Les were there, too. They will be charged."

"What a huge mess!" exclaimed Eva. "But I still don't understand." Her forehead creased in concern. "Dad didn't touch her! Why go to all the trouble of bribing Jim to protect him, when he hadn't done anything wrong?"

Mack's lips tightened. "He knowingly walked away from a dying woman."

"True. But he didn't actually kill her, and he likely didn't even know she was dying." Eva persisted, looking for an answer. "It was an accident."

"Yes, it was. But Eva, nobody walks away from a bleeding person." Hannah spoke sadly. "If he'd called 911, she might not have died. I guess he didn't want anybody to know he was even there."

"Tanbark ruined that plan," Bird pointed out.

"I'll guess Kenneth didn't want to add to all the trouble he was already in," speculated Paul. "His insurance fraud case is coming up in August. I bet he thought another scandal would prejudice the jury against him."

"He misjudged it badly if that was his aim," said Mack. "I've never seen such a blatant case for telling the truth and taking your medicine."

Paul nodded. "The cover-up made it far worse."

Mack agreed. "The cover-up is what he'll be spending time in jail for."

"Think about it," said Stuart. "He would have been embarrassed about leaving the scene, but it would've lasted one day if he'd just called an ambulance and faced it right then."

Hannah agreed. "If he'd told the truth about what happened, Pierre wouldn't be clinging to life in the burn ward of Sunnybrook Hospital."

"If he'd told the truth, Pierre would be fine, and Cliff and I would never have gone through what we did," added Phil. The sound of his voice made Bird realize how quiet he'd been until now. "The entire community became vigilantes. It wasn't pretty."

Patty put her arm around his waist.

Stuart asked, "How's Pierre doing?"

"Better every day." Mack seemed pleased to have some good news.

"That's good," said Paul. "And very lucky for the Justice for the Innocent gang. That would've been a murder charge for them."

Stuart had another question. "Does all of this hinge on Tanbark's eyewitness account? I mean, he's homeless, and mentally ill."

"Which is very convenient for my grandfather." Bird suddenly felt exhausted. She sat on the tire-well of the trailer, still holding Sunny's reins.

Mack turned to her. "It doesn't matter now that the Wells have confessed. Their story backs up Tan's. But we still need to speak to him right away. Bird, do you know where he is?"

"No. But he's around. He won't come in unless he knows he's safe."

"Nobody can hurt him now. Kenneth Bradly is going nowhere."

Bird gazed levelly into his eyes. "Then I'll try."

"Thanks." Mack studied her fondly. "You're a remarkable girl."

Bird was deep in thought. "How awful for Tanbark. He came here to find his family, and he walked right into a boiling vat of deception."

Hannah shivered. "How right you are. His timing could not have been worse."

"For Tan, but perfect timing for Kenneth!" Paul exclaimed. "To think he might have pinned the whole thing on his own son!"

"He gave it a good try, that's for sure." Mack straightened. "Thanks, folks. Now, I must be going. I have an interrogation to do."

"Thanks for filling us in, Mack." Paul shook his hand.

"My pleasure."

Bird stood and rubbed Sunny's face. He was dozing in the afternoon sun, bored by the human-talk. "I'm glad that my grandfather is where he can't cause any more trouble for people."

Mack nodded. "There are people who only look at life from their own perspective. Your grandfather, sadly, is one of them."

"He just doesn't care about other people," said Eva. "He wants what he wants, and heaven help anyone standing in his way."

"He's always been that way," agreed Hannah, linking arms with her sister. "That's why it's taken us so long to be able to stand on our own two feet."

"You've both certainly learned how to do that!" teased Paul.

"I'll second that," chimed in Stuart. "And in Eva's case, feet shod in Manolo Blahniks!"

The drive home from the show was very quiet. Hannah, Bird and Julia had the truck to themselves. Liz had gone with her mother and Phil, and Lavinia had taken Kimberly to the Malone's farm, where they were working out the details of Moonie's sale. Eva and Stuart had gone home to unpack their clothes, and were coming to Saddle Creek later for dinner and to pick up the girls. Paul had headed off to a horse emergency.

Bird lay down in the back seat. Her head was full of what Mack Jones had told them. She could scarcely believe that her grandfather had actually tried to set up four innocent men. Justice for the Innocent. How ironic.

A quotation from English class floated into her mind. "Oh what a tangled web we weave, when first we practice to deceive." She sighed. That poet really knew what he was talking about.

Bird had just started to doze off when Hannah jammed on the brakes. The horses clattered and bumped in the trailer as they regained their footing, and Bird rolled off the back seat onto the floor.

"What?" Bird blurted, jolted awake. "What happened?"

In the front seat, Julia trembled. Her hands covered her mouth and her eyes bulged. Hannah's knuckles were white as they gripped the steering wheel.

"What's wrong?" Bird demanded.

"Stay where you are." Hannah opened the truck door and stepped out.

Bird pushed the seat forward and jumped down from the truck. What she saw caused bile to rise in her throat.

The body of a small grey coyote lay on the road at the end of the Saddle Creek lane.

"No!" screamed Bird. "Nooooo!" She fell to her knees on the gravel and felt for a pulse. The coyote was still warm. She licked her wrist and put it near his nose to feel his breath. There was no sign of life. "Cody! Oh my dear Cody." Bird sobbed. "Did we hit him?"

"No," answered Hannah. "He was already here."

This had to be a dream, thought Bird. It was impossible that Cody was dead. She bent her head to his prone body and buried her face in his fur. "Cody! This can't be true."

How could this have happened? Cody was too wary to fall in a trap. He would never have been hit by a car. He never ate food left out, so he couldn't have been poisoned. A hunter? A brush wolf? Natural causes?

Bird pushed her fingers through his fur and felt for a gun shot or teeth marks. Nothing on the body. She worked her hands up the animal's neck and felt his skull.

There, between his eyes. Something small and round had hit him hard, causing a deep skull fracture that must have killed him instantly.

"I hope you didn't suffer, my friend." Bird snuffled and wiped her dripping nose and tears on her arm. "I can't believe this."

Hannah reached down and put her hand on Bird's head. "I'm so sorry, Bird."

Julia knelt down beside her. "We'll have a funeral. Remember when Hector died last summer? His funeral was lovely. We'll have a lovely funeral for Cody, too."

A sudden terrible wail from the bushes beside the road interrupted the quiet moment. Somebody was there, gasping for air and sobbing.

Bird knew it was Tanbark.

Slowly, horribly, things started to come together. Tanbark … Tanbark hunted his food in the wild, and he did that with a … slingshot. A slingshot. Bird's fists clenched and her jaw locked. That's what had killed Cody. The hole in his skull, right between his eyes, had been made by a rock flung from a slingshot.

She stood up, seething with rage. "Tanbark Wedger, you come out here right now."

Hannah gasped at Bird's sudden anger. Julia huddled close to her aunt, and together they watched what transpired next.

Tanbark emerged from the shrubs and walked slowly to the lane, head down and shoulders slumped. "I didn't mean to kill him. I promise, Bird. I didn't mean to kill him."

"Then why did you?" Bird shouted. "Why did you kill him if you didn't mean to?"

"I wanted food. You said Cody would bring me food! I saw him and I followed him and I kept asking him for food. He looked at me like I was crazy! I lost my temper and pulled out my slingshot."

"Cody didn't have any food for you, Tanbark! How could he have? Even if you'd come around the house, like we agreed, I was gone all day, so he couldn't tell me! If I'd been here, I would've sent him to you with food, but I wasn't!"

"He should've had food for me! I was hungry and you said he'd bring me food! I was mad!"

"So mad you killed him? Did you mean to kill him, Tan?"

Tan's shoulders slumped even further. "I knew it was wrong as soon as I did it."

"I never should've helped you! Everyone is right. You're crazy —and now Cody is dead!" Bird sank down on the ground beside the dead coyote and cried. "You killed Cody!"

Tanbark crumpled, completely deflated. He covered his head with his arms. "I'm sorry," he whispered. "I'm sorry." His voice became louder. "I'm sorry!" His body heaved with sobs. "I did something very, very bad."

Bird girl.

Bird raised her head slightly and studied the dead animal on the ground beside her. What was this? Was Cody speaking to her, even in death? *Cody?* She gently patted his fur, ignoring Tanbark's cries.

Yes, it's me.

Did it hurt much?

What?

The stone to your head?

I know not of what you speak.

Bird sat up. Something was very odd. *Where are you, Cody? Beside you, in the cover of brush.*

Are you alive?

Very much.

Show yourself.

There are many people, but look now beside the tree.

Bird looked. There was Cody, in the flesh, peeking back at her from the bushes! She stared at the dead animal on the lane. Then she stared back at Cody. Alive.

I thought this was you, Cody! Dead. On the lane.
No. That's a wild coyote. Not a nice one. He stalked the wild man.
Why?
He thought the wild man might lead him to food.

The picture was becoming clear. The coyote wanted food from Tan and Tan wanted food from the coyote. And he'd gotten angry when the coyote didn't understand. But Bird still was furious; Tan had thought the coyote was Cody, and he'd killed him anyway.

"Tan, I will never forgive you for this."

"I couldn't stop myself, Bird. I got so upset."

"So why do you continue like this? Look at yourself! You know you need help. You told me so when we were down in the cave."

Tan gnawed on a fingernail. "I know," he whispered. "I know."

"Will you get help now?"

Tan's teeth chattered, and he wrapped his arms around himself. He looked utterly, completely miserable.

Bird asked the question a different way. "What do you think I mean by getting help, Tan?"

"I'll go to a doctor. I'll take medicine. I'm so confused! I feel afraid and out of control, and I don't like it! I've done something horrible and I know it. I'll go to a doctor if you want me to."

"It doesn't matter that I want you to." Bird allowed her voice to soften. There was no reason to yell any more. "This will only work if you do it for yourself. You have to want to get better."

Tan stood up and placed his hand over his heart. "I want to get better, Bird. I never want to do a thing like this again."

"I have witnesses, Tan. Hannah and Julia heard you say that."

"I know. I mean it. I want to get help."

"Today?"

"Yes. If that's what you want."

"No, Tan! It has to be *you* who wants help today. Not me."

"Then I want to get help today."

"You won't run away like last time?"

"I won't run away."

Bird relaxed a little. "Then we have a deal. Go with Aunt Hannah to clean up and get some clothes." Hannah nodded in agreement. "Julia and I will bury the ... body of our ..." She didn't know what to call the animal now that it wasn't Cody.

Julia finished her sentence. "The body of our dearest coyote friend." She began to cry again.

Hannah and Tanbark climbed into the big rig. Hannah carefully steered it around the dead coyote and drove up to the barn.

Bird waited a moment before speaking, then she confided in Julia. "This is not Cody."

Julia didn't say a word. She stared at Bird, then at the dead coyote, then back at Bird.

Bird tried again. "Seriously. This is not Cody. Cody is in the bushes." *Show yourself to Julia, Cody.*

Cody's head popped up again.

Julia gasped. "I can't believe it! Cody's alive!" She jumped in the air gleefully and hugged Bird. "Cody's alive!" she repeated. Then she stopped. "Did you know all along?"

"No! Would I have hugged a wild coyote? Especially a dead wild coyote?" Suddenly both girls realized that they could be covered in germs. "Yuck! I need a bath!" Bird exclaimed.

"Me, too!" Julia paused. "But why didn't you know it wasn't Cody?"

Bird wasn't sure. "I assumed it was Cody. Same size, colour. It didn't occur to me that it could be any other coyote, I guess."

Julia shrugged. "Same with me."

"Let's bury this poor animal, then soap up in the wash stall."

"Good idea! We don't want to bring cooties into the house. Where should we bury it?"

"In the hole behind the barn where we thought we'd bury Saul."

Julia nodded. "The horse that never dies. He's thirty-four, isn't he?"

"Yes. At least. Aunt Hannah got the hole dug years ago."

Julia nodded. "There's plenty of room in there for this little guy."

"You take his back feet, I'll take his front. Look sad as we pass the house."

"It is sad, Bird! This coyote didn't deserve to die."

The two sisters began their journey to the barn, carrying the body.

"Are you going to tell Tan the truth?" Julia asked. "He's miserable."

"I need to figure that out. He meant to kill Cody." Bird was quiet for a few paces. "I think that's why he realized he needs help."

"Because it shocked him? That he could do that?"

"It might have made him understand that he really can't control himself."

Julia considered this. "Weird, isn't it, how his mind works."

Bird nodded. It certainly was.

35
HELP

Tan let the warm water of the bath surround him. He had no feeling left. He didn't care if he lived or he died. Bird had meant something to him. He could relate to her, and she'd cared enough about him to seek him out, listen to his story, clear his name and save his life. Nobody except his mother had cared this much about him. But Bird had cared, and now she hated him. And Cody. His soulmate. He'd killed him with his slingshot. It had taken Tan four tries—the animal was quick—but he'd gotten him with the fourth rock. Between the eyes. And he'd been happy about it. But only for a moment.

PAUL ARRIVED AT THE BARN as Julia and Bird were scrubbing themselves, fully dressed, in the wash stall. Soap was everywhere. They were wearing rubber scrub gloves on their hands and singing "Rubber Ducky" at the top of their lungs to break the tension.

Both saw Paul at the same time, and gasped guiltily at his expression.

"It wasn't Cody," explained Julia.

Paul's puzzled expression intensified. "What wasn't Cody?"

"Sorry!" Bird said. "One minute while we rinse ourselves off." They stood under the shower until the suds disappeared, then Julia turned off the water. Bird grabbed two big towels and handed one to her little sister. She told Paul how Tan had shot a coyote with his slingshot, a coyote he thought was Cody. "He feels so bad," Bird explained, "that he actually said he wants to get help."

Paul listened carefully. "This could be a very significant event."

Bird nodded. She certainly hoped so. "Do I tell him that it was a wild coyote?" she asked. "If he knows he didn't kill Cody, will he decide he doesn't need help?"

Paul thought about it. "I see your point."

"But we have to tell him sometime," said Julia. "Otherwise he'll never trust us again."

"I wasn't going to not tell him. It's just when and how."

"Let's see how things are going at the house," suggested Paul. "Then we can decide how to deal with it."

Bird inhaled deeply as they headed down the lane, taking in everything around her. This was her last day at Saddle Creek.

She admired Sunny and Charlie as they grazed contentedly in the front field together. Bird felt at peace amidst the rolling green fields, the scent of the vibrantly coloured flowers and the sound of birdsong. She thought of all the things that made her happy. Winning at the horse show with her beloved horse, being surrounded by people whom she loved, having helped solve a mystery. Knowing that Cody was still alive. Knowing that Tan was going to get help. She sighed again.

We really showed them today, Bird.

I had a great time. Thank you.

I like to win, Bird. I'm glad we won.

Me, too.

You admit it now?

Yes, of course! But we'll never win if we forget why we're out there.

I know, I know. To have fun. You're getting boring.

When they entered the house, Lucky jumped on Paul and wagged his tail. "Down, boy," he commanded.

Why do you still jump up on Paul, Lucky? You know better.

Because he expects me to.

He tells you not to.

He doesn't mean it.

Bird smiled and patted his head. Smart dog.

Hannah was at the sink making a salad. "Wash up, folks! Eva and Stuart will be here soon." Then she saw Julia and Bird, soaking wet. "Oops. I guess you girls don't need a bath."

"We washed the dirt and coyote germs off," said Julia.

Hannah stopped what she was doing and turned to face her. "Coyote germs? That's a little insensitive, Julia. Cody was far more than a coyote, he was like a pet."

Julia didn't say anything. Bird looked around the kitchen. "Where's Tan?"

"Upstairs in the tub. Why?"

Bird told her about the mistaken identity.

"Thank heavens," said Hannah with a huge smile on her face. "That sweet animal. We would've missed him so badly."

"But here's the problem. How do I tell Tan?"

"Good question," Hannah answered. "We have to do this right. Mack Jones is dropping by shortly to talk to him."

"Did you call the hospital?" Bird asked.

"Yes. And they've been in touch with CAMH, the Centre for Addiction and Mental Health in Toronto. They'll take him in. Alison Wedger has been wonderful, too. She'll be here tomorrow morning to drive him down to the city."

"Is Tan okay with all of this?" Bird worried.

"He knows it's the right thing, and the right time."

"I'm glad he's getting help." Bird choked on her words and wiped away a tear.

"We're all glad." Paul turned for the stairs. "I'll go up and make sure Tan knows what socks to wear. He can't have my argyles."

"I'd never give him your argyles!" Hannah teased.

When he'd gone, Hannah's expression turned wistful. "You're going home tonight, girls. I'll miss you both. I've loved having you here with me."

Bird and Julia hugged their aunt tightly.

Bird was deeply sad to leave. She loved Hannah. Hannah was a good and kind and strong person. She'd looked after her and raised her while Eva was learning how to look after herself, and had always done her best for Bird, even through very difficult times. This holiday had reminded her how much she felt at home here among the horses and the farm work. Life in the country suited her.

"Can you babysit us again some time, Aunt Hannah?" Julia asked.

"Of course! I want you here every chance I get," Hannah answered. "Maybe you girls can stay forever. Oh my heavens, I will miss you!"

Hannah and Bird and Julia were locked in their hug when Stuart and Eva walked through the door.

"I guess my girls weren't too much trouble," Eva said with a sniff.

"Aren't we lucky?" Stuart quickly put his arm around her waist. "We can go on holiday anytime, and never worry."

Eva smiled tensely. "We are lucky. I'm glad Julia and Bird love their Aunt Hannah so much."

"We love you, too, Mom," said Bird, recognizing their mother's insecurity.

"We love you more," Julia enthused.

Paul came down the stairs and greeted Eva and Stuart. Then he turned to Bird. "Please come upstairs. Tan needs to talk to you. Now."

Bird took in Paul's expression with a sinking feeling. Something was very wrong. Julia would have to deal with Eva's issues alone. She ran upstairs and went straight into the bathroom. Tan lay in the tub, covered in luxurious bubbles. His eyes were red and swollen.

"Bird," he said, as soon as he saw her. "Cody was a wonderful animal. He should be alive right now, and I should be dead."

Bird put the toilet seat down and sat. "Tan, listen to me."

"No. There's nothing you can say." Tan's voice was oddly calm—not like the other times he'd been angry or upset. "Paul said not to worry, but I can't help it. It's over. I don't want help, Bird. I'm too tired. I don't have the energy."

Bird gazed at Tan's haggard, ravaged face. She felt his exhaustion. She could only imagine how daunting the prospect of rehabilitation was for him.

"Do you have the energy to go back into the woods?"

"No."

"I understand, Tan."

"I don't know how you can."

"Trust me, it's one thing I'm good at."

"But I killed Cody."

Bird hesitated before she spoke. "Tan, you did an awful thing. You were mad at Cody, and you aimed your slingshot between his eyes, where you knew a stone would kill him."

"You're right."

"And you told me you'd get help."

"Yes."

"Because you can't control yourself, right?"

"Right."

Bird took a deep breath and plunged in. "It turns out that it wasn't Cody that you killed."

Silence.

"You killed a wild coyote."

Silence.

"An innocent, wild coyote. He followed you around, thinking that you'd lead him to food. You thought he was Cody. He wasn't."

Silence.

"You killed a coyote, Tan. Just not Cody."

"I killed a coyote, but it wasn't Cody?" Tan blinked, trying to understand. "I didn't kill Cody?"

SHELLEY PETERSON

"You did not kill Cody."

"He's still alive?"

"Yes."

"It wasn't Cody, and you didn't tell me!" Now Tan was shouting. Oddly, Bird much preferred this emotion to the flat, lifeless tone he'd been using before—at least he cared enough to yell.

He continued. "I can't believe you'd be so horrible. Cruel, Bird! You let me think I killed Cody and you knew I didn't? I hate you!" Tan thrashed angrily in the bubbles, sending soap all over the bathroom.

"I thought it was Cody! I didn't know until later."

"When did you find out?" Tan peered at her disbelievingly.

"When Cody showed up. I thought it was his ghost."

"You didn't!"

"I did."

"That's stupid! There's no such thing as ghosts!"

"Well, I thought it was his ghost, and then I realized it was him."

"You're crazy."

"As crazy as you?"

Tan became quiet. He made circles in the water with his hands. "I am crazy. I've been crazy for a while. I don't know why."

"But you're going to get help, Tan. Your mother is coming."

Tan began to cry. "I want to see her. I haven't seen her in a long time."

Bird noticed someone at the bathroom door. It was Hannah. Bird quietly moved to the door and whispered, "Mrs. Wedger should come tonight."

They looked at the bathtub, where Tan was quietly crying.

Hannah nodded. "She's on her way from Toronto. Paul had the same thought, and already called her. Mack sent a cruiser, and he'll ride back down to Toronto with them."

Bird turned back to Tan. "Hang on," she said softly, as she

returned to her perch on the toilet. "I'll wait with you until she comes."

Alison Wedger arrived within the hour. Her tired face was kind and intelligent, Bird thought. And beautiful.

Tanbark stumbled to her as she walked in the door.

"Mom," he cried as he buried his face in her shoulder. "Mom."

Alison held him tight.

"Please sit down Alison, Tan," said Hannah after a minute. She pulled out two chairs. "Make yourselves comfortable until Mack comes. Tea?"

Alison nodded. "That would be lovely."

Paul sat with them while Hannah busied herself at the counter. "Alison, I'm Paul. That's Hannah over by the sink."

Hannah waved.

"And this is Bird."

Bird smiled at her. She noticed the worry lines around Alison's eyes.

"Hello, everybody. I'm a bit of a mess right now. I hope you understand." Alison kept her arm around Tan, whose head was bowed. "I haven't seen Tanbark for so long." Her voice cracked, and Hannah brought her a tissue. "I wondered if I'd ever see him again."

Paul nodded. "Of course. I'm glad you could get here so quickly."

"I just dropped everything. I'm so glad he's safe and wants to get help." She couldn't say anything more.

"Tan is lucky to have a mother like you," said Bird, "who has always cared so much for him, through everything."

Alison looked at Bird directly for the first time. "Thank you, Bird. I cannot count the sleepless nights." Her smile looked intensely sad. "You're the one who found him, aren't you?"

"I guess. But really, he found me."

"But you understood that he was good. That means a lot to me."

Bird chuckled softly. "Tan and I've had a few trials, that's for sure."

Alison stroked Tan's forehead and smoothed his unruly hair. "He wasn't always like this, you know."

Hannah brought the cups to the table. "I remember him when he was fifteen or so. He was on top of his game."

"What a difference." Alison sighed. "Tanbark was the best at everything. Smart. Athletic. Popular. Then came the chemical imbalance."

"It can happen to anyone," said Paul.

"And it does," answered Alison. "It came as a complete surprise to me."

Hannah poured the tea. "Milk? Lemon? Sugar?"

"Just clear is perfect." Alison smiled at her hostess. "The good news is that a chemical imbalance can be treated successfully once the ill person decides to get help."

"But how do you know you need help," asked Bird, "when you think that you're fine and it's everybody else who needs help?"

"That's the big problem," Alison smiled sadly. "I guess something finally happens to make a person sit up and see what the people who love them have been seeing for a while."

Bird thought about the dead coyote. At least he'd given his life for a good cause. "Do you think Tan will get better? Will he be like he was before?"

Alison cocked her head in thought, and smiled. "That's what they tell me, and I want to believe it!" She tightened her grip around her son's back. Her eyes held conviction and strength. "I'm told that once the person has admitted that he needs help, which is now, this disease can be mastered. It won't be easy. With treatment, counselling and hard work, it'll take some time, but we've begun the healing—thanks to all of you."

Mack Jones arrived as they were drinking their tea. "It's best we get to CAMH as soon as possible," he said after introductions were made. "There's a room all made up for him. They're waiting for us."

Bird studied Tanbark. He was holding on to his mother, his face still buried in her shoulder. It must be scary to be him, she thought. She considered how brave Tanbark was. His greatest fear had always been confinement. Now he must face that fear, and many more.

"Goodbye, Tan. I'll miss you." Bird gently touched his trembling arm and said, "I'd like to visit you sometime."

Tan turned his head and squinted, his eyes blurry. He said, "Yes! Visit." He bent his neck and rested his head on his mother's shoulder.

"Time to go," said Mack in a quiet voice. "The car's waiting."

Without a backward glance, Tanbark, with his mother and Mack at either side, walked out to the cruiser and got in. The tires crunched on the gravel road, and they were gone.

Bird let the tears fall down her cheeks.

36
ALL GOOD THINGS

Tan leaned on his mother's shoulder in the back of the cruiser and dozed. He was so tired. Tired of hiding. Tired of running. Tired of avoiding people. He didn't want to think about anything. All he knew was that his mother was here to help. He repeated silently—I need help. I need help. This time, he was going to get it.

BIRD AND JULIA QUIETLY SET THE TABLE in the dining room, while Hannah and Eva bustled in the kitchen. Pete and Laura had been invited, and were expected at any moment.

The sound of a vehicle attracted their attention. Bird recognized the truck first. "The Piersons are here."

"Come on in and sit down!" Hannah was warm in her welcome. "Tanbark and his mother just left for Toronto. We need some cheering up."

Laura nodded. "I know exactly what you mean, dear. It's very sad, but he'll be fine, I have faith. He's young." She smiled kindly. "He's in the best of hands. He'll soon respond, with the right medication. You'll see."

Hannah hugged her elderly friend. "I hope you're right."

All around the dining room table, faces glowed with goodwill. Bird looked at each person, one by one: Laura Pierson, bubbling with energy and love; old Pete, intelligent, tough-minded and perceptive; Aunt Hannah, hard-working, honest and caring; Paul, trustworthy, kind and generous; Julia, funny, sweet and earnest; Eva, insecure but good-hearted and loving; Stuart, attentive and sensitive. Bird loved them all.

Paul carried a tray of champagne flutes—two with ginger ale for the girls—and set it down on the table. Everyone took a glass. Paul held his in the air. "I propose a toast." He cleared his voice and said:

"Fear less, hope more.

Eat less, chew more.

Talk less, say more.

Whine less, breathe more.

Love more.

And all good things will be yours."

"Beautiful!" exclaimed Laura.

Pete held up his glass, then drank. "That's an old Scandinavian proverb, isn't it, Paul?"

"Indeed it is, sir. To honour your Norwegian heritage."

"Let me add this," said Pete, "to honour my Canadian friends and family. To truth, love and life. And to hard work and good luck."

Under the table, Lucky's tail thumped. *To me? A toast to me? Yes, Lucky. I'm sure he meant you.*

After the dinner dishes were done, while everyone else sat around the fire chatting about the recent adventures, Bird quietly slipped out the kitchen door. She walked through the moonlight, filling her lungs deeply with the fresh night air. She savoured the aromas of earth, newly cut grass, wild leeks and young pine.

Later that evening, she and Julia would go back to the house that Stuart and Eva had bought when they got engaged. Tonight, she'd sleep in her new bed, in the bedroom that she'd helped decorate. But before she went, there were two things she needed to do.

Sunny?

Here.

Can you come to the fence? I want to rub your ears before I go.
No. I'm busy.

Bird snorted wryly. This wasn't how she'd imagined their parting. She climbed over the fence and stumbled on a rock in the dark.

Ouch. Dumb horse. I just want to pat you one more time. Why do you make everything so difficult?
You'll be back. I know it.
Of course I'll be back, but aren't you even a little bit sad that my holiday here is over?
Maybe. Okay, I am. Okay, I'm really sad. Do you feel better?
I do.
So you feel good when I feel bad, and that's good?
I feel good that you like having me around.
Well, I admit it. I do.
I love you, Sunny. You're my best friend.
You're my best friend, too. I never knew what that was until I met you.

Bird hugged his smooth neck with both arms, and Sunny's chin pressed into her back.

May I interrupt?

Bird turned to see Cody, standing beside them in the dark. *Hello, little friend.*

I come to say goodbye. Is it true you must go?
Yes, Cody, but I'm not far away. I'll be back soon.
Much has happened in the time you've been here.
That's for sure.
I will look for you when you come again.
Thank you, Cody. I'll look for you, too. You have a very special place in my heart.
I trust you, Bird.

This was high praise indeed from the coyote, and Bird was flattered. *I trust you, too, Cody. May I pat you?*

You may.

She rubbed Cody's furry ears with her left hand, and stroked Sundancer's soft nose with her right. She felt immensely lucky.

Then, as stealthily as he'd come, Cody was gone.

Sundancer silently moved away, and resumed his grazing.

The night was still.

Slowly, Bird walked back through the field toward the farmhouse, with all its windows warmed with light. She stopped on a grassy rise. From there, the house looked welcoming and safe. Like a perfect family lived inside, with no troubles at all, only laughter and joy.

She wondered how it must have looked through Tan's eyes, as he lurked around peering in windows. Did it appear forbidding and claustrophobic? Or did he worry that he wouldn't fit in? Perhaps he was drawn to it, but couldn't find a way to belong. Bird didn't know. But both times that he'd been in the house, he hadn't stayed long.

Bird sat on the sweet-smelling grass, deep in thought. Tanbark. Her uncle. She could only imagine what he was about to face. For sure, his loss of freedom would be difficult to overcome—if he could manage it at all. His distrust of people would also be a challenge. Bird's stomach tightened on his behalf. Dear Tan. Right now he was in a car on his way to a completely unfamiliar world. She so wanted him to be all right. Hopefully he'd come to realize that people cared about him, and that he was not an outcast. She crossed her fingers and made a wish for him.

Bird rose from the ground and stretched herself tall. The pungent, earthy smell of the summer night tickled her nose— she loved that aroma. She stared into the sky, where the moon and stars were beginning to appear. Bird smiled. In the end, they'd been able to look past the bright moon and see the stars, as Paul had mused that night. The truth had been obscured by her grandfather's conniving, but they'd figured it out.

Bird sighed. She would never understand why her grandfather did the things he did. Life would be so much better for him, and the people around him, if he'd just face his mistakes instead of plotting and making them worse. At least he was a good example of what not to do. Those lessons were useful, too.

Suddenly, the screened kitchen door slammed with a mighty whump. A tall male figure ran across the driveway toward her. He jumped the fence with one hand on the top rail and a graceful sideways leap. Bird stared. Could it be? She blinked and stared again.

Alec!

Bird's hands flew to her mouth and she gasped in surprise.

Run to him, Bird, urged Cody.

Run to him, teased Sundancer, *before he gets away again!*

They met halfway across the field. Alec grabbed Bird around the waist and twirled her before setting her back down.

"I missed you, Bird," he said softly. "Nobody in the world comes close to you."

"Have you been looking?" Bird asked slyly.

"What do you mean?" Alec jumped back, startled.

She took pity on him. "I missed you, too." She looked up into his beautiful clear eyes and took his hand. "I really did."

Alec smiled shyly. "You're amazing."

Bird felt happy from the bottom of her feet to the top of her head.

"Have you been keeping busy?" he asked.

Bird began to laugh. "Just a little."